Tom Bodett made ~~...~~ e
spokesman for the Mo ~~...~~ *light on*
for you") and as a commentator for National Public Ra-
dio. Millions across the country enjoyed his weekly broad-
cast from

THE END OF THE ROAD

They're a motley, friendly, more-or-less wholesome crew. Doug McDoogan, local miscreant, teller of tall tales, and con artist—whose ingredient list includes just a bit more "artist" than "con." Mayor Richard Weekly, grand marshal of the End of the Road Days parade, who gives the blue ribbon to a dump truck. Argus Winslow, junkyard tycoon. Ruby and her Video Roundup. Tamara Dupree, the animal rights activist who finds herself in the most uncomfortable position of having killed a cat. And Ed Flannigan, whose wife is less than convinced when he suddenly, suspiciously, converts from Willie Nelson to that "twinkle ding-dong music" from Windham Hill. . . .

"Tom Bodett's sharp-eyed accounting of life's perpetual disorders is one of those all-too-few gems that really make you laugh out loud."
    —Bob Elliott, the Bob of Bob and Ray

THE END
OF THE ROAD

TOM BODETT

BANTAM BOOKS
NEW YORK · TORONTO · LONDON · SYDNEY ·
AUCKLAND

Acknowledgments

A warm and specific thanks to my friend and partner, Johnny B. I wouldn't have done this book without the radio show, and I couldn't have done the radio show without him. Thanks to Steve Hibbs and Sharon McKemie for holding it all together at Free Flight, and thanks to Bob Lindner, Dick Brescia, Dave West, Rich Wood, Susan Kernes, and Robert Hyland for getting it off the ground.

Thanks to Gary Thomas and Lance Petersen for the good ideas, and the radio show cast, crew, and supporters for all the help and good times.

And my warmest personal regards to all the folks of Homer, Alaska, who continue to keep me honest just by living well.

Contents

PART THREE

Introduction

LIVING and working in such a beautiful place as Homer, Alaska, has many advantages, the most significant one being that it is very close to The End of the Road. The End of the Road is a remarkable little vicinity that I particularly enjoy because it seems to be plugged full of familiar people. Familiar in the way that they all tend to remind us of someone we've known before. A genuine and unaffected regularity that can only be imitated, never reproduced.

My job here was to introduce you to these folks, but I've never been good at introducing strangers. How do the standard ones go at parties? . . . "Meet Clayton, he's an accountant." As if accountants are extruded in a factory somewhere all the same except for body styles and color options. Clayton, whoever he is, is surely more than an accountant just as the Ed Flannigan you're about to meet is more than a road-grader operator, and Doug McDoogan is less than a liar.

I like to let my guests mingle at these parties and speak for themselves. So, if you'll forgive my rudeness, I'll leave you folks alone to get to know one another. Treat them kindly, please, they're friends of mine.

Similarities between the characters in this narrative and individuals either living or dead doesn't seem at all surprising.

—T.B.
Homer, Alaska

THE END
OF THE ROAD

PART ONE

—·—

1

The Big Bazaar

LABOR Day was not a good day for our mayor, Richard Weekly. His two decades as mayor has had its ups and its downs, but few days were as downright interesting as the big End of the Road Days celebration last Monday.

The festivities kicked off with the parade at the corner of Main and Clearshot in the center of town and headed out to the A&B Gravel Pit.

The first thing to go wrong was with the parade. As always, Mayor Weekly was the Grand Marshal and responsible for awarding the blue ribbon to the entrants. There were five entries this year, up one from recent years, but it was the same old things. A pickup truck with the Chamber of Commerce waving in the back. Fanny Olmstead, the preacher's wife, dressed up like a clown passing out religious pamphlets. The Boy Scouts ambled by proud and disorganized. The fire truck was there all waxed up, and Ed Flannigan, a new entrant, brought up the rear in a brand-new, bright orange State Highway Department dump truck. After giving out awards for twenty years to the same four outfits, the mayor decided to give this year's blue ribbon to Ed Flannigan and his dump truck just because it was fresh.

Well, as it turns out, Ed and his truck were actually on their way to the gravel pit to get a load of rock, and weren't in the parade at all. They were just following it.

The day sort of disintegrated from there.

Every year for years the mayor's been the judge for the pickled herring contest and has never been able to admit he can't stand pickled herring. But these women take great pride in their pickled herring skills, so he treats it with a sort of nauseated respect.

The problem on Monday was that he couldn't for the life of him remember who got the prize last year because he can't tell one jar of that yuck from another, and he accidentally gave it to the same woman. A woman who was as embarrassed as he was. This was such a social misdemeanor that rumors began to fly he'd been bribed. For the first time in his political career the mayor started to worry about the upcoming election.

He couldn't worry about it too much right then, though, because he had to officiate the Salmon Throw, which ended up being won by Doug McDoogan because he bent the rules. What the Salmon Throw is basically is that contestants pair off and throw a dead fish back and forth until they can't stand it anymore.

McDoogan cheated, they say, by wearing a full set of rubber rain gear, but he was, the mayor insisted, the last person holding a fish.

The losers called foul because they were completely slimed out, stinky, and peppered with scales while Doug slipped out of his rain gear fresh as a daisy. Mayor Weekly settled it by saying there wasn't any rule book on this stupid contest and if that was a problem, maybe they shouldn't be doing it at all, which is what he really wanted in the first place. There's something about grown men tossing a fish back and forth in a gravel pit that unsettled the mayor.

Letting Doug McDoogan take the contest was not a popular decision for the mayor mostly because McDoogan has managed to pester or alienate just about everybody in town. You see, he is just about the biggest liar that ever walked the Earth. They say to take everything Doug tells you, divide it by three, subtract six, and don't believe the rest. A person with a reputation like that just shouldn't be winning no community contests. Mayor Weekly was really starting to think his political grip was slipping.

Trying to muster some of his hard-core support, he wandered over to the soup table where Pastor Frank of the First and Last Baptist Church was dishing out bowls of homemade chowder with his wife Fanny, who was still dressed in her clown suit. Pastor Frank Olmstead is what you might call a black-belt fundamentalist, and he was in a pretty poor humor that day because Reverend Saffire was at the next table doing tarot card readings.

Mayor Weekly just wanted to chat with the pastor because he knew if he stayed in the good graces of the great Frank Olmstead, he'd be in the good graces of his entire flock, and that was a considerable number of registered voters in this small town.

The mayor didn't get his chat, though. All he got was a sermon about the devil's work going on next door while Fanny bobbed her rubber nose up and down in agreement, and Mayor Weekly consented to talk with the Reverend Saffire about the problem.

Reverend Saffire isn't what you'd think of as a righteous "reverend." Actually, he drives a school bus, but he is what you might call a "self-anointed mystic." He believes that we all originated from cosmic dust, which is not a new idea, but he claims to be a first generation. He thinks he fell out of the sky and just sort of gathered himself up on the beach somewhere.

The mayor walked over to ask Saffire to move his tarot operation to the other side of the pit by the beer tent, but all the strange reverend did was in the nicest way lean over and ask Pastor Frank if he would like a reading.

Richard Weekly the man might have stayed to re-solve the argument that ensued, but Richard Weekly the mayor had to attend to a problem with the pistol-shooting contest.

It seemed that Argus Winslow, the local junkyard tycoon, had forgotten to bring the old headlights he always supplies as targets for this event. He refused to go get them only because Bud Koenig was the first person to tell him to.

Bud and Argus haven't agreed on anything except cheap whiskey for forty years, and if Bud thought that Argus should go get the headlights, Argus, by nature, thought it should be the last thing he'd ever do.

No one has ever quite figured out why Argus and Bud, who homesteaded this area together, get along so poorly, but everyone agrees they must like it because they really work hard at it. Whenever they're seen in public they're usually together, nose to nose, shouting about something and trading pulls on a bottle of the worst whiskey money can buy.

And so it went at the End of the Road bazaar's "Blast for Cash" pistol shoot, until the offended women from the pickled herring tables—in an act of symbolic martyrdom over the mayor's handling of the taste contest—volunteered their jars of herring as official targets.

This is going to leave a heck of a mess is all the mayor was thinking as he wandered over to the beer tent to see what the trouble was there.

Tamara Dupree, our local vegetarian activist, lover of all living things but most men, and a new-age missionary among the Northern barbarians, was in a heated discussion with a couple of our barbarians. It seemed that Tamara had set up a petition table to protest the trapping of fur-bearing animals complete with graphic pictures of the consequences of leg-hold traps. The men had misread the posters as advertisements and had tried to buy several dozen traps from her.

Mayor Weekly would like to have stayed for the debate but couldn't because the pistol shoot was being held up by Ed Flannigan and his blue ribbon dump truck that came back for another load of gravel.

Mayor Weekly directed the truck through the audience and held them back as Ed went to work with the loader.

Ed got his load and tooted his horn to the crowd gathering around the hopeful marksmen drawing beads on the pickled herring.

The field of contestants was quickly narrowed after one firing. The rules are simple: if you miss once, you're out. Among those eliminated was Doug McDoogan, who claimed that his gun misfired, and then that he'd actually hit a duck that flew past just as he shot and stopped the bullet, and finally that he hadn't fired at all and it was Argus's shot they heard when he took an out-of-turn crack at the flag on top of the beer tent.

Mayor Weekly put his arm around Doug, escorted him gently out of the group and told him quietly that he'd better shut up as long as there was live ammunition on the premises.

The six final contestants included, as always, Bud Koenig and Argus Winslow, who were without a doubt the best pistol shots going. One or the other of them always walked away with the hundred-dollar cash prize.

Six more herring jars were set up on the target table and everybody missed but Bud and Argus, who got their jars just before a stray shot knocked a leg off the table which fell down and broke the rest of the jars except one which just rolled over and spilled.

The mayor, being the official of this auspicious event, was elected to go put things back together. The target area was every bit the mess Mayor Weekly envisioned it could be, with pickled herring stuck to every rock, table, and piece of glass in sight, but he sucked in his breath, calmed his stomach, and made the announcement that there was only one target jar left.

Argus Winslow immediately declared that they should bring out some plastic beer cups to shoot at for the prize, which Bud Koenig, naturally, disagreed with. Claiming that you can't change targets in the middle of a contest, Bud said that the whole thing should be called off, which Argus disagreed with at some length, while the crowd grew impatient and just wanted to get the darn thing over with so they could go home.

Pastor Frank stepped forward and said that the prize money should be given to the church for missionary work. Tamara Dupree announced in no uncertain terms her disgust with the whole idea of guns and said the prize money should go to forming a local Animal Protection Society, which Reverend Saffire agreed with, but only if soil conservation were included. Doug McDoogan said that the whole contest was invalidated and they should start all over with new targets because he claimed someone had tampered with his gun sights and it's no wonder he missed. Fanny Olmstead took off her clown nose and told Doug to shut up, while Mayor Richard Weekly stood in the middle of it all wondering what to do.

Finally, mustering every last bit of political wit at his disposal, he thrust out his chest, straightened his shoulders, stepped grandly forward, and compromised.

He gave fifty bucks to Bud, fifty bucks to Argus, told everybody it was a draw, and would somebody please start picking up the paper cups and plates because it was getting late.

He hated to end the party, but he'd had about enough of it. Judging by the willingness that everybody started folding up tables and such, they had too.

Reverend Saffire pulled up to the beer tent with his school bus and collected those who had no business driving themselves back to town, and Mayor Weekly helped the Chamber of Commerce group take the tent down.

When all was packed away in the pickup truck, the good mayor drew a fresh cup of lukewarm beer from a lone keg and sat on the tailgate. He watched as the crowd of constituents made their weary way out the entrance to the pit.

He saw Saffire pull away with his merry load of revelers. And Pastor Frank walking with his arm around Fanny, who'd pulled a sweater over her clown suit. Tamara Dupree and Ed Flannigan were carrying a trash can together. Doug McDoogan leaned up against Ed's dump truck, still examining his pistol like there was something wrong with it.

He could hear Argus and Bud arguing over at the pistol range. They were sitting on big rocks, facing each other with a bottle between them. To his relief, it looked like the guns had been put away.

"These people are going to drive me crazy." He watched as the tired backs of the last tired citizens disappeared along the road to town. He laid back on the folded tent in the pickup and his next thought was involuntary.

"Dear God help me . . . I love this town."

2

Ed Again

ED Flannigan is changing and nobody seems to know why. The roughneck road-grader operator, softball pitcher, sportsman, and scrapper that everyone knew and loved is leaving us day by day for some new guy. Actually, some "new-age" guy. "Ed Again" is what people are starting to call him.

"He's getting to be *so* nice," some of the women are saying in great admiration.

"He's getting to be so *nice*," some of his old friends are saying with an equal amount of revulsion.

The women are giving the credit to Ed's wife Emily, and the men are handing her the blame. Emily is a little different from Ed. No, she's a lot different. She was many things before she met Ed and was swept off her feet by his rough good looks, granite physique, strong will . . . and steady job.

She'd been a poet, a painter, and a Radcliffe scholar with a passion for art and artists. But four years of living with a starving screen writer in Los Angeles eventually brought her to the End of the Road for a reprieve. Now, three kids, two dogs, and half a duplex later, she's watching as her man transforms before her very eyes.

His Willie Nelson tapes are getting dusty and he's listening to her Windham Hill records; "twinkle dingdong music," he used to call it. He bought her a wind chime for their anniversary. The first anniversary he'd remembered in eight years. She caught him reading a book, *Insight into Intimacy,* and embarrassed him one night. Now he looks at it right in front of her and reads little pieces of it out loud. He's becoming gentle in bed, patient with the kids, and turned down a moose hunt with his buddies over Labor Day weekend so he could go with Emily to the back-to-school sales in Anchorage. "What in the heck is going on around here?" she says at least six times a week.

How it all started was when an old college friend of Emily's came around last year. She claimed to be one of those channelers. You know, a mystic sort of fortune teller. Said she could become the spirit of some old Egyptian architect or something and tell your future and stuff.

Well, as you can imagine, Ed had a pretty good time around the dinner table with this one and got a few hoots with it over coffee down at the shop. "I saw her do it for Emily," he'd tell the boys. "She'd roll her eyes back in 'er head and start talkin' like Moses in one of those Jesus movies. Told Emily she used to be a nun in Constantahoople, or Cincinnati, or someplace like that."

Yeah, there was a lot of laughs, but Ed got corralled one night by Emily and her friend to try a "reading," as they were calling them. "Oh, come on, Ed," Emily said. "At the very least it'll give you something to make fun of." Ed pretty much agreed with that, so he and this channeler went into the kitchen by themselves so the kids wouldn't see.

Ed wasn't laughin' when he came out a half hour later. "What a bunch of crock!" he shouted at the whole room, his face red and his thumb pointed over his shoulder to the kitchen. "Tell that mystic friend of yours to get her Egyptian road show out of this house . . . now!"

Emily was not the sort of person to take direct orders like this from her husband, and normally Ed wasn't the kind of person who gave them. There was something in his tone, though, something in his eyes, that told Emily she'd better ride along with him on this one.

She went in and asked her friend what had happened. The friend said she didn't know. Channelers, she said, don't remember what they say while in their spirit body. Emily said she'd better leave in the morning, and she did.

Ed never told Emily what happened. He never told his buddies about it either. But it continued to bang around in his head, and like a loose wheel bearing, that's all he could hear.

When Ed had sat down at the kitchen table across from this woman, he watched with a big smirk on his face as she rolled her eyes back in their sockets, entered her trance, and started talking to no one in particular in a throaty voice.

"We have with us this day a lost and lonely soul. A soul who carries much anger within himself," she began. "This is a soul with the potential for little in this walking on Earth, but with great hopes."

She went on and on in an infuriating monotone for thirty minutes about how Ed was put on this Earth as a punishment for horrible things he'd done to people in former lives. He'd been a murderous mercenary and an inept and cowardly leader. He'd been a cannibal and sexual deviant. His life this time around was to be made up of shattered dreams, painful relationships, and to have every good thing that ever happens to him ripped away. Including his children.

Ed's smirk had been steadily melting away through the whole reading, but when she mentioned the thing about his children being taken away, he lost all expression. He sat staring at the whites of her eyes and a hate began to build and rise up out of his stomach. A pure red, white-knuckled hatred of a person who could sit and say such things about a man's life. Ed slammed his fists down on the Formica table, which almost tweaked the woman off her chair, and he left the room.

It was over a year ago that happened. For a while Ed seemed a little testy about things in general, but particularly about things spiritual. "Biggest crock ever invented." "Damn fakers oughta all be arrested for fraud." And on and on. Ed made it pretty clear what he thought of this stuff. But he kept a secret. A scary secret.

The secret was that he half believed the stuff the woman had told him. He didn't admit it, of course, but he couldn't get it out of his head. He was supposed to be miserable, she told him. By golly, he *felt* miserable.

He would lose his wife and his children, she'd said. Somehow he knew he would. They didn't seem like his family sometimes. He barely noticed them, really. They were more something to bring a paycheck home to than anything else. A reason to work, he guessed. A guy's gotta work.

And that job. He hated his job. Heavy equipment was loud, dangerous, and boring. Ed should know, he'd been working with it most all of his life. Draggin' that road-grader blade across the same old roads week after week. Listening to the same old hackneyed jokes back at the maintenance shop day after day. He didn't know what kind of job he wanted. Just a quiet one would do for now.

Ed went on and on with this for a few months. Pinpointing every little thing about himself that had gone stale, and ending up with little left over. It might have been the end of him, just as the channeler had predicted, except something very fortunate happened. Another channeler came to town.

This one arrived on the arm of Tamara Dupree, our local new-age missionary. She and an unfamiliar woman friend were sipping tea down at Clara's Coffee

Cup when Ed happened to sit down to breakfast one morning.

Ed was overhearing their conversation without really meaning to when he heard the word "channeler" being applied to Tamara's friend. He dropped his fork into his two over easy and let his jaw hang in mid-stride on a piece of side pork.

His first impulse was to reach over and choke this person. Ed had been having homicidal fantasies about Emily's friend for months, and being three feet away from one of her ilk was almost too much for him. But he fought back the urge.

Then something came over Ed that was relatively rare in his life. Something sweet and unexplainable. Something unique to the human mind. Ed felt the rush of what can only be described as divine inspiration. The solution to the problem that'd bugged him for the last several months leaped into focus. All he had to do was lie.

Ed's reasoning gets a little complicated here, but that's the nature of divine inspiration, so let me try to spell this out.

You see, Ed's big problem was that he was half believing a bunch of bad news about himself that came from a source he couldn't reasonably trust. So if he could completely discredit his source, he could let go of all this stuff that he figured had to be bunk in the first place. There, that's clear enough.

So what Ed's inspiration told him to do was talk with another channeler, only this time pretend to be somebody else. This way whatever was told to him, good, bad, or indifferent, would show that these spirit people could be fooled, and if they can be fooled, they must be fools, and who cares what a bunch of fools think of you.

Inspiration having its divine limitations, it never occurred to Ed what would happen if he got the same story as before, proving that all this was for real, but he was pretty sure of himself on this one.

So what he did was swallow the last of his side pork, put on his best "have a nice day" smile, lean over and tap Tamara on the shoulder. "Excuse me for inter-rupting," he said, trying to sound like that Grasshop-per guy in the old kung fu TV show. "My name is Ed and I couldn't help but overhear that your friend is a fortune tell—er . . . channeler. I'm trying to get in touch with my spirit body, and I wonder if you can help me."

Clara, behind the counter, caught some of this talk and looked at Ed like maybe she should take his tem-perature. Ed ignored her. He was on a mission.

"I would like to have a reading," he said, looking evenly into the eyes of this unsuspecting woman with Tamara. I won't bore you with the spiel he embarked on to sell his point, but let's just say it had something about the poetry he'd been reading lately giving him a low energy, and he felt he was coming out of balance with his karma and every other darn thing he could remember ever hearing his wife talk to her old school friends about when she thought he wasn't listening.

Ed got his reading, that day. He met Tamara and her friend at Tamara's cabin and sat across the table from the channeler while Tamara smiled knowingly from the woodbox. Ed had already run out of weird things to talk about, so he just got quiet and tried to smile the way everybody else was.

The channeler went into her trance much the way the other one did, only to Ed's relief, she didn't roll her eyes around, she closed them, and she didn't change her voice. She talked in a lilting and relatively normal tone, even if she was using some strange ways of say-ing things.

Ed smiled knowingly at the end of her nose as she started in.

"We have before us one of great energy and loving. There is much nurturing in this soul. It is an old soul who has walked on this Earth many times in love and in caring. In this life this one has come for his rewards. All things that he shall desire shall be his so long as his love and his caring remain in constant force . . ." And on she went for forty-five minutes about what a won-derful guy he was, what a wonderful life he has ahead of him. A life full of riches, serenity, security, and true love. She spent a lot of time on his capacity for love, and especially his love of children and helpless things.

Ed's knowing smile nearly turned into a smirk. *It's working,* he thought, *I fooled her.*

But as all this good news went on and on and on, his face relaxed and he began to start picturing this person she was talking about. A calm, happy person in a quiet place surrounded by people who cared about him. *Nobody's that lucky,* he thought, but he never interrupted, and let her go all the way to the finish.

Ed was uncomfortable in the silence that followed, but Tamara broke into it with offers of camomile tea all around. Ed had never had a sip of herbal tea in his life, but he took it, feeling unusually polite all of a sudden. "Very good," he said to Tamara, as if comparing it to all the other camomile teas he'd been drinking lately.

I'd be understating it to say that Ed walked out of there a little bit confused. His divinely inspired plan had gone exactly according to Hoyle. He'd fooled them. He knew that. But he couldn't shake the fact that he liked the sounds of this new deal. He thought, *Well, maybe in the mood I was in before, I'd fooled that other channeler.* Ed didn't feel like spending much time with this thought. He had other things to think about.

For the first time in almost a year, he didn't have a bad thing in his head. Foiled dreams, rotten jobs, broken marriages. It was replaced by riches, serenity, and all those other things that played back so much nicer.

Ed still doesn't know what to think of it. And most folks around here don't know what to think of Ed these last couple months. He walks a little slower. Listens when you talk to him, but seems almost distracted by something. The boys are getting a little worried, wonder if maybe the exhaust on his road grader is leaking or something.

Ed takes the ribbing with a smile. Sort of a knowing smile, like there's some kind of clear, sweet music playing back in his head. Good music. The kind you want to listen to.

3

Tamara and the Cat

TAMARA Dupree hasn't had the easiest time of it since she reached the End of the Road. It's not surprising, though. She came in with such a chip on her shoulder, she was bound to run into trouble sooner or later. What's funny, and kinda sad about it, is that most of the trouble she's had, she's done to herself.

Tamara came in from California, or maybe it was Oregon. She's what you might call a vegetarian activist. If you get behind her in line at the grocery store with a pack of hamburger in your cart, she starts makin' little gaggin' noises in her throat and tries to move away from you.

That's when you're lucky, 'cause Tamara's not shy with her opinions and like as not she'll start rummaging through your groceries, lecturing you on which vital organ functions are going to fail if you eat this, that, or the other thing. She has not endeared herself to very many folks this way, and a lot of us have taken to putting Ding Dongs and Nutty-Buddies on top of our carts just to get a rise out of her.

Tamara blew her credibility as a champion of all God's creatures right off the bat. She wasn't in town a month before she organized a local Prevention of Cruelty to Animals group, then promptly got arrested for cruelty to animals herself.

It had to do with that dog she's always got with her, "Karma" she calls it. Tamara, in some unexplainable leap of logic, decided that if she was going to be a strict vegetarian, her dog should be too, and promptly put him on a diet of tossed green salads and whole grains. She darn near starved that poor thing to death before Floyd, our dogcatcher, caught wind of it and gave her a citation.

As you can imagine, Tamara felt pretty bad about this and mostly sulked around town leaving her dog at home until he got some meat back on his frame.

Tamara might have recovered from this experience with grace and dignity, and gone back to her crusade against hunters, trappers, and meat-eaters in general, if she hadn't been blind-sided by yet another moral quandary. One that just might change her for good.

This quandary came in the four-legged form of a cat. A stray cat. Tamara was strolling back out to her cabin one day when she heard this thing singin' the blues in the bushes like only a lost and hungry cat can. Determined to vindicate herself for screwing up so bad with her dog, she decided to take this cat home with her and feed it.

You'll have to know a little more about Tamara to appreciate what an act of courage and contrition this really was. You see, Tamara was allergic to cats. Insanely allergic. This stemmed from something that happened to her as a little girl.

One morning as she was entering the school building to go to second grade, a stray neighborhood cat followed her in. Tamara never even knew it was there until the big heavy metal and glass door caught the cat by the tail.

The cat let out a shriek like some horrible banshee movie she'd seen on Walt Disney. Little Tamara stood stock-still. Her hair stood straight up and she turned around just as the trapped cat yanked its tail loose from the door.

What happened next plays back to Tamara only in her worst nightmares. The cat, still screaming, ran straight at Tamara, climbed up her dress, and bit her smack dab on the end of the nose. Then it leaped to the floor and careened down the hall like some hideous whirling dervish, bouncin' off lockers and screaming the whole time.

Tamara became completely and immediately allergic to cats. Doctors were never able to explain it, but from that day on, the presence of a cat would cause her to break out in itchy hives, her lips would swell up, and she'd plunge into an anxiety attack. Anxiety attacks not altogether different from the one she was having as she made her way up to this hungry stray cat in the weeds.

She was absently rubbing the tiny scar on her nose as the words never before spoken parted her already swelling lips, "Here, kitty-kitty-kitty."

You gotta hand it to Tamara. There are few of us who would do such a deed for the sake of ideals. But little did Tamara know at the time, but this cat would cause her to violate just about every value she ever had.

By the time Tamara carried the cat into the cabin, her values were already starting to wane. She'd had to walk with it in her arms for a full half mile, and with every step she could feel her lips pump one notch fatter, and a new itchy hive would spring to life somewhere under her clothes or on her face. The whole time her anxiety level was building to a fevered pitch, so as she walked through the door her big lips were quivering and tears were rolling down her blotchy cheeks.

She set the cat down with relief, but there wasn't to be any relief. No sooner had the cat's feet touched the floor when it spotted Tamara's dog Karma curled up in the corner by the woodstove. The cat arched its back, let out a painfully familiar shriek, and pounced square in the middle of the dog's back.

What happened next cannot really be described. Some things are best left to history, and dim memory. Because that's all that Tamara had left of the experience. When the dust settled, she was sitting on the floor with her legs sprawled in front of her, the chimney knocked loose from the woodstove, leaving soot on her quilted bedspread. And the apothecary jars along the drain-board counter full of her prized beans, herbs, and grains were a shambles.

All was quiet except for the faint tinkle of glass coming from a new hole in the front window. A hole about the same basic size and shape that a thin dog with a cat attached to its back might make.

Looking back on it, it wouldn't be quite clear to Tamara where the terrible thought entered her head. It might have been as she picked glass from her garbanzo beans. Maybe when she tried to brush the chimney soot from her handmade quilt. Maybe when she cut her finger taping cardboard over the broken window. Or when trying to suck on that particular finger, she was reminded of her swelled lips and realized her little cabin was awash in toxic cat hair.

Whenever it was the thought entered her head, it would be a thought she hadn't felt such conviction for since she decided to picket the Fish and Game offices for issuing moose permits. LICENSE TO KILL it said on her sign. "Kill is right," she said to herself now. She knew if she ever saw that cat again, she was going to murder it.

Tamara, of course, was only able to come to this conclusion by the sure notion that she never would see the cat again. At least not as soon as she did.

Her dog Karma came limping home about an hour after the melee and the two of them hugged each other in front of the stove, Tamara apologizing to her dog the whole time about bringing such a demon into their lives. Karma seemed to accept the apology only after being fed a double helping of Gravy Train, curling up once again for a long evening by the woodstove.

As if on cue, the demon cat appeared in the front door and let out a shriek. A shriek that sent Tamara up to the ceiling and the dog out through the cardboard that now served as a front window.

Tamara landed on her soiled quilt, facing the cat in the doorway, who stood its ground. It let out one long hollow yowl that sent goose jiggers running from Tamara's tip to her toes. It seemed to be saying, "You brought me home to feed me, so feed me."

Tamara felt compelled by this haunting cat to do its bidding, and she went to her ice chest to retrieve some cheese and raw fish scraps she'd been nursing her dog back to speed with. Hypnotically she went about her task while the cat stood in the doorway and watched her.

Tamara could barely see through her watering eyes as she laid the bowl down in the middle of the room, but as she saw the cat jump for the food, an instinct took hold of her she'd never felt before. A murderous instinct.

Slowly, gently, she eased the door shut. Then, mumbling "Nice kitty, good kitty, eat your supper now . . ." she made her way casually over to her pillow and removed the slipcover.

Tamara had learned from a lifetime of vulgar stories that the way to get rid of a cat had something to do with a burlap bag and a pond. She had a pond not fifty yards from the cabin, and a chimney-sooted pillowcase would have to do as well as a burlap bag any ol' day.

As graceful and fixated as any good predator, Tamara made her wary way behind the feeding animal. With itchy arms poised, fat lips pursed, and watery eyes dilated, Tamara pounced on her prey with the pillowcase.

It was a good shot. With the dexterity that can only be accomplished with the adrenaline rush of the attack, she scooped the cat into her bag and commenced to kneel on it so she could get the end tied shut.

She had him. A sort of mechanical will took over now. The cat got strangely quiet in the bag after only a moment's struggle, which made it easier for Tamara to slip on her boots for the short march to the pond.

When she got to the edge of the pond, Tamara did not even stop to consider. With a far-off look and a deep satisfaction, she took two big heave-ho's and sent the bagged demon cat out to its certain end.

She never looked back as she walked peacefully to the cabin. With every step she could feel some relief. She could feel her lips again, she could see clearly through dry eyes, and the itchy hives were disappearing a step at a time.

By the time she reached the front door, she felt completely herself again and was delighted to see Karma back in the cabin, happily eating what the cat didn't have time to finish.

It wouldn't be until later that night, after the lamps were turned off and she'd curled up in her blankets and relaxed with sounds of the dog's snoring, that it would all hit her. *I killed a living thing,* she thought to herself. *Me, Tamara Dupree, champion of life, protector of the innocent, conscience of a society, and a darn concerned eater . . . I* killed *something.*

She cried into her bare pillow and tried to come to grips with this. She thought back to the cold-blooded act she'd committed only hours ago. How she'd so easily trapped the helpless creature with a cunning that could only have come from somewhere deep inside her. A place she's tried to overcome all her life. She thought of the dazed and deadly walk out to the pond, and the cruel toss. She wept harder and harder at the thought of the whole terrible evening.

Then she thought of something else; something she'd forgotten. In all those vulgar stories she'd ever heard about cats and burlap bags, there was another element she'd overlooked in her fevered acts earlier that night. Rocks. You're supposed to put rocks in with the cat.

Her heart started to throb with the realization. She started to itch under the covers, and once again, right on cue, a long moanful yowl came from the front porch.

Tamara froze. Her heartbeat was screaming in her ears. Her lips puffed, her nose ran, her feet hit the floor . . . and every value she held dear fell to bits.

She grabbed the broom on the way through the door and was momentarily stunned at the scene on the porch. The cat had chewed or clawed four holes in the pillowcase and worked only its legs out. It was standing there in the dim light like a spook and screaming like a banshee in some Walt Disney movie she'd seen.

She took off after it with her broom as the cat careened through the woods like some hideous whirling dervish bouncin' off trees and screaming the whole time—like a scene in a school hallway a long time ago—with Tamara and her broom right on its tail. Swingin', and swearing, and stumblin', and reaching deep down in her heart to find the strength to get through everything that was in her way.

Fanny Olmstead, wife of Pastor Frank Olmstead of the First and Last Baptist Church, was rushed to the hospital emergency room Wednesday night after attending a public debate on evolution vs. creation. It seems Ms. Olmstead pursed her lips so hard during the evolutionist's talk that she dislocated her jaw. She was treated and released with a stern reminder from her doctor that the foot-pounds of force applied during lip pursing of fundamentalists is equivalent to that of most great white sharks.

A local youth feared drowned after falling from the family fishing boat was found hours later perched safely on a single piling left standing from the old Salmon Bay Cannery. Twelve-year-old Norman Tuttle was reported in good condition and high spirits after having spent six lonely hours in the darkness.

4

Missing Youth

NOT many things come easy to a twelve-year-old boy, but Norman didn't have much trouble falling off his dad's fishing boat. Actually, he was fairly well made for the stunt. Having grown over six inches in the past eight months, his arms and legs were stretched into territory he was not entirely familiar with. His misplaced head bore the lumps and scuffs of many poorly judged doorframes and sudden moves on deck. Norman was a klutz. It was only temporary, his mother had assured him, but this offered little consolation at the moment of contact with the black icy waters of Southeast Alaska. A contact which, in itself, was a study in awkwardness.

Norman had come out on deck to "answer nature's call," as they say. He propped his legs against the low boat rail in the dark with his too-long shins, and his feet simply went out from under him. His brief moment in midair was spent desperately trying to put himself away rather than concentrating on any graceful form of entry. If you've ever felt the chill of Alaskan waters, you might better understand his choice of subject on the way in, and let's face it, there is just no pretty way to fall off of a fishing boat.

Landing face first, mouth open, is also no way to prepare oneself for the next step. Namely, hollering for help. During what seemed like the eternity it took for Norman to clear the saltwater from his throat enough to scream for help, he watched as the boat chugged steadily away in the darkness.

"DAAAAD!

"DAAAAAAAD!!

"UNCLE STU!"

Norman could still feel the throb of the propeller pulsing against his body.

"DAAAD! WAIT! DAAAD, Dad, oh no, oh God."

Norman tried swimming after the boat, stopped once to slip out of his deck shoes, and when he looked back up, he'd lost sight of the single white stern light. He could still hear the prop in the water, but it had no direction. Nothing had direction. The overcast sky was black, the water was black, the shoreline that they'd been following couldn't be far off, but it could have been not-far-off any way he pointed.

Twelve is an uncomfortable age to be in a situation like this. Too old to cry, too young to swear, without even much of a life to have flash past. Norman was stunned, but only temporarily. There's a call for action built into all of us, no matter how old, that often comes into play at these times. This is our God-given ability to panic, and Norman proceeded to do exactly that.

Clawing at the water like a drowning man (and not being too far out of character), Norman thrashed his way toward what he knew must be the direction of shore. Panic not lending itself to well-thought-out scenarios, it never occurred to Norman he might be swimming out to sea. Which was just as well, because he wasn't.

As he made his way along, his adrenaline calmed and his wasteful strokes became long and even. He knew he was moving at a good pace now. As he started to think again, the first thing he thought was, *Boy, it's cold*. He was already losing feeling in his legs, and his throat was getting a knot in it like he'd just eaten ice cream too fast. *I'm going to freeze to death, and die,* he thought. Then he laughed, and gulped a mouthful of water in the process. *You dummy,* of course *if you freeze to death you die,* and he laughed again. The cold was taking its toll on Norman's mental process, and just as he was about to let it all go while listening to his own garbled laugh through the rhythm of his stroking arms, he heard, "BONK!" Then he felt it.

"Ouch," he said, grabbing his forehead.

Although Norman would later be teased that only he could bump his head in the wide ocean, it was the most welcome goose egg he'd ever awarded himself, or ever likely to. Reaching his arms out in front of him, he felt the exquisite scaly surface of a barnacle-covered piling.

It was standing straight up and down in the water, and after wrapping himself around it in welcome embrace, he realized that it wasn't floating. The piling was attached to Earth, Norman was attached to the piling, and for a minute or two life seemed good again. He cried with relief at the notion he'd swam in the right direction.

Norman's flow of thought was getting pretty sticky by this point, so it took a while for it to sink in that he was still going to "freeze to death, and die," even if he was in the company of several hundred well-grounded barnacles. Venturing a look up the piling to see what it might be attached to, he saw that it was, in fact, attached to thin air. Only inches above his head it stopped short of any expectations of holding up a building, and far short of salvation.

Reaching up, he felt the flat top of the piling, and with considerable grunting managed to haul his own wet self onto it. While draped over the top belly down, Norman's bladder reminded him he had not finished the business he'd went out on deck for in the first place. It felt warm—secretly wonderful—and he cried again at the thought of it.

The damp late-summer air also felt warm compared to the water, and although Norman was shivering uncontrollably, he managed to sit up straight on the piling and let the feeling come back to his legs.

If it had been light enough for anyone to see him, Norman would have been a sorry sight. A gangly, quivering creature swaddled in wool and mounted on a stick like some child's toy waiting to be brought to life. If you pulled a string at the bottom, he might raise up and wave, or dispense a candy.

But he didn't rise, wave, produce candy, or any other such thing. Norman just sat—shook, and worried. He knew that his dad and Uncle Stu hadn't seen him go out on deck. They were in the pilot house drinking coffee and gabbing like they always did at the end of a trip. Norman was back in his bunk looking at dirty magazines, as he always did at the end of a trip. Unless one of them decided to go back and look in on him, they wouldn't know he was gone until they got to town, which was still hours away. They wouldn't look in on him. Norman knew that for sure.

Norman was mostly tolerated and largely ignored on the boat. His dad and Uncle Stu had fished together since they were kids. They always did the same things, they always said the same things, and a bashful boy who couldn't walk a straight line on land or sea did not fit into their routine. It was his mother's idea to send him along on these summer trips. "It will be good for Norman," she said.

"It will be good for Norman. It will be good for Norman, but what is Norman good for?" his dad had snapped back to her. Norman was not supposed to hear that, but like most things you're not supposed to hear, that's what stuck in his head.

It was still stuck in his head as he sat on his piling in the dark. *What is Norman good for? What is Norman good for?* He wrapped his arms as far around himself as he could and tried to think of two things he was good for.

He was good for chopping bait, but then he was

always cutting holes in his gloves, and that made his dad mad. "Those things cost money, ya know," he'd say, and toss Norman a fresh pair that he always managed to fumble and drop.

He was good for coiling line, he thought. That's about the only other thing they ever let him do. But then a lot of the lines he coiled went off the deck in a big tangled wad when they tried to make a set. "When you going to learn to turn a coil, Norman?" his dad would say. "Fixing your messes takes time. Time is money, Norman."

Norman settled on the fact that maybe he was only good for costing money. And here he was doing it again. He fell off the boat, and his dad would have to turn around to come find him. It never occurred to Norman that his dad would be anything but angry about this. He pictured him pulling up on the boat to rescue him. His face red, his head shaking. He'd pull him on board without a word then mumble on his way back to the pilot house, "Try to stay with us this time, all right?"

Norman decided he hated his father, and cursed him out loud to the dark water. The sound of his own voice startled him, and he looked around. The tide was going out. His stocking feet were a good four feet from the water, when just a while ago they were nearly touching it. The sensation almost made him fall over, and he became panicky with the realization that the tide had probably another twenty feet to go before it ebbed.

Norman was terrified of high places. His dad had sent him up the mast once to replace a fitting. He only got halfway before he had to stop. He clung to the rigging like a little bear and cried until Uncle Stu climbed up to get him. His dad never said a word. Just stood there with that red face and shaking head.

That's how he'll find me, Norman thought. *Shaking, and crying, and holding on to this piling.* Norman wanted to fall in the water and simply float away. But the thought of it made him even colder. His shivering had become convulsive, and it was likely he would knock himself back in the water with his own quaking and twitching.

"I've *got* to stop shaking," he said out loud, and he heard his dad in his voice. It suddenly sounded unavoidable.

"I'm *going* to stop shaking," he said louder. He liked the sound of it, and tried different ways of putting it. "I'm going to *stop* shaking." "*I'm* going to stop *shaking*!" "*I'M GONNA STOP SHAKING,*" he yelled into the night, and listened as the sound evaporated from his ears.

When all was quiet again, he became aware of himself. His hands were on his hips. He was sitting tall and firm. And he wasn't shaking.

"Well, I'll be," he said, now enjoying the company of his own voice. "It worked." He smiled and did a little dance with his shoulders like he'd just shot a tin can out of the air. A lucky shot, sure, but let's take *some* credit.

"Okay everybody, listen up!" Norman assumed an admiral's posture and swung his head from side to side so all of nothing could hear it. "I'm gonna sit on top of this pole, I'm not gonna shake, I'm not going to fall in the water, I'm not going to cry, and I'm not going to do it all night long if I have to." He snapped his head forward in his best *so there* way and thought of other things to say.

"Oh yeah, and when my dad gets here I'm going to sit this pole like it's never been sat. It's going to be, 'Look at Norman. That boy can sit a pole, now, can't he?' You bet I can, ol' man. This is Norman speaking. The boat fallin'-offest, cold water swimmin'est, pole-sittin'est little clod you ever saw."

He paused for a long time. He'd never heard his voice used with such conviction before. It lent an importance to what he was saying, and Norman felt compelled to say important things.

"I been doing some thinking up here on this pole, ol' man." Norman posed like a thinker, fist on chin.

"An' I been thinking none of this would've happened if you paid a little more attention to what was going on around here."

What came into his mind to say next brought a lump to his throat, so he stopped, shook it off, and yelled even louder, "None of this would have happened if you paid a little more attention to . . . *me!*" He let the word ring in the air then repeated it softly with a hand on his chest, "Me."

The tears came again, and he couldn't stop them. They leaked from his clenched eyes and were wiped clear by his clenched fists. "DAMN YOU!" he screamed, opened his eyes, and almost fell off the piling.

The water was now better than twelve feet below him. It made him dizzy, and he groped the empty air for something to hold on to. Finding nothing, he swayed and clasped his legs as if to keep them there. "I'm-not-going-to-fall-in-the-water," he said deliberately. "You left me here, and I'm-going-to-sit-right-here." And sit he did.

He might have sat there all night. He might have sat there all the next day, too, if he had to, but he didn't. No sooner had he assembled and locked himself into his permanent sitting position—hands on knees, head straight, eyes forward—when he saw the searchlight come around the point. It was his dad and Uncle Stu. He could hear them.

"Nooorrman."

That was Uncle Stu, thought Norman.

"Normy!"

That was Dad.

Norman didn't feel like hollering anything just yet. *Let them look a minute or two more,* he thought. Then it struck him. *Normy?* His dad hadn't called him that in years. Not since he was a little kid wrestling on the living room rug. Not since Dad taught him how to ride a bike. *Normy.* Norman's string was pulled.

"HERE, DAD, I'M OVER HERE!" Norman raised up and waved his arms in the air just as the searchlight met his eyes. He heard the engine roar and saw the boat swing toward him. His dad was on the bow holding the light.

"Normy, are you all right?" His dad's voice sounded odd. Was he mad? No, Norman knew too well what he sounded like when he was mad. It was something else. Worry? Relief? . . . Something. The sound of it washed over Norman like a warm wind.

"Yes, of course," Norman said, "I'm okay, Dad." He could hear his dad talking to Uncle Stu at the wheel.

"Easy, easy now. Don't hit the piling. Easy, Stu! Darn it! You'll knock him off of there. Norm, can you climb down?"

"You bet." It seemed that "Norm" could, in fact, do things that Norman couldn't. Forgetting his fear of high places, he shinnied down the piling and stepped gingerly onto the deck. His knees started to buckle, but he stopped them, and let them quake for a second or two. Then he straightened up to look his dad in the face for the first time.

When Norman saw the tears come to his father's eyes, he had to look away. When he felt the big arms come around him, he stiffened, but the arms stayed.

"Oh Normy, Normy," his father was saying in his ear. "I thought I'd lost you."

Norman just stood and cried. He took his father's warmth and sound and smell, and wrapped it around himself like the blanket Uncle Stu was pulling over his shoulders.

His dad gave one last big pull and stepped back, wiping at his own tears—curious about them, and surprised.

Norman took one step back, tripped over the hatch cover and fell into the full hold of fish. His dad and Uncle Stu lunged to catch him but only got the blanket. As Norman lay on his back looking up at their terrified faces, he felt a flush of blood coming to his cheeks, as it did every time he let his father down. His dad's look of terror melted away and his head began to move back and forth. That familiar shaking head. Familiar, but changed. In place of the scowling red face was a face adorned with a smile. A smile as wide and warm and full of promise as that hold was full of fish.

5

Tamara and Ed

HOW Ed Flannigan and Tamara Dupree got together is a mystery to almost everybody. Ed, a reforming roughneck, and Tamara, champion of the new age, were an unlikely couple. But recent events in each of their lives make it not so unbelievable. Ed had a brush with mysticism, Tamara a collision with murder.

It was about three weeks ago Saturday Ed was driving around by himself on Far Road, as he's been known to do lately, just thinking, dreaming, and admiring the countryside, when he spotted Tamara coming out of the bushes with a crazed look on her face, dragging a broken broomstick.

He knew Tamara only slightly, but well enough to see she didn't look herself, so he stopped to see what the matter was.

The matter was, but he didn't know it yet, that she'd just single-handedly beat the life out of a stray cat who had spent the better part of that day terrorizing her and her dog.

Had he known, he never would have said what he did as she stood there in the failing light, dazed and determined not to talk.

"Whatsa matter? Cat gotcher tongue?"

Ed was still standing there with that irritating smirk men get on their faces after they think they've said something clever, when Tamara swatted him alongside of the head with her broom handle. She was rared back to have another go at him when Ed jumped forward and got both his arms around her.

Ed was a good-sized man, and thrash and kick as she might, Tamara couldn't get free. Pretty soon she relaxed, and Ed felt her sobs start to come about the time the broomstick hit the road.

He stopped *holding* her, and just *held* her for a long time. He didn't know what he was doing, or why, but it seemed important at the moment. Later, all he would remember of this whole encounter was the way her hair smelled.

They spent most all the rest of that long night in Tamara's cabin. Drinking herbal tea and talking. Tamara told Ed all about her insane allergy to cats and what had prompted her to murder this poor stray in cold blood. How the cat had attacked her dog, wrecked her house, soiled her bed. How she'd tried to drown it in the pond in a pillowcase, only to have it escape and come back again. Finally, how she'd chased it down in the woods with her broom and beat the bejeezus out of it in the bushes just before Ed found her.

Ed didn't entirely understand how a vegetarian activist and dedicated animal protectionist could be driven to such a deed, but he listened, sipped his tea, and they both laughed—just a little.

Ed told Tamara about how he got his nickname, "Ed Again." How he was starting to suspect that there was more to life than huntin' moose, hittin' softballs, and bangin' around all day in a State Highway Department road grader. How he'd been reading some "books 'n' stuff," as he put it, on some "stuff" this mystic channeler had told him about. This "sensitivity stuff." How he didn't know just what all this was about yet, but that's what he was cruising around on Far Road lookin' for when he saw Tamara.

Tamara smiled, took Ed's cup, and told him he'd better get home to his family before the sun came up. Ed and Tamara parted company with that delicious and dangerous feeling of having shared secrets with a new friend.

Ed's trouble started before he even got home. Emily had begun to worry about him around one in the morning. That's about as late as Ed ever stayed out on his poker night, no matter how well the game was going. And in the last few months, since Ed's strange and gentle behavior, he was more likely to be in by ten. She called her best friend Kirsten Storbock, whose husband Stormy was Ed's best friend, to see if she'd heard anything of the boys.

What she'd heard was more than a little upsetting. Not only had Stormy been home for over an hour, but he'd mentioned seeing Ed's truck parked along Far Road by Tamara Dupree's little cabin.

Emily's whole world came crashing in on her. She sat down on the couch white-lipped and thought the whole terrible thing through. The past few months flashed before her. It was just like she'd seen on *Donahue*. Wives can tell if their men are having affairs by a few simple observations. First they do things they've never done before. Emily thought of the wind chime Ed got her for their anniversary last month. The first anniversary he'd remembered in eight years of marriage.

Donahue also warned about husbands coming home with unfamiliar vocabularies. Emily thought of how Ed had hung the wind chime outside their bedroom window. Said they reminded him of little faerie voices in the night.

She'd laughed about it then, and so did Ed, but now she thought, *Faerie voices? Ed Flannigan, my Ed Flannigan, using the term faerie in anything that wasn't a bad joke?* Oh, she felt so stupid.

Erratic changes in behavior. That was another warning sign. She thought clearly of how just a month ago Ed had given up a moose-hunting trip with Stormy so he could go shopping with Emily and the kids in Anchorage. How she suddenly seemed so attractive to Ed, and how tender he'd been becoming after the children had gone to bed. Just as she was about to fall in love again with her own husband . . . this.

Ed wouldn't know for a long time what mental process had gone on in Emily's head, but when he drove into the driveway of the duplex, he saw the wagon was gone and the lights were blazing in the house. The seedy pre-dawn sky was depressing enough, but not near as depressing as what he found inside.

All his Willie Nelson tapes were pulled apart and strung around the living room. His bag of "don't touch 'em these are Dad's" Doritos was in the sink, made into a sickly goo with his last four beers.

He poked his head into the kids' rooms upstairs and was not surprised to see them gone. In his and Emily's room he saw the closet flung open and the dresser drawers pulled out and ravaged. Then he turned around and saw the most depressing sight of all.

Fastened to the wall was one of only three things he'd ever asked Emily not to touch; his first edition 1987 Ducks Unlimited poster he won at the Firemen's raffle last fall. It had a long message written on it in Magic Marker, but Ed hadn't gotten to that yet because what the poster was attached to the wall with was one of the other things he'd asked Emily never to touch. His prized four-power Leupold hunting scope, driven through the poster and into the Sheetrock apparently by his six-hundred-dollar Smith & Wesson target pistol with the hand-carved cherry grip: the third and final thing he'd ever asked her not to touch. It laid on the carpet below the message, with the snot beat out of it. Ed sunk to his knees to hold it, then looked up to read a little note from his wife.

"Dear Granola Lips," it started.

Uh-oh, thought Ed. *I probably should have called.*

> *I hope you and your hairy-legged sweet-heart had a good time tonight while I laid in bed worried sick about you. But did I have anything to worry about? Nooooooo, you were being well-tended by your organically grown chicken out the road. I'm heading north with the kids and dogs. Tell your little friend that I intend running over every small animal I see along the way.*
>
> > *Emily*

Ed called Emily's sister in Anchorage to see if she was there yet. Her sister hung up on him.

At least I know they got there safe and sound, thought Ed as he lay back on his bed, listened to the wind chimes dinging in the window, and passed out with confusion.

It was a long week for Ed Flannigan. Every time he tried to call Emily, they'd hang up on him. He tried to get off work to go talk to her, but they had him working overtime cleaning out culverts along the highway. Getting ready for the big fall rains.

Every night Ed would come home only to reread the terse and undeserved message from his wife. He wiled away the hours trying to spool his Willie Nelson tapes back on the cassettes with a pencil eraser. They all ended up twisted, and none of them would play again.

Ed was getting mad. He carried it around in him

all day and slept with it every night. A knot in his stomach and a crease across his forehead. It gave him a headache. Really, the only reprieve he ever got was when he'd spot Tamara Dupree coming or going with her dog.

First he'd feel anxious and guilty, then he'd feel sorta giddy. Almost boyish. His face would flush and he'd remember what her hair smelled like and the glint of her deep blue eyes as she sat across the oil lamp from him that one long night.

Then one morning Ed woke up, looked at his Ducks Unlimited poster stuck to the wall with his four-hundred-dollar scope, and thought, *The hell with it. If I'm going to be in this much trouble, I might as well do something to deserve it*. He decided right then and there to ask Tamara Dupree out on a date.

Fortunately, and because it moves the story right along, Ed got his opportunity that very Saturday. He was in town headin' to the beer store when he spotted that skinny dog of Tamara's tied up in front of the Natural Food Coop. Ed pulled up before he could have any second thoughts and wandered inside.

It was his first time inside the place, and he poked around the aisles lined with bulk-grain bins, trail mix, and unfamiliar packaged foods. Finally he spotted what he took for malted-milk balls and measured out a couple handfuls in a bag.

Nearly to his relief, he never saw Tamara in the store, but when he got outside she was there leaning against his truck, drinking on a juice can and smiling sort of sadly at him. "I'm sorry about your wife," she said.

"How'd you know?" Ed faced her, taken again with those blue eyes.

"Small town." Tamara shrugged. "What are you going to do?"

Ed looked at Tamara for a long while, then to kill some more time he opened up his bag and put a candy in his mouth. He was about to speak when a pained look came across his face and he spit a spray of chewed candy on the ground.

"What *is* that stuff?" he said, wiping his tongue off with his shirt-sleeve.

"Carob balls," Tamara said, laughing and offering a drink of her juice.

"God, I thought they was milk balls," he said, looking into his bag. "Why do they even bother with these?"

Tamara didn't answer, she just stood there smiling while Ed took a swig of juice, made another face, and handed it back to her.

Before a pall of silence could drift back between them, Ed blurted out the single intention he'd arrived with.

"Wanna go bowling?"

Tamara started laughing again, only harder. Ed watched with frustration and some embarrassment as she giggled her way through untying her dog, gave him one long gorgeous wet-eyed look, and started to walk away. Ed didn't know what to do. What to say. He just stood there and watched her make her way across the parking lot. His heart began to settle into resignation just as she turned around and said, "Why don't you just come out to the cabin. We'll talk some more."

Ed was nervous. This wasn't a new sensation for him, but definitely an uncommon one. All his life he'd been tall, good-looking, agile, and competent. He'd had very little cause for nervousness in anything he'd ever done, but then he had to admit, he hadn't done all that much either.

He took a shower and dressed. Thought the better of his choice and dressed again. He splashed on a bunch of Old Spice, thought better of that too, and took another shower.

By the time he reached Far Road in his truck, it was already dark. There was a light breeze blowing and he could hear the pie tins clanking around Tamara's garden in the direction of the light coming from her cabin window.

"Time to take those pie tins down now that the

garden's in," Ed said as an opener on his way in.

"I will," Tamara said. "Eventually. The sound kind of keeps me company out here."

"Don't see how a woman like you would have much trouble keeping company," Ed said back, and it was the perfect launch for a perfect conversation that lasted, once again, the whole night through.

Tamara talked of her causes and convictions and how it got in the way of her relationships sometimes. She talked about old boyfriends. Ed talked about Emily and the kids. They sipped mineral water and told weird-parent stories. They laughed at their childhoods and laughed at themselves. Tamara showed Ed books she admired and lent him a few. She laughed at his cynical and playful observations: "I suppose if the French didn't bottle and sell this spring water to Americans, it'd just be running all over the ground someplace."

The morning drew close, and so did they. Leaning over the wooden table, in the light of the oil lamp they talked on and on, eye to eye, heart to heart, until they got too ringy from lack of sleep to say anything new.

"You'd better go home now, Ed," she said. Ed got up from the table not disappointed.

They hugged each other in the doorway as friends would, but the smell of Tamara's hair made Ed feel a little guilty. He blushed—and she blushed—and they said good night.

That morning as the sky began to widen with that depressing predawn light, Ed Flannigan and Tamara Dupree lay in their respective beds, wide awake. A brisk fall wind made its way the six miles from Tamara's cabin to Ed's duplex.

Tamara laid in bed listening to the cheap sound of pie tins banging in the breeze. Ed listened to his wind chimes like faeries in the woods. The two sounds together would be just noise. Like the competing battle drums of rival armies. Like dead branches on church bells. Like the sound of the wrong people falling in love.

———— • ————

The End of the Road Rotary Club delivered a fat $200 check to the Volunteer Fire Department to go toward the new pumper truck. They raised the money through their recyclable can bin on Main Street. The donation along with the $900 raised during the End of the Road Days Bazaar brings us within $27,500 of the goal.

It's raining sideways on the ridge, northways down the river, and all over town. The creeks are rising, the snow line is creeping down the mountainside, and the forecast calls for more of the same. If not worse.

The state troopers remind us that running into moose on the highway is a really bad idea, and to keep an eye peeled for our goofy forest friends when driving.

———— • ————

6

Argus
and Bud

THERE was an interesting picture on the front page of the local paper this week. It featured our very own Argus Winslow with his mouth wide open, his face flushed, and his hair sticking straight up in the air. The caption read, "Local man unhurt after one-car accident." The photo credit went to Bud Koenig. Not a big deal really, but there's a funny little history to these two guys, Bud and Argus, that makes that picture worth a little more than it might to the casual observer.

Argus Winslow and Bud Koenig have an odd association. Nobody around here can quite figure out what goes on there. They've known each other nearly forty years. They both homesteaded here about the same time, and in many ways are a lot alike; hardworkin' old-timers who share a love for their country, the countryside, irreverence, and an occasional bump of cheap whiskey. They both have that square-backed countenance and even stride of men who've worked hard all their lives. The skin of their hands is scarred leather gone gray by years of dirt, grease, blood, and bad deals.

You'd think they'd get along like a couple thieves, but that's not the case. They report to hate each other's guts and nobody's quite sure why.

After overhearing enough of their marathon arguments, it appears that there is an old debt between them in the amount of about five hundred dollars. It's not clear who owes whom, or even if the men themselves are certain anymore. Regardless, they use this as a reason to disagree on just about everything except irreverence and cheap whiskey.

Argus is by far the more colorful of the two men, and most verbal as well. He owns the junkyard here in town and enjoys playing the role of his own junkyard dog. He's crotchety, opinionated, and stubborn as an old rusted bolt. He refuses to dicker price with his junk customers, which you think would not be a good posture to take in that particular business, but he gets away with it.

Someone might ask him what he wants for an old water heater leaned up against the shop. "Twenty dollars," he'll say, and this is where he usually turns his head and spits tobacco juice on something. "Will you take ten dollars?" the uninitiated customer might ask. "Sure I'll take ten dollars, but not for that water heater, you weasel-lipped little dipstick, I just told you twenty."

Argus loses a lot of his new customers like this, but had the person gone ahead and bought the water heater, he would have discovered that it was indeed worth the twenty bucks. Argus has a keen sense of the market value of every piece of junk in his yard, and he's always right. Just ask him.

The other thing that works against Argus on a business level is his language. He never cusses, in fact he's known to take great exception to profanity, sometimes violent exception if there is a woman present. No, Argus never swears, he just always sounds like he does. He has a way of stringing biting little nonsense words together that can offend the sensitivities of even the most seasoned bystander before they realize what he said. "Weasel-lipped dipstick" is one of his favorites, usually reserved for Bud. "Soggy toast on two legs." "Rachet-brained she-goat." Argus's opinions of other people are made painfully and colorfully clear. He has a lot of "cornstarched" difficulties in his life, as in "that cornstarched truck of mine don't run," and most of his adversaries come in the form of "bags"; sleaze-bag, slime-bag, grease-bags, and so on.

Oddly enough, underneath all this bluff and bluster is a heart of solid gold. He likes to scare the bejeezus out of the kids who hang around the junkyard, but then pretends not to know when they come to sell him his own scrap metal that they've taken from the back of the yard where the fence is broken down.

Argus can identify every little piece of wood or metal on the place, including date of acquisition, who brought it, where it was, and, of course, what it's worth. He likes to see the kids thinkin' they're gettin' away with somethin' until he figures out the best way to trap 'em and teach 'em a lesson.

Always by his side is his dog Barney, who adores Argus. Argus insists that Barney is a coyote to anyone who cares, which is another of his eccentric flukes because Barney is clearly a black Labrador retriever. No doubt it's Argus's way of covering up any affection he might accidentally reveal in regards to poor Barney.

Argus is famous and loved for giving out his homemade corn biscuits he always has in a bag nearby, even though no one other than Bud Koenig has had the guts to tell him how terrible they are. "Worse things ever invented," says Bud. "I think he gives 'em out to people just to watch 'em suffer through one."

Bud Koenig is a fairly gentle soul in comparison to Argus, but most people are. Bud is a semiretired logger who runs the local saw shop. He's mostly known for being a trouble faller. That is, he's the guy everybody calls when they gotta drop a tree between the garage and the outhouse, or keep a bad leaner out of the powerlines. It's said that you can place a wooden stake anywhere around any tree and Bud can drive the stake with the fallen trunk.

Bud always carries a camera with him to take the before and after pictures of his trouble trees, and his saw shop is papered with photos of him standing on this tree next to that house, that tree next to this high-voltage vault, and whatnot. Some of his falls are actually spectator events, and his most famous ability is being able to make a leaning tree turn around on its stump and fall the other way. Nobody's ever figured out how he does it, and Argus accuses him of being a "cornstarched chain-saw witch," which doesn't quite hide his admiration for Bud's skills.

So anyway, that's Argus and Bud in a nutshell, and might better explain how Argus ended up on the front page of the paper after he drove off into the ditch last week.

Ya see, Argus was on his way out to the Storbock place to pick up some old barbed wire when a moose jumped in front of his truck. Argus, knowin' that running into a moose is usually a losing proposition, veered off the side of the road and wound up upside down in the tall grass. Luckily, Argus is a religious seat-belt wearer, after many of these such road moose encounters, so he wasn't hurt. Just sorta stunned, more'n a little angry, and left hangin' upside down in the cab with Barney standing on the ceiling and licking his face.

"Get the French dip away from me, ya corn-starched coyote," he was yellin' just about the time Bud Koenig happened upon the scene. Bud was on his way back from a trouble fall out the road, and saw Argus's pickup in the ditch with one wheel still turning.

Bud could hear by the tone of Argus's voice that he wasn't hurt, so he took his sweet time gathering up his camera and saunterin' down to the wreck. "Hey, Winslow," he yelled just about the time Argus spotted him comin', "there's a thousand-dollar fine for litterin' in this state. Oughta keep your junk outta the ditches."

"Just my cornstarched luck," grumbled Argus. "Coulda broke my neck and had it done with, now I gotta hang here and listen to your half-baked wit."

"Don't talk to me about half-baked. I told ya if you didn't stop eatin' them things you pass off as biscuits, that you were gonna get top heavy and tip over one day."

"Cut it out and unhook me, Koenig. All the blood's goin' to my head, and the cornstarched buckle's stuck on this rig." Argus was wigglin' around in his harness, but with all his weight against the belt catch, he couldn't spring it loose.

Bud just squatted down beside the window and shook his head. "Boy, I dunno, Argus. You're not supposed to mess with accident victims until the ambulance gets here. Hate to get myself in a lawsuit over this."

"Oh, give it up, Koenig. You know I ain't hurt, just danglin'. Hurry up and let me loose before my eyeballs bug out."

"I dunno, Winslow. Looks kinda good on you. Maybe I oughta get a picture of this. Remind you one day what you look like with somethin' other'n air in your head."

Argus's eyes nearly did bug out at the sound of this, and just as he opened his mouth to give Bud a piece of his throbbing mind, Bud snapped the picture, reached in—popped the seat belt loose, and ran for the hills.

It wasn't until he got the film back from the drugstore a few days later that Bud figured he really had somethin'. Everybody in town was more'n a little familiar with Argus's temper, and if a person turned the upside-down Argus right side up, there couldn't have been a more poetic portrait of the man.

Fritz down at the paper wouldn't normally have run a shot like that on his front page, but his only other option that week was a picture of the Rotary Club handing over a commemorative check for two hundred dollars to the fire chief toward the new pumper truck. It seemed to Fritz he'd run a similar shot of the Elks

Club handing over a bowling trophy to the Lame Moose Saloon team not long ago, and decided some variety was in order.

It'll sell papers, thought Fritz, *but it's sure gonna raise hell with Argus.*

When the papers came out on Thursday, everybody in town thought the same thing. There was sort of a hush over the community as it waited for Argus to come erupting out of his junkyard and head straight for Bud's saw shop with murderous intent. Chief of Police Peter Bindel even stationed himself diplomatically along the flight path just in case a little peacekeeping might be in order.

No one would have been alarmed at all, though, had they known just a little more about Bud Koenig and Argus Winslow. At that very moment while the town laid in wait, Bud was in his shop chuckling to himself and pasting his front-page photo alongside the cash register. He looked into the bulging eyes of his old friend and said out loud, "Argus Winchester Winslow, you are a piece of work."

Argus Winchester Winslow sat in his aluminum house trailer not entirely discernable from the rest of his junkyard and held the front page of the paper on his lap. The paper jumped up and down with the laughter coming from deep inside his big belly.

"Barney," he said to the dog, who didn't care. "That cornstarched character Bud Koenig cracks me up."

The two men went about their separate days chuckling mostly to themselves and admiring one another from afar—like friends do.

A lot of residents are getting ready for their annual Hawaiian vacations by laying around the tanning salons. You better get your name on the appointment list if you're headed to the tropics. Although pretanning is not required, it certainly is the polite thing to do, as anyone who's seen an Alaskan's first day on the beach will agree. There is so little pigment in an Alaskan's skin that many of us don't even cast shadows on the sand until after the first week. So give the other tourists a break, and get a little color before you go.

Fourth grader Stanley Bindel won the Young Buck's Science Fair Blue Ribbon for his project titled, "Why Plants Need Water." When asked by the judges about his conclusions, the young scientist replied, "Because if you don't water your plants, they die." Second-place prize went to Stanley's little sister Nicole, who brought a hamster.

7

Tamara and Ed Go Bowling

YOU couldn't actually say that a hush descended over the bowling alley when Ed Flannigan and Tamara Dupree walked through the door. But it did get about as quiet as a bowling alley can.

Tamara and Ed were just about the oddest alliance ever assembled. Tamara was dressed in an all-natural-fiber hand-woven Mexican poncho, oversized muslin peasant blouse, jeans, and hiking boots. Her hair was pulled tight around her head and trailed down her back in a long braid. She carried a woven-basket handbag about the size of a seat cover in a small truck.

She walked ahead of Ed, who had on his Bud's Saw and Chain league bowling shirt, a Caterpillar baseball cap, and personalized bowling bag with LUCKY EDDIE written down both sides of it in sparkle paint. About all they had in common, to look at them, was blue jeans and boots, and the evening would prove that to be the case.

Tamara and Ed's little fling was only a week old,

and everybody in the place was talking behind their hands and giggling into their beers as the two made their way down to lane three with their shoes.

Their short week as friends was precipitated by a traumatic and homicidal experience with a cat on Tamara's part coinciding with a momentary rift in Ed's marriage to Emily. Emily was gone to Anchorage, cooling her heels with the kids, while Ed and Tamara had spent a luscious week of long evenings talking over tea at Tamara's little cabin, getting to know each other and filling the hole that each of them had in their lives at the moment.

This night, though, when Ed went out to the cabin for another long and, I don't mind telling you, *innocent* conversation, Ed had a better idea.

"Listen, Tamara," he said over the first cup of tea, "I'm always out here drinking your herbal tea, listening to your twinkle music, and talking about your shelf of books. Why don't we do something on my territory tonight."

It was that notion that found our pair lacing up bowling shoes on lane number three and attracting more attention to themselves than was comfortable, or deserved.

Ed's good buddy Stormy Storbock was on the next lane with a few of the boys, pretending to be absorbed in the scoring of their series. Stormy and his wife Kirsten were Ed and Emily's best friends, and if Ed was feeling awkward, Stormy was becoming downright stricken.

Stormy went up to the snack counter for a pair of long-neck beers and darned near ran right into Ed when he turned around.

"Couple'a those brewskies would hit the ol' spot, wouldn't they, Stormbocker?" Ed was trying to sound offhand, like things were as they should be, but his exuberance gave him away.

Stormy brushed by Ed and said with knives in his voice, "Get your act together, Flannigan."

Ed said after him, "She's just a friend, Stormy."

But Stormy had already reentered the din and either didn't or wouldn't hear him.

Ed got a pair of beers himself and returned to Tamara and lane three, already feeling a little uneasy with the evening. Tamara didn't help his uneasiness much by refusing the beer and reaching into her seat-cover purse to pull out a jug of papaya juice. Then she began proudly peeling an avocado on the scoring table with her Swiss army knife.

"Want some?" she offered.

"Thanks," Ed said, now glad he had the two beers to himself, "no."

Showing Tamara how to bowl was an equally awkward and annoying experience for Ed, mostly because Stormy and the guys on lane four were constantly stealing glances, glares, and leers every time Tamara walked up for another try. As is typical with almost any novice bowler, Tamara's first half a dozen tries were gutter balls.

"No-no," Ed would say patiently. "If you throw with your right hand, you lead with your right foot." "Don't look at your feet, look at the pins. Aim just to the side of the head pin." "Tamara, God, you don't even have your thumb in the ball. Whatsa matter with you?"

"I'm afraid it'll tear it off," Tamara said, getting a little exasperated herself.

"It's not going to tear off your thumb. Just be sure to let go of it."

Tamara stuck her thumb in the hole of the ball and was so afraid of getting it stuck that on the next throw she let go on the back swing and cracked Ed square in the left shinbone.

Stormy and the gang next door howled and blew beer while Ed just winced and said quietly to Tamara, "You can hold onto it just a little bit longer than that."

Now self-conscious in the other direction, Tamara's next ball flew down the lane like a meteor over Texas, describing a perfect arc to mid-alley and crashing down to Earth with such a bang that even Larry behind the snack counter looked up. That says something because if you'd worked in a bowling-alley environment for as long as Larry has, you wouldn't be looking up at just any ol' bump in the night.

"Better get that ball away from her before she wrecks the place and kills us all," Stormy managed to yell over the cackles coming from lane four

I need more beer, Ed thought to himself as he left for the snack bar.

As for Tamara, she'd had just about enough ridicule for one night. She turned to the boys next door with her arms folded across her chest and gave one of those looks that only a woman of Tamara's particular strength of character could deliver. One of those *you mess with me one more time and I'm going to be on you like laser beams through pudding pops* looks. You know the kind. They work.

When Ed got back with his *three* fresh beers, things were pretty quiet on ol' number four and Tamara was busying herself at the scoring table making what looked to be a salad sandwich.

"Oh, darn it," she said, reaching into the big bag all the way up to her shoulder. "I forgot to bring my wheat-grass paste."

Ed frisked himself in mock concern. "Boy, I'm fresh out too."

Tamara ignored this and without looking up offered again. "Want some?"

"Naw, thanks. I got a chili dog comin'." Ed walked toward the ball return. "You wanna try your hand at this again?"

"I'll eat first. You go ahead, and I'll watch. Maybe I'll see what I'm doing wrong." Tamara sat back in her chair while Ed stood concentrating on the approach.

His first ball flew down the lane, came unnervingly close to the gutter, hooked back and blew all ten pins away. Tamara raised her eyebrows, and Ed looked over at Stormy, who looked away just in time. Ed took another big pull from his beer while he waited for his ball and set up for another one.

An instant replay of his first shot, Ed got his second strike. When he went up to take his third, Stormy Storbock pulled up even with him in the next lane. Only incidentally the two strained friends slid their toes to the foul line together and their balls raced down the lane together, forming a neat and simultaneous pair of strikes.

The men never looked at each other or anybody else as they dried their hands over the blower and waited for their balls. Ed's came up first so he used up the difference by gulping down the rest of a beer and starting on another.

Again the two men set up together, released together, and blew another twenty pins into chaos. Ed didn't even see Tamara gawking at him in astonishment. Stormy couldn't hear the rest of the boys hooting and encouraging the silent competition.

Ed guzzled yet another beer, snatched up his ball, and one more time he and Stormy stared down the lanes together. Both men were still teetering on one foot when Ed saw his fifth strike go down. Stormy left a widow in the corner, cussed at it and looked at Ed for the first time. "Lucky, lucky Eddie," he said, and couldn't hide the smile. Ed grinned back, and in that moment a stricken friendship was repaired.

Ed walked back the approach beside Stormy and said, "You pick up that spare, and I'll lay twenty bucks on the next three strikes in a row."

"You're on, partner." Stormy stood drying his hand and waiting for the ball while Ed wandered back over to Tamara, whom he'd forgotten all about.

Tamara was sitting back with a look of pure horror on her face that momentarily shook Ed. Then he spotted the chili dog Larry had delivered while he was bowling sitting right in front of Tamara's face and having no less effect on her than if it were the severed head of her own dog.

"That's disgusting," she hissed when Ed sat down next to her.

"No, it ain't, it's a chili dog. *That's* disgusting," Ed said, poking his finger straight into Tamara's avocado and waving it around in the air. "Looks like a big moose booger or somethin'." Ed clowned like he was pulling it out of his nose, to the delight of Stormy, who had indeed picked up his spare and was waiting for the contest to resume.

Encouraged by Stormy's goofy attentions, Ed carried the prank a little further by pretending to be shaking this "moose booger" from his finger, which he did in fact do, sending the avocado straight onto Tamara's white muslin peasant blouse. "Oops," he said with a stupid grin that seemed to fit him well at that moment.

"Ed Flannigan, you're drunk," Tamara hissed, like only Tamara can hiss, as she spread green goo all over her front trying to wipe it clean.

"Tamara Dupree, you're right," and Ed picked up his dripping chili dog, took an oversized bite, and let the juice ooze out the corners of his mouth, looking his date full in the eye the whole time.

"You're a vulgar and ridiculous person, Ed Flannigan." Tamara began madly stuffing fruit and vegetables back in her saddle bag. "Where's that sensitive new man? Where's the person who wanted to find his heart? Where's that changing gentle soul I've been talking to all week?"

Ed swallowed his food and pulled his sleeve across his face, taking with it the dregs of the chili dog and his mischievous grin. "Tamara," he said, serious now, and maybe even the slightest bit sad. "This gentle soul—went bowlin'."

Tamara picked up her boots and left without saying anything. Ed looked after her for a while, then Stormy came up behind him. "Boy, she's a pretty one, Eddie."

Ed snapped to and got up, reaching into his pocket and pulling out a bill. "Cut it out, Stormy, twenty bucks, let's bowl."

The two renewed friends went at it in earnest. Strike after strike after beer after strike after beer. Each time they'd cue up together. Each time they'd slide down to the foul line united. The pins would scatter in harmony. The balls would return in close rank, and everything made sense to everybody.

The twenty bucks was won by Ed and spent on Stormy. They sat around the snack bar with their last-call beer as Larry turned the lights off on the lanes.

Ed looked toward the entrance and brought up the subject for the first time. "Stormy, what am I going to do about Tamara?"

Stormy dug in his pocket, pulled out twenty cents and pressed it into Ed's hand. "Eddie, ol' pal. What you do about Tamara is you go right over to that pay phone there, you call your wife Emily and beg her to come on home with your kids. That's what you do."

Ed wrapped his hand around the two dimes and started coming up with the words.

Tamara was so mad about Ed she was almost halfway home before she realized she was still in rented bowling shoes. She sat down on the shoulder, changed into her boots, and pitched the shoes into the weeds.

Tamara didn't make friends too easily, and to have a new one snatched away so quickly cut deep. She tried to walk slowly, working to pace herself with her heartbeat. She was gradually calmed by the crisp air that smelled of burning wood. She could hear the sound of the wind in the spruce tops blending with the surf along the shore to one side of her.

She felt, more than heard, an owl sweep over her head and take something in the grass up ahead. *It's as it should be,* she thought. The fire, the wind, the water, the natural order of things; Tamara's home. Where everything is as it should be.

———— • ————

There was a minor accident at Main and Clearshot between two departing motor homes on Wednesday. It seemed that Gladys and Seymour "call me Sam" Prentergast from Des Moines, Iowa, had stopped to take a picture of a moose just about the time that Fred "just Fred" Phillips of Muncie, Indiana, rounded the bend looking over his shoulder to see what his wife Elsie was making all the fuss over in the kitchen. Fred and Elsie's "Winnebago Explorer" hit the rear end of Gladys and Sam's "Vagabond" at a high enough rate of speed that it put Sam and Gladys in the back bunk together for the first time on the whole vacation and put a considerable amount of Elsie's tuna salad onto Fred's driving sweater, which Fred regretted, but expressed relief that no one was injured in the accident. The two couples met, reconciled the damages and agreed to travel as far as Edmonton together, or maybe Calgary, depending on the weather.

Police Chief Peter Bindel reported that local ne'er-do-well Doug McDoogan was fined $100 for operating an illegal gambling concession out on the Spit Road. Mr. McDoogan is contesting the citation based on the fact that he lost all his money on the deal. The case is pending the return of the magistrate from a bird hunt across the inlet.

———— • ————

8

Jenuwine McDoogan

I WANNA tell you a little bit about this Doug McDoogan guy before I get into the fiasco out on the spit last Sunday.

Here's a guy who's been a carpenter for the last fifteen years, worked eight years as a logger down east of Crater Lake in Oregon, was wounded twice in three different tours of duty in Vietnam, and knows women better'n any man, due to his five unsuccessful marriages.

There he stands, all twenty-eight or -nine years of him taking up a past that a pair of twin senior citizens would be hard put to verify. In short, Doug McDoogan is the worst liar to come down that pike since the last election. No, I can't say that. He's not the worst liar, he's the *best* liar.

Doug's the kind of liar who can believe himself. He'll fight with honor and determination when accused of stretching the facts some. Big lies, drawn-out lies. Long complicated stories peppered with so many jokes and braided events that unless you listen closely, ring so true you can't help but buy another beer and beg for the details.

He'd stick his thumb in this hollow spot he has between his eyebrows and start in, "Yeah, I got this dent in my forehead down south. I was loggin' at the time near Chiloquin. Lotta rattlesnakes in the brush around there. I hate snakes. Scared to death of 'em. All my buddies knew it and whenever they killed one, which they were always doin', they'd sort of keep it around me every chance they had.

"One time they knotted one around my choker and sent it out to me knowin' I'd have to untie the thing to hook my log. Crazy kooks. Anyway, I was goin' after this one big ponderosa musta been six foot at the butt, and I had to get right down on my belly and scoot under it a little at a time to reach the end of my choker. You know what a choker is, don'tcha, is a piece'a heavy cable you sling around a log to drag it outta the weeds. Anyway, after I gets all wedged in under this log butt, what do ya figure is layin' right in front of me? You bet. The biggest darned timber rattler anybody'd ever seen, lookin' me right in the eye. I put 'er in reverse and tried to scramble out when this dern snake commences to bitin' on me right there."

He'd stick his thumb back in the dent, take a short pull from his beer, and go on. "I got all hung up on the brush and he musta bit me five or six times, me screamin' bloody murder the whole while, before the hook tender on one foot and the riggin' slinger on the other finally drug me out from under there.

"Well, I was just about dead by then, they figured, so they got right to cutting up my head to bleed out the poison. That's how come the dent; loggers not bein' known for their finesse at such things.

"Those two old boys sure saved my life. Did it just to laugh at me later, though, I suspect. I finally had to quit that job. Got so tired of finding snakes everywhere by those guys. In my lunch bucket, under my bunk, on my seat in the crummy. Disgusting people those Oregon loggers can be."

It was a good story to be sure, except he had to keep his audience straight to make sure no one was there from his Vietnam rendition of the head dent.

"Viet Cong used to reload a lot of their own ammo, ya see, an' sometimes they didn't get enough powder in 'em, or they'd misfire . . . yep, they shot me right between the eyes. Just kind of stuck there . . . knocked me cold, but that was about it. . . ."

He'd usually tell the logger story at the Lame Moose Saloon and save the war ones for the Yahoo Club. But that doesn't always work, even drunks bein' ambulatory at times.

Sooner or later someone would stand up and call him in the lie, there'd be a big stink with pushing and shoving, and pretty soon ol' Doug would come rolling down the front steps. This gives a person a good idea where that dent probably did come from.

There's a certain amount of admiration you gotta give to a liar of Doug's proportions. He doesn't even know what he likes to eat anymore. When a waitress asks him what he wants for breakfast, he always lies to her, and I guess he's just gotten used to that. He eats a lot of "logger's specials" down at Clara's Coffee Cup when a hot biscuit with fruit jelly would have tasted pretty good all by itself. He lives in a world completely of his own design, and it doesn't always treat him kindly.

Doug McDoogan is usually a victim at his own hands.

You see, Doug fancies himself a bit of a con artist. Unfortunately, for a con to be successful he has to command some confidence from his audience and have a pretty sharp wit. Natural gifts which, unfortunately, Doug lives without. But that doesn't keep him from trying.

Doug lives out on the beach in a driftwood shack he threw together, and most of his business endeavors have to do with things that float in on the tides. Doug spends a lot of time wandering up and down the beach looking for an angle.

He got the grand idea one time to sell "Genuine Alaska Rocks and Shells" to the tourists. He thought with the proper display that he could charge money for the stuff that people could walk twenty feet and pick up on their own. His idea of a proper display was an old packing crate with an army blanket over it, and a hand-lettered cardboard sign declaring JENUWINE ALASKA ROCKS AND SHELLS YOUR CHOICE, $5.

Besides all the obvious flaws with this endeavor, Doug was also only semiliterate. Having "genuine" spelled J-E-N-U-W-I-N-E didn't make any sense to anybody. He did get a few people to stop, though, probably thinking that a *jenuwine* Alaska rock might be some kind of agate or crystal formation. Doug sat beside the road in the rain two days with that one, until his cardboard sign finally got soggy and caved over.

His next venture was just as ill-inspired and even less successful. He picked up a bunch of driftwood planks and boards laying around and billed them as "Alaska Water Logs" which not only proved uninteresting to tourists, but unsalable as well. Doug didn't even get anyone to stop for that one.

Then he found a bunch of washed-up salmon skulls that had bleached in the saltwater and figured he might be able to bill them as "Alaska Dinosaur Skulls." He went through most of a cardboard refrigerator box struggling to spell "Dinosaur," then gave up and settled on "Lizzard" with two Z's, then wrote "Skulls" correctly but didn't like the looks of it, scratched it out and wrote "Heads" instead. So the bill of fare at the McDoogan establishment for three more days was "Alaska Lizzard Heads," which made a fool of nobody but Doug.

In between all these enterprises, Doug would work now and again sliming fish over at the salmon cannery to support himself. This is where he raised the capital to embark on his most recent undertaking, which left him not only dangerously in debt, but got him a hundred-dollar fine to boot.

One night Doug had worked late at the cannery and picked up a six-pack of beer on the way back home. When he came over the bluff to the beach, he saw before him, not a hundred feet from his shack, a huge bundle of culverts. Culverts are those big metal tubes that go under roads and driveways to let the

water through. They must have fallen off a barge somewhere out in the gulf and found their way to
McDoogan's beach.

Doug went and looked them over. There was a
dozen of them, about two feet across and maybe
twenty feet long, all strapped together as pretty as you
please. Doug sat down in front of them, fascinated.
This was the most spectacular and unusual debris he'd
ever chanced across, and he knew there must be a way
to turn a profit on it.

It never occurred to Doug that he could just lay a
salvage claim on the bundle and sell them to a con-
struction company for a couple hundred apiece, but
then a lot of things never occur to Doug.

He sat in the sand in front of the culverts, gulping
down bottles of beer in his excitement, and analyzed
the options. He thought maybe he could rig doors on
each end of the tubes and rent them out to other cannery workers as sleeping quarters. He figured you
could lay them three to a tube, head to foot, times
twelve is thirty-something by, say, two bucks a head
per night, is around sixty bucks a night. He climbed
inside one to test the accommodations and discovered
to his great dismay that it felt a lot like sleeping in a
culvert.

Doug sat back in the sand and studied. You can't
draw water from a dry well, and try as he might, Doug
McDoogan could not get another idea about this deal.
He threw down the last gulp of his last beer, cussed to
himself, and threw the empty bottle at the open end of
the culvert bundle. It hit the edge of one of the culverts
and broke into pieces. Doug felt challenged by this. He
wanted to throw it through a culvert, not against it. He
picked up another bottle and tried again. Again it
smashed against the edges.

Doug eyed the situation again, or I should say
"cross-eyed" the situation, as that six-pack was starting to take its toll on him. Looking at the open ends of
twelve two-foot culverts, a person sees mostly air and
very little culvert. A person might think you could
throw an object at it with his eyes closed and hit a hole

by pure luck of the draw. Doug grabbed up another bottle, took careful aim, and once again broke it against an edge. "That ish really deceiving," Doug slurred.

And then the seed of an idea began to germinate in his head and bloom. He picked up another bottle. Crash. Another, crash. One more, crash! By God, he had it! He'd make a contest out of it. There ain't a man in the world wouldn't think he could throw a bottle through one of those holes at this range. Doug guessed a guy would bet five dollars he could. And only one man, Douglas G. McDoogan, knew better. And Doug went to bed, already flushed with success.

The next morning, when the Sunday crowd was headed out the Spit Road for their weekend outings, they were greeted by Doug's biggest and boldest sign yet, BECHA CANT, $5, was all it said.

The first to stop was Ed Flannigan and Stormy Storbock, who were headed out to do some fishing. They walked up to Doug, who was grinning like a mud shark and surrounded by dozens of empty bottles he'd been up since dawn collecting.

"Bet we can't what?" Stormy asked.

Doug put on his most challenging sneer and said grandly, "I betcha can't heave a bottle from here through the open end of one of those culverts."

"Five-buck limit?" said Stormy, already reaching for his wallet before Ed could get his out.

"We'll see," said Doug, handing Stormy a bottle. "I'll hold the money, you take your best shot."

Stormy took a grip on the bottle and without a second thought tossed it neatly through the end of a culvert. It rattled down the inside and fell out the other end. Doug's jaw dropped a notch, but he recovered, thinking, *That's good if the first one gets lucky. That'll bring in even more suckers*. Doug paid out five dollars from his own pocket and traded Ed a bottle for a fiver.

Ed leaned forward like the softball pitcher he was and underhanded his bottle straight through a culvert without even touching a side. "Boy," said Ed. "That's fun. Pay up and give me two more bottles easy money."

To be merciful to Doug, I won't describe the sad

scenario that followed. Ed and Stormy took most of Doug's money and would have cleaned him out if they hadn't had a softball game that afternoon and wanted to save their arms.

By the time Ed and Stormy left, there were a dozen other people waiting in line. Doug was down three hundred bucks and nobody had missed once. He was more than perplexed. He was shocked. He felt cheated. By whom was unclear to Doug, but most things are. Never once did it enter his mind that the six misses he'd made the night before had anything to do with the contents of the bottles he was throwing.

He ran out of money long before he ran out of bottles, and when everyone had finally left, Doug had given out two hundred dollars in IOU's, Argus Winslow now owned the bundle of culverts, and Chief of Police Bindel had issued him a hundred-dollar citation for operating an illegal concession.

Doug went back to his shack bitter and defeated. He thought of the long miserable morning over and over, and as his mind was apt to do, some embellishment was allowed to creep in. Suddenly that monotonous string of perfect throws was being interrupted by the occasional shattered bottle. Then another. Then twenty busted bottles in a row crashed in his head as the glass flew and the money poured in. His pockets were swelled with fives and tens, and Ed Flannigan lost his whole truck to him, and Doug was cruising up the highway with Tamara Dupree slid over on the seat next to him, listening to loud music and heading out to look at the new house that Stormy Storbock had put on the line for one last desperate throw.

Doug McDoogan leaned back in his driftwood shack and grinned like a mud shark. *They're never going to believe this down at the saloon,* he thought to himself. And that was the first thing he'd been right about in a long long time.

PART TWO

Mayor Richard Weekly was reelected to his tenth con- secutive term. He received 563 votes running unopposed, as he has for twenty years. When asked about his consis- tent political victories, Mayor Weekly said, "I don't figure that it's because they think I'm such a good mayor. I just don't think they want to take the time to break in a new one."

Traffic slowed to a standstill on Pioneer Avenue Monday when a flatbed truck carrying fish entrails from the can- nery overturned on our busiest street. "It was slicker'n a soaped oyster out there for a while," said a disgusted Mayor Richard Weekly. "We dumped a bunch of sand on it, and it sort of set up on us. I don't know, it might be easier to build a new street rather than clean this one up."

Emily Flannigan and the kids are back in town after an extended visit to her sister in Anchorage. She remarked that the rumored split between her and Ed surprised her and didn't we have anything better to talk about.

Tamara Dupree announced to her contact group at the Natural Food Coop that she was taking a two-week yoga retreat in a yurt near her cabin and would the group please see that her dog was fed and her mail collected.

9

The Storbock Fire

KIRSTEN and Stormy Storbock had been in their new house just a few months. You'd think that might have made the emotional trauma of being burned out a little bit lighter than, say, if it'd been the old family homestead or something, but it didn't.

You see, Kirsten and Stormy had most of the last ten years invested in that place. They'd bought the land before there was even a road to it. They cleared the site themselves on weekends. Stormy, with a lot of occasional help from Ed Flannigan and other friends, had done all the work himself. He'd dug the basement, laid the block, pounded down the floor, raised the walls and rafters. He and Kirsten wired, plumbed, insulated, Sheetrocked, and painted.

They did what they could as money and time would allow. Both of which were in constant short supply. Stormy had a good job as a machinist at the boat yard. Kirsten took in bookkeeping work for various small businesses around town. Some years were better than others, but it always seemed that when there was money there was no time, and when there was time they were broke.

It took them so long that there were already two additions to the original plan, accommodating the children they'd had in the meantime. No, it was more than just a new house. It was darn near an obsession.

But probably even more important than the house was what it housed. All their stuff. They'd put nothing but their best into the new place. They'd weeded out all the dregs when they moved from town, and had the garage sale only a week ago. What remained was the cream. A tough thing to lose, and made tougher by the fact that every item in the house had been so recently touched, cleaned, packed, unpacked, and positioned in the new place.

How the fire started is no great mystery. It happened due to a combination of a brand-new electric stove, a measuring spoon, and Stormy's famous garlic bean dip.

Kirsten had fried some bacon for herself and the two kids after sending Stormy off to work. She'd always cooked with gas in the old house in town and still wasn't used to the electric burners, even though it's what she always wanted. With a gas stove you can always tell when the burner's lit because you see it. On Kirsten's new deluxe electric it was a light on the control panel that told when a burner was on. She never did get in the habit of paying attention to that little light, and she certainly didn't the morning of the fire.

She'd taken the plate of bacon down to the kids, watching *Woody Woodpecker* in the TV room. She had a cup of coffee for herself and thought she might curl up in the afghan and watch a little Woody too. She'd barely got her legs covered when the smoke detector went off upstairs.

"Oh, that darn thing," she said. "Goes off every time I make toast. I'm going to have Stormy disconnect it."

The kids were glued to their cartoons and paid the blaring beep of the alarm no attention at all except to move a nudge closer to the TV set. It occurred to Kirsten halfway up the stairs that she hadn't made any toast. She grabbed another gear in her stride about the same time the smell of scorched bacon grease reached her.

When she looked into the kitchen she saw the fire in the fry pan and time seemed to fall completely to pieces. The shrill bleep of those smoke detectors lends a certain air of disaster to the calmest of situations, but when coupled with a real fire it's bound to curdle your nerve endings.

Kirsten of curdled nerves rushed into the kitchen. She'd dealt with grease fires before, but this one was threatening to stain her new wallpaper. She turned off the burner with one hand and reached for the baking soda with the other. Husband Stormy was an active volunteer fireman and they always kept a box of baking soda in the cupboard next to the stove for this very reason. But this time it wasn't there.

Kirsten rifled through the cupboard, throwing out cereal boxes, bowls, cups, and cookies. She found the meat-loaf pan she'd been looking for all week and the cap to Stormy's thermos bottle, but nothing to put a fire out with. She'd forgotten that Stormy had made his notorious garlic bean dip for Ed and Emily's re-union party the night before and the box of baking soda was at that moment working a different shift as a deodorizer in the refrigerator.

By the time she pulled her head out of the cup-board, the cabinet above the stove had caught fire. She knew better than to throw water on a grease fire, but the cabinet seemed like the more immediate concern, so she went to the sink.

When she turned on the water, the stream from the faucet landed in a measuring spoon left over from her delicious scratch pancakes' fixings, shot in a perfect arc across the kitchen, and fell right into the flaming fry pan. The grease roared like a machine gun at her as it escaped the pan on the film of water, made its way across Kirsten's "Plum Delight" Formica counter and up her washable "Country Morning" vinyl wallpaper.

By the time she grasped the reality that this fire was out of control and she'd better call for help, the flames had already reached the kitchen wall phone. The only phone in the house.

Panic has a nice way of keeping your mind occupied, and the very next thing Kirsten occupied hers with was her children.

She pulled herself together on the bottom step to the basement and entered the room as calm as a singed mother in a burning building can be. "Jason, Jennifer, the house is on fire. We have to go get in the car."

"Ummm-hmmm," the kids said, moving yet another nudge closer to the television.

"Oh, screw it," she said, grabbed the kids by the napes of the neck, hauled them up the stairs and out the door to the garage. The kids stopped squirming as soon as they smelled the smoke and saw the kitchen full of fire.

As Kirsten loaded the kids in the car, little Jennifer said, "Is Daddy gonna come and put out the fire?"

"I hope so, honey." And Kirsten did hope so. More than she hoped for anything in her life as three quarters of the Storbock clan sped down the narrow road to the neighbors.

The fire call sounded just about the time Stormy got to work. He did a U-turn, headed into the fire hall, and barely got into his gear in time to grab hold of the fire truck on its way out the door.

"Where's it at?" he yelled to Ed Flannigan, alongside him on the rear step.

"Flat Back Ridge," Ed yelled back, with a look acknowledging it was Stormy's neighborhood. Stormy held on tighter and looked to the direction of his home. There were only five houses on Flat Back Road and his was one of them. It was a twenty-five-minute drive up the hilly roads, and even a small stack fire can do a lot of damage in twenty-five minutes. Stormy would not believe it could be his house, and at the same time could not wish the fire on any of his neighbors. All he could do was hold on.

When they cleared the ridge and started down Flat Back Road, all the men could see the thick black smoke. It still could have been anyone's house from that angle, but when they passed the Tuttles' place, their nearest neighbor, Stormy saw his kids waving to him from the front porch, still in their pajamas, and his heart fell. They rounded the bend to his driveway just in time to see the roof collapse.

Stormy didn't see her at first because she was so still. But Kirsten stood in the front yard in a pink housecoat, ankle deep in snow, holding some things in her arms.

Stormy ignored the flurry of activity around the truck and ran to his wife.

"Kirsty, are you all right?" Stormy stood in front of her, holding her shoulders. He could see she wasn't hurt, but she had the strangest look on her face. He looked at the things in her arms: his softball glove, their wedding picture, and the kids' toothbrushes. He realized she must have ran through the house and grabbed anything she could. She looked to be in shock, but not really. There was something goofy about her expression. Like she was baffled. Baffled by something important.

"Stormy?" she finally said, looking into his face for the first time.

"Yes, honey."

"Where did you put the baking soda?"

It was a long and difficult morning for the Storbocks. The house was a total loss. When the roof collapsed it took both floors with it all the way to the basement. The only salvageable item they could find was an electric Weed Eater the kids must have drug out sometime, which revealed itself when the heat from the fire melted the snow back.

Stormy and Kirsten didn't stay to watch the firemen water down the remains of their home. They had a few other things to attend to. The first and foremost concern of where were they going to sleep that night was taken care of by Ed Flannigan, who insisted they move into the empty half of his duplex.

The second concern, and it was a close finish between one and two, was what were they going to wear, which led to what were they going to eat, what were they going to cook it in, how were they going to bathe. And with each question a jagged piece of themselves was torn away.

"Stormy," Kirsten said on the quiet drive with the kids out to the duplex. "We don't even own a bar of soap."

"We can buy soap." And attempting to add some levity to the situation, Stormy added, "At least we have some toothbrushes."

This added nothing. In fact, it's what finally broke Kirsten into tears for the first time that day. What played through her head in a continuous loop was her mad dash through the smoke-filled house that morning. How she was trying to save their most precious things and couldn't decide. She'd picked up Jennifer's favorite doll, then dropped it to grab Jason's big stuffed horse. A practical instinct overtook her and she ran crouched into the kids' bedrooms, gathering up clothes. Clothes were money, and when she thought of money she dropped the clothes and went into the master bedroom to get the cash out of the dresser.

Once in there she remembered Stormy's gun collection, which was worth a lot more money than what was in the drawer, and she started to gather them out of the cabinet as the smoke in the room got lower and lower. On her knees and struggling with the dozen or so heavy rifles, she made one attempt to throw them straight through the bedroom window outside but missed, and they fell to the floor in a big and dispiriting tangle of hardware.

She had no more time. She went back to the

dresser on all fours and reached blindly into the top drawer. She grabbed the first thing she laid her hand on, which turned out to be their wedding portrait. She dropped back down and headed for the door. On the way out she spotted Stormy's softball glove in the corner and grabbed that. Passing the bathroom she noticed the kids' toothbrushes laying on the edge of the sink and shagged them just out of reflex. There was no more she could do. She crawled out the front door into the snow to watch her dreamhouse burn down.

"Grandma's doilies," Kirsten said out loud in the truck.

Stormy understood and added, "High school yearbooks."

"My journals for the kids."

"The wagon I made for Jason."

"My blue dress with the straps you like."

"Six bowling trophies."

"My recipes."

"Your basket collection."

"Your guns."

"Your beautiful house."

All four Storbocks were in varying degrees of tears when they rolled up to Ed's duplex.

"What in the heck is all this about?" Stormy said, pulling himself together and stopping short in the driveway behind at least six other cars.

There was a frenzy of activity around the house. Pastor Frank Olmstead and his archrival the mystic Reverend Saffire were on either end of a sofa sleeper, trying to get through the front door. Frank's wife Fanny led a procession of ladies from the First and Last Baptist Church carrying grocery bags and cardboard boxes.

A herd of wild children careened around the front yard begging Jennifer and Jason to come play as Kirsten and Stormy made their way into the house.

Emily Flannigan was washing out cupboards in

the kitchen, and right behind her was Francine Tuttle situating plates, bowls, and other tableware she was producing from a large box on the floor.

Sissy Tuttle was gabbing incessantly while cleaning out the refrigerator, and Ed was getting a pot of venison stew going on the stove.

Kirsten, still in her housecoat, and the two pajama-clad kids were swept up the stairs by the church ladies and their boxes. The kids were back down within minutes in nice-fitting but unfamiliar clothes.

Stormy made his way up the stairs wide-eyed and speechless. Bud Koenig and Argus Winslow were in the bathroom arguing over the proper height to hang a shower curtain. Mayor Richard Weekly was struggling with the frame to a bunk bed in the smaller bedroom.

Ed peeked in the larger room to see three cooing women producing slacks, skirts, and blouses out of their boxes. Kirsten held some of them up to her front, and when she met Stormy's eye, she just shrugged once and grinned.

Back down in the living room Pastor Frank and Reverend Saffire were carrying in a coffee table followed by Doug McDoogan, who walked straight up to Stormy with a loose wad of old clothes.

"Here's all your old shirts and stuff I bought at your garage sale last week. They never fit me anyway." Doug turned on his heel and walked back out the door.

Stormy couldn't for the life of him think of a single thing to say or do. All he could manage was to stand and fight back a lump in his throat and try to wish away the mist in his eyes.

Ed Flannigan, stirring the stew in the kitchen, got a look at Stormy's face as he walked outside and decided to go out and check in on him.

Ed found him leaning on a pickup truck with his arms folded, watching the kids run circles around each other in the snow. Ed sidled up next to him and folded his arms. Men share some of their most intimate moments leaning against vehicles with their arms crossed looking at anything but each other.

Nothing was said until Ed saw Stormy's hand reach up to wipe at his face. "Sorry you lost your home, Stormy."

Stormy turned and looked at Ed, then to the house with the strangest combination of people ever assembled coming and going, wiping windows and unpacking boxes full of food, clothes, towels, and toys. He caught a flash of Kirsten's bare back as she tried on blouses in the upstairs window just before a new curtain went up.

Stormy looked back at Ed and finally found his voice. "It was a house, Ed. Just a house."

Ed and Stormy leaned back against the pickup and watched the kids. Jason and Jennifer were the center of attention. Stormy could tell they were describing the big fire to an admiring audience by the way their hands moved up in big dramatic gestures and then down again with mean and ugly faces. Stormy started to fall back into the loop. The endless loop of precious things up in smoke. Then he took another look around and stopped himself short.

No matter what he lost, and he knew he'd be continually missing new things for months to come, he also knew one thing, and that was for sure. He knew that everything he really needed, everything that counted, was alive and well within a hundred feet of where he stood.

10

A Lucky
Break

A LOT of us have been blind-sided by life at one time or another, and Doug McDoogan has probably taken more than his fair share of swats. But these things that appear out of nowhere aren't always so bad. The good surprises are called "windfalls" or "lucky breaks." But what they really are is the answers to prayers we haven't thought to pray yet. At least that might best describe Doug's recent good fortune.

Doug McDoogan, if you'll recall, is our local End of the Road ne'er-do-well. He lives in a driftwood shack out on the beach, where he goes from one ill-conceived scam to the next, trying to make his fortune with as much foolishness and as little work as possible.

He's at different times tried to sell tourists beach-rock souvenirs, old fish skulls, soggy driftwood, and any number of other scams and swindles he usually lost on. Doug's latest endeavor, which eventually led to his windfall, also involved some things the tide dragged in.

Doug was set up in his usual spot beside the Spit Road, sitting on a stool next to a packing crate with a variety of dirty bottles arranged on it. His hand-lettered cardboard sign read RARE BOTTLES, $5. It seemed like no matter what Doug was trying to sell, it cost five dollars. Even these supposedly "rare" bottles, some which still had labels on them, and most stamped NO DEPOSIT NO RETURN, with twist-off tops.

The tourists were mostly gone for the season and Doug didn't expect much out of his bottle business, but he was bored. If he was going to be sitting around anyway, he figured he might as well sit around with a chance of selling something.

He was wrapped up in his rain poncho against the damp wind and whittling on a piece of driftwood with a jackknife, as he always did. Today he was making a sea lion. Doug always made animals with his whittling, or at least parts of animals, because he never has finished a carving.

About an hour into his sea lion an elderly blue-haired lady with a walking stick and a camera walked up behind Doug's concession. "Excuse me, young man. But what are you selling?"

Doug, with his typical flare for sales, said without looking up, "Bottles, rare bottles. Five bucks if you want one."

The lady looked the bottles over and laughed out loud. "These aren't rare bottles. Look, this one still has the ketchup label on it."

Unaffected by criticism, Doug just shrugged. "Be rare some day, maybe. Better get 'em while they're still cheap."

Where most people were repulsed by Doug and his enterprises, this woman was charmed. She leaned into her walking stick and beamed curiously at the top of Doug's head as he struggled with a particularly tough slice of his knife in the driftwood.

"May I ask you what you're carving?"

"You might ask, and I might know, but I don't. So far it's a sea lion, I guess."

"May I see it?" The lady held out her free hand,

and Doug readily turned it over to her without making eye contact. Doug never made eye contact. He'd told so many lies to so many people and led such a life of complete insincerity that eye contact with another person would most likely cause him to explode.

"This is a beautiful piece of work, young man. When will you finish it?"

"It's finished now if you want it to be. I never finish 'em. I just whittle 'em for a while and leave 'em go. Somethin' to do, I guess."

The woman turned the partial carving over in her hand to admire it. "This *is* beautiful," she repeated.

And it was. The piece of driftwood was roughly the shape of a reclining sea lion to begin with, and Doug had formed the head and upper body nearly perfectly. It appeared as if the sea lion were emerging from the wood.

"You have a remarkable eye for shape. And the detail you get with that little knife . . . this is exceptional. I'd like to buy this from you."

Doug almost fell off his stool. "Buy? That? What for?"

"I own an art gallery in Anchorage and I display Alaskan talent. With some lacquer on it, this piece could be quite nice just the way it is. How much would you sell it for?"

Doug didn't have to think about this too long. "Five bucks," he said. The only price he knew of.

"It's worth much more than that," said the blue-haired lady, putting down the carving to reach into her pocket. "I'll give you twenty for it. And I need to know your name."

"Doug. Doug McDoogan," he said, in awe of the bill he held in his hand. Then it dawned on him. "Hey, lady, I got lots more of this stuff in my shack. Wanna see 'em?"

"Why yes, I certainly would." And as Doug scrambled over the bluff ahead of her to his shack, his heart was flying. This, he thought, had to be his best scam yet. *Twenty bucks, can you believe it? Twenty bucks for a whittled-up stick. Eeee-hoo.*

Doug burst through the blanket that served as door to his home and started sifting through the various chunks of driftwood he kept by the fire pit. One, with a dog's head partly on it, was half burned, but it looked okay. He found about a dozen more of varying sizes and species in his woodpile or holding down pieces of plastic around the hut.

By the time the blue-haired old lady got there, Doug had arranged his wares on the sand floor. Doug was in a state of complete but elated confusion. He'd never given a single one of his "whittlin's" a second thought before. He was dumbstruck watching the woman move her head quietly back and forth in admiration of what laid before her. She stooped and picked them up one at a time.

There was the dog, and a fish, clearly a salmon. There was a harbor seal, and a wolf carving as different from the dog carving as the real animals are. There was the head of an eagle just barely let out of a piece of wood that by itself suggested an eagle. Every piece was like that. Suggestive. Doug seemed to do just enough carving on each one to make clear what the potential was. As if every creature were caught in a stage of transformation from lumber to life.

Finally the woman spoke. "You, young man, are an artist of uncanny ability. You have an eye that few do, and a sense of completion that is truly your own. I will give you eight hundred dollars for all of these, and fifty dollars each for any more I take in the future."

All the ability, good eye, and completion stuff went completely over Doug's head, but he understood the eight-hundred-dollar part perfectly. Doug could have died and gone to heaven on the spot.

Doug carried the carvings to the old woman's car, blabbering the whole time. "I can make three of these a day, hell, I'll make six. I'll get a new knife. I'll make real big ones if you want. Maybe you don't want, heck, I can make 'em smaller too. Real small. I'll carve bugs or worms, or I know what, you tell me what you want me to whittle and I'll whittle 'em. Fifty bucks, heck, I'll *finish* 'em for fifty bucks."

The lady just walked and listened until he got to that part, then she stopped him. "Doug, you're a unique talent, but you're dumber than a post, no offense, dear. I want you to just keep doing what you're doing. Whatever you do, don't change that, and don't finish them. Stop 'whittling,' as you say, when *you* think they're finished."

The lady gave Doug her business card and eight hundred dollars in twenties and fifties. She got into her car and pulled away with a curt wave and a grandmother's smile.

Doug held the money in his hand and his knees went weak. He'd never had this much money before in his life. It was *real* money. The kind of money you still have something left from the next day. He counted it again and stuffed it into his greasy pants pocket.

He turned to walk toward town with a bounce to his step like he'd never had. And the closer he got to town, the warmer that money got, and the warmer it got, the bouncier went his walk, until finally he was half running down the shoulder of the road, laughing out loud and relishing the feel of the big wad of bills now burning a hole right through his pocket.

Doug's "windfall," of course, was getting a big wad of cash out of the clear blue sky. His "lucky break" was something entirely different. You see, Doug McDoogan and money were a dangerous and irresponsible combination. Doug had very little sense to begin with, but his most wanting area of sense was financial. It was inevitable, and in his nature, that he'd spend his dough on the very first thing he came across that was for sale.

If it'd been a car, he'd own a car. If it'd been a bar, he'd own a hangover. A boat, a bike, a pile of lumber. It didn't matter. If it was for sale, it was sold to Doug McDoogan. Doug's lucky break was that the first thing he saw he could spend his money on was a FOR RENT sign in an apartment window.

It wasn't much of a place. Anybody could see

that, but Doug. What Doug saw when the landlord opened the door was something just short of Buckingham Palace, not that he knew where or what that was.

It was one room with a bed, a table and chairs, and a little kitchenette with a bathroom off it. Doug hadn't been under a real roof since he came to the End of the Road, and he hadn't ever had one to call his own. He'd been pitched out by his folks when he was sixteen and had lived pretty much like a stray dog ever since. Probably the only reason he's stayed around here as long as he has is because the road doesn't go any farther and it hasn't occurred to him to turn around yet.

The landlord didn't have much to say. He just stood in the doorway with his arms folded across his gut and watched Doug. Doug turned the light off and on about six times and chuckled. He turned on the water in the kitchen, waited for it to get hot, and chuckled some more. He disappeared into the bathroom, flushed the toilet, and came out laughing. Then he dove onto the bed, put his arms behind his head, and looked at the man in the doorway. "How much?"

"A hunert and fifty, first and last months' rent, and a fifty-dollar damage deposit. All utilities paid, no pets and no parties."

Doug looked thoughtful for a moment—I stress that he only *looked* thoughtful—then asked, "How long can I stay here for seven hundred and fifty dollars?" He paused a second, then added, "In advance."

The landlord considered for a moment. "For cash I'll give you the rest of November free and you can stay through April."

April . . . the word hung in the air for Doug like a sweet perfume. *April.* That was *next year.* That was springtime. A winter away. A whole long dark winter indoors. It might as well be ten years from now.

Doug went to the table and slowly counted out the money.

"When can I move in?"

"Soon's ya want. But no pets, and no parties."

"Can I whittle?" Doug asked with genuine concern.

The landlord looked at Doug, tried to make sense of the question and couldn't, but with the self-importance that landlords grace us with, he had to respond. "Don't be carvin' up the furniture," and he left.

Doug closed the door then leaned back against it. He turned the light off, then back on, then off, then on. He went to the oil heater on the wall and turned it up. He sat at the table and looked at his kitchen for a while. Then he turned and looked at his bed. He went in the bathroom and flushed the toilet again. Then he turned on the shower, waiting again for the hot water.

When it came he stood back and watched the steam roll out. He felt it on his face and held his hands in it. Even though the mildew had grown halfway up the sides and he could see daylight through the drain hole, it was the prettiest thing he had ever laid his eyes on.

Doug ran back to his beach shack to get his things, which amounted to a pot, a cracked mug, a small wad of clothes he wrapped in his army blanket, and a variety of beach junk which he left. He was able to situate everything into a pack on his back and used his free arms to pick up a load of whittlin' material.

His high spirits had him talking out loud to himself as he wandered along the beach selecting chunks of small driftwood.

"Here's a goat. And that's a bear. Oh look, a deer's butt just as plain as day. I can't believe that old lady's going to pay me fifty bucks for this stuff. God, it's just *laying* here. Now there's a mink, and oh, hold the onions, a little baby's face. Never found no babies before . . ."

And Doug got back to his new digs with an armload of creatures that only he could see. He laid his blanket out on the bed, put his pot and mug in the kitchen cupboard, and arranged his whittling on the table. He addressed them on his way out the door again, "Okay, all you guys, hang tight. I'm going to go down to the store and buy me the biggest steak I can carry, and some beer, and some soap. I'm gonna take a hot shower until I can't stand it anymore, then I'm going to let you out of your wood."

Doug's light was on late into that night. His room was up to eighty degrees but he wouldn't back the heat off. He sat naked in the delicious stench of a fried steak, ankle deep in wood chips, and let his mind hang where it usually did, in neutral.

On the table at his elbow was the proud partial head of a mountain goat staring into the hindquarters of a deer backing out of a chunk of spruce. Doug never looked back to them after he'd set them down. It meant nothing more than fifty dollars to him. Every so often he'd look up at his toilet, or over to his bed, and he'd beam and wonder what he did to deserve such a lucky break.

And in his hands a piece of sun-bleached wood was changing itself into the face of a baby. Its eyes were closed in peace, and its lips were slightly parted in a sleepy-wondrous innocence. And the baby's face, like the artist who held it, stopped only halfway out of the wood.

Argus Winslow was the winner of the Turkey Pull at the Lame Moose Saloon this weekend. Pairs of contestants place their bets on who will walk away with the bigger piece of a cooked turkey with one solid tug. Mr. Winslow got everything but a drumstick, which was left in the hands of a disappointed Bud Koenig. "It really leaves a mess," said Mayor Richard Weekly, who officiated the event. "I don't see why they just can't pull wishbones like they used to." Proceeds from the contest went this year to the Kirsten and Stormy Storbock Fire Fund, and the mayor is drafting a petition to ban this contest along with the annual Labor Day competition in the Salmon Throw.

Monday also starts the Christmas mailing season, and the Post Office wants to remind us to get those packages off early. Being aware that most of our Christmas shopping is also done through the mail, in a time-saving maneuver the postmaster has announced that you should go around the back and pick up your own mail. She says just keep your hands off the machinery, don't be reading other people's postcards, and try not to play around with the hand trucks so much like last year.

11

Norman's Thanksgiving

NORMAN Tuttle had a good Thanksgiving. The best. It became one of those sort of momentous occasions that, even at the age of twelve, he knew would stay with him, no doubt, for as long as he lives.

The day started out quietly enough. Norman and his dad worked together in the basement most of the morning, putting away fishing gear and cleaning up to accommodate the houseful of relatives due that afternoon. Norman's mother was in the kitchen cooking and running herd on the three younger brothers and sisters who were going slightly crazy with the anticipation of what was obviously a special day. Even though they had no idea what the occasion was.

Norman knew what it was, but he didn't care, or even much care to think about it. He was enjoying the time with his dad in the basement. Ever since the accident on the fishing boat two months before, Norman and his dad had something special between them.

Norman had fallen off his dad's boat in the dark on

the way back to town, and no one had seen him go. He'd sat on an old dock piling he'd managed to bump into for most of the night, waiting for his father to notice he was gone and come find him.

When his father did notice he was gone, he thought Norman *was* gone. Lost, drowned . . . gone. During the six hours of what he thought was aimless searching, the elder Tuttle had made a pact with God. He swore that if he got his boy back, he would never not notice him again. He wouldn't belittle him. He wouldn't keep expecting impossible things from the poor clumsy kid. And he would love him. Standing on the deck that dark night holding his soggy son in his arms, he knew that it was a pact he would keep.

And he was keeping it. He took him hunting. If he was going down to the store, he'd remember to ask Norman if he wanted to tag along. He taught him how to play cribbage, and they played a lot. Well into the damp dark nights of November the elder Tuttle men could be found at the kitchen table counting score, "Fifteen-two, fifteen-four, run for three is seven and a pair for nine."

"You missed your nobs, pay attention."

"I'm winning. *You* pay attention."

"Don't talk to your dad like that."

"You're jealous."

"You're grounded."

"You're joking," and so it went. They were becoming the best of friends.

And as these best of friends were cleaning up the basement, Norman listened while his dad told old Army stories. Norman liked these the best because they were always illegal. His dad would stop sweeping and drop his voice. "Don't you ever tell your mother about this, but one time when I was stationed at Fort Lewis, me and a few of the boys got into some moonshine, and as you know I don't drink, and I didn't then either, but there was these three dancers, see, and . . ." On he'd go on some story that usually only made half sense to Norman, but it didn't matter because his dad seemed to enjoy the telling, and that was plenty for Norman.

Norman's day took a decided turn for the worse when they finished up in the basement. "Well," his dad said, with his arm over his shoulder, "that oughta give you kids plenty of room to play. Better go get cleaned up. It's Thanksgiving, bub. Company's comin' soon." And his dad walked up the stairs not knowing he'd just burst his boy's bubble.

Kids, Norman thought. *It's always "you kids." I'm twelve goin' on thirteen. They're kids. I'm a . . . well, I'm, uh, Norman.*

Norman, of course, was overreacting to something his dad said, but that's well within the rights of a twelve-year-old boy to do, and besides, it was supported by the Thanksgiving history of the family.

Thanksgiving in the Tuttle household was an overrated and predictable affair, to Norman's way of thinking. It was always the same thing year after year for as long as he could remember.

Grandma and Grandpa Tuttle always came, which was no occasion because they lived in town and they saw them almost every day anyway. The only difference was that Grandma wore her Thanksgiving dress and Grandpa wore his tie. Same dress, same tie, every year. "What a pretty dress, Mom," Norman's mom would always say at the door, and, "Pop, don't you look dashing today," to Grandpa. Same lines every year.

And Grandpa would always have in his hand a bottle of wine. Thanksiving was the only time Norman ever saw alcohol of any kind in the house. All Norman knew was that it was for the Thanksgiving toast that his dad made every year.

Then Uncle Stu and Aunt Sissy would show up. Uncle Stu was his dad's brother and fishing partner, and Norman saw him every day too, but he never saw Aunt Sissy much. Aunt Sissy was a pain in the pants, and everybody knew it, including Uncle Stu and possibly herself because she was never around much.

All Aunt Sissy did was talk, and she never said anything. The first thing she always said to Norman was, "My, look at you. How you've grown into such a little man." Norman had been growing into Aunt Sissy's little man for eight years that he could remember and possibly longer, because she was saying the same thing to Norman's youngest brother, who was only two.

She'd go on and on about almost anything that came to mind without taking a breath, and it didn't seem to matter if anybody paid any attention to her or not, and they usually didn't. She just liked to listen to herself. A lot more than anybody else did.

On top of Aunt Sissy and Uncle Stu, and Grandma and Grandpa, always came Uncle Elmer and Aunt Edna. They were okay, Norman thought, and they didn't see them much because they lived across the state. What Norman dreaded about the arrival of Elmer and Edna was the five kids they brought with them. The whole chemistry of the house changed when they poured in the door.

Norman's mother would turn into a staff sergeant and start barking orders. "Shoes off, everybody. Norman, put the coats in the bedroom. Has everyone said hello to Grandma and Grandpa? Norman, I said put away the coats . . ." Everyone would be in the kitchen for a while saying hello while babies crawled around people's feet, toddlers cried, and everybody talked at once over Aunt Sissy.

The adults would allow this cacophony to continue for an appropriate time and then Norman's mom would finally issue the order that he'd come to despise. "Okay kids, we need room in here. Everybody down to the basement to play until dinner." And that would be it. They'd all go downstairs and invent games, or watch television, and generally be just kids. There would be no more contact with the grown-ups for the rest of the day.

When dinner was ready they'd be set up at card

tables in the other room so that the adults could enjoy their meal, and told to hush when it came time for the toast, which was always a long-drawn-out thing thanking the Lord for good fishing, or good health, good food, or whatever. When they were done, Norman and the rest of the kids would be sent either outside to play or back into the basement.

The adults would adjourn to the living room to talk in low tones about important things that Norman had no inkling of. Norman wasn't sure he belonged in the living room, but he knew he didn't belong in the basement.

All his cousins, like his brothers and sisters, were younger than him. It used to be okay, but somewhere along the line Hide and Go Seek, Cooties, and Crazy Eights had lost their luster for Norman. He was a commercial fisherman, sort of, and he beat his dad at cribbage. That should be worth something to somebody, but at the age of twelve going on thirteen there are a lot of "should be's" and too few somethings and somebodies.

The extended Tuttle clan arrived on schedule and according to formula. Grandma and Grandpa showed with dress and tie and ceremonial bottle of wine. Uncle Stu came with Aunt Sissy whose mouth hit the deck running. "My, Norman, you've grown into such a little man." And of course the grand finale, Aunt Edna, Uncle Elmer, and tribe arrived in full bloom.

The kitchen sounded like midweek on the New York Stock Exchange if everybody brought their children to work. Babies crawled between legs, toddlers cried, Norman was ordered to put the coats away, and everybody was told to kiss their grandparents.

Then, just as the din reached a fever pitch, Norman heard the despicable announcement. "Okay kids, we need some room in here to breathe. Everybody to the basement so we can get dinner ready."

Eight young Tuttles made their jovial way down the basement stairs to pursue their silliness in private, while one half-young Tuttle lingered by the kitchen table swiping olives from the relish tray Aunt Sissy was preparing. "Norman, you'll spoil your dinner," she said.

Norman's dad was talking and laughing with Uncle Elmer in the corner. When he heard Aunt Sissy, he glanced to Norman absently and said, "Norman, your mother said 'kids to the basement,' go now."

Norman looked at his dad and his heart fell into his socks. Hadn't he just been telling him dirty stories in the basement not two hours ago? How could he possibly go back down in that room now and play tag with a bunch of, a bunch of . . . *kids*.

Norman's tail was draggin' and his head was drooped to the limits of physical reason as he left the room. Whether on purpose or not, or if it was coincidence, or divine providence, Norman did a very fortunate thing before he disappeared down the stairs. He stopped and took one short hurtful look back to his father, who at that very moment looked up from his discussion and saw it. It passed as quickly as it came and nothing was exchanged, only acknowledged.

Norman went down amid the din of younger Tuttles and pretended to busy himself arranging things on his dad's workbench. The other kids had four games going on at once, each one less interesting to Norman than the one before, and they paid him as little attention as he gave them.

Meanwhile his dad upstairs was having some thoughts of his own. He'd seen that Norman was put out about something, but he couldn't figure out what it was. He knew the kid was sensitive, but he couldn't believe he'd be upset by getting ratted on for stealing olives. So, he sent him downstairs. Big deal. It was Thanksgiving. That's where the kids go on Thanksgiving.

It wasn't until just a little while later, when Norman's dad watched Grandpa Tuttle, his dad, pouring the wine into the glasses before dinner, that the problem came clear to him. He remembered the year, and it wasn't that long ago, that his dad had handed over the responsibility of the Thanksgiving toast to him. "Frank," he'd said, "it's your house, and you're the boss. Would you do us the honors, sir."

And an honor it had been to stand and lift his glass and recount the Tuttle blessings as he saw them. The Tuttles were teetotalers, which is a lot harder to say than it is for them to do, so having the wine at dinner was a lot more glamour than appeal. No one has ever really asked where the tradition started, and no one has ever finished their glass of wine either, but the tradition endures.

Thinking about the toast and puzzling over Norman, Frank Tuttle made a grand decision, and quietly set another place at the big table complete with wineglass.

When Aunt Sissy called the kids for dinner, Norman was the last body to slink up the stairs. He was looking at his feet as he walked past the big dining table and didn't see his dad until a hand reached out and touched his shoulder. "Norm," his dad said. "Why don't you join us?"

Like I said. There are just a few occasions that we're allocated in this life that are going to stay with us all the way to the end, and this was certainly one of Norman's. For as long as he lives he'll remember standing for the first time with the grown Tuttles, with a mysterious half glass of dark red wine in his hand, and listening to his father's benediction.

He thanked the Lord for the good fishing season, and he thanked Him for good health, and a year of peace. And he thanked Him for his healthy children. And he looked Norman full in the face, and thanked his Lord most especially for bringing his oldest boy back to him to grow into such a fine young man.

And Norman clinked his glass with his father's and sipped the strange wine and wondered, as he always would, how something that tasted so bitter could leave such a sweet and lasting taste in his mouth.

———— • ————

The State Highway Department's effort to identify rural roads for the sake of emergency services was a failure, and the computer-generated street signs will be removed. The intersection of 45th Avenue and B Street will return to its original name of "the Old Dump Road at the Hooper Place," and newly dubbed "C Street" will continue as "Busted Axle Road."

The local Organization of Fishermen's Wives at their last regular meeting this year considered a motion to change their name to "The Organization of Fisherpersons' Spouses." The new unisex title was rejected after lengthy debate because it had too many S's in it and they didn't think it would fit on their Halibut Derby banner anyway.

———— • ————

12

Every Little Boy's Dream

THERE'S nothing like a tragedy to get people motivated. Our most recent motivating tragedy was the house fire at Stormy and Kirsten Storbock's new place. We've been trying to raise the money for a new fire truck here for the past year, with limited success until that happened.

Even though it's admitted that no amount of fire equipment would have reached that particular house in time, it got people into a "fire consciousness," and before that sorry week was out, the volunteer fire department had received the remaining $27,000 in grants and donations necessary to acquire the new pumper rig.

Mayor Richard Weekly, who doubles as our fire chief, had been in contact with the truck manufacturer in Ocala, Florida, for several months, and when he called them to say we'd raised the necessary money, he got some good news. Although normally it took up to a year to have a fire truck made to order, they had a last-minute cancellation on a truck that met the End of the Road Volunteer Fire Department's specifications and they'd let it go, as is, for a hefty discount if someone came to pick it up.

Ed Flannigan was selected to go by a straw lottery, and Stormy Storbock won second-in-command through a series of pool games with the other fire fighters and the fact that he wanted to pick up some furniture from his grandma's house in Peoria, Illinois, to help replace what they lost in the fire.

By the time the boys climbed off the bus in Ocala, their tails were draggin'. They'd taken a small plane from home to Anchorage, flew all night on three different airliners, got a commuter from Jacksonville to Gainesville, and finally hopped a Greyhound for the last leg to Ocala.

"I can't believe we can still be in America after all that," Stormy said.

"Well, if this ain't the *other* end of the road, it's gotta be close," Ed offered, wiping sweat from his face with his Caterpillar cap. "The hell of it is we came down at six hundred miles an hour. We gotta take the low road home."

"We'd better get started." Stormy clapped Ed on the back, shouldered his duffel, and pulled out the address of their truck dealer.

Both men were privately elated at what lay ahead. To drive a brand-new fire truck all the way across the United States. The envy of the turnpike. The pride of all. Every little boy's dream. I don't think there's a man in America who didn't spend at least a year of his young life sure he would grow up to be a fireman.

Some did. And two who did were recovering all the energy they left on the buses and airplanes as they walked through the door to the truck plant. It was little boy heaven. There were pictures of delicious red fire trucks on every wall in the entry office. Big ladder rigs, little horse-drawn pumpers. Bright red and chrome. Proud. Reliable. Sanitary. The works.

They were met by the sales manager and shown out to the lot to meet their new truck. When they rounded the corner and followed the arm of their guide to the truck, their little boy smiles hit the asphalt. You wouldn't have boxed the looks left on their faces and sent them to your worst enemy.

"I'm gonna call the mayor," Ed said, backing away from the lot.

"Me too," Stormy said and followed Ed, leaving a somewhat perplexed fire-equipment sales manager in the hot Florida sun.

"Mayor Weekly?"

"Yes?"

"It's green." Ed was holding the phone out from his ear so Stormy could hear too.

"What's green?"

"Our truck. The new truck's green."

"I know. It's supposed to be green."

"Whadya mean it's supposed to be green? It's supposed to be *red*. Fire trucks are red. This one's green."

"Calm down, Ed." The mayor assumed the patient, weary tone he often uses in explanatory situations. "That color green is the latest in safety features. Red turns black in the dark, but the green stays visible."

"Mayor Weekly, with all due respect, we'll have four lights flashing, the siren howling, and an ambulance following us. Do they really have to see the whole truck?"

"Ed," the mayor said calmly, "just bring the damn truck home. And don't forget my butter cookies." And the mayor hung up.

"What'd he say?"

"He said it's supposed to be green, and don't forget his butter cookies." Ed put his arm on Stormy's shoulder in resignation. "Looks like we got ourselves a lime-green fire truck. C'mon, bub. We got a lot to do."

And they did have a lot to do. Being that almost everybody at the End of the Road was from someplace else, they had a long list of stops to make on behalf of friends back home. They had to run through Bloomington, Illinois, to get a bunch of butter cookies from the mayor's sister. Then they had to go to Peoria to pick up the furniture at Stormy's grandmother's, then Omaha for some stuff for Frank and Fanny Olmstead. Scottsbluff to visit Ed's in-laws, up through Montana to Bud Koenig's people, and on and on to Seattle, where they were to put the truck on a sea barge and fly the rest of the way home.

The first thing the boys discovered about driving their fire truck was that traffic was not going to be a problem. Things started to ball up on I-75 outside of Gainesville just about the time Stormy was playing around with the switches on the dashboard, looking for the windshield washers.

When the lights went on and the siren lit off, the traffic parted before them like the Red Sea. "Oooweee, that's gonna be handy," Stormy said and settled back into his seat as Ed guided the truck at record speed around Gainesville and off into the night.

Two big kids in a green fire truck hell-bent for Peoria sounds a heck of a lot more exciting than it is. Stormy slept most of the way through Georgia, then Ed slept stretched out on the co-pilot's seat until Stormy pulled over at a burger joint outside of Lexington, Kentucky. The boys ate somebody's idea of an English muffin, filled their thermoses, washed their faces, and changed drivers again.

"Where's Peoria?" Ed asked, putting it in gear as Stormy pulled his jacket over his head.

"Take a left at Cincinnati." And that was the last Ed heard of Stormy until he had to hit the siren to get through a bit of a backup outside of Indianapolis.

When they got to the outskirts of Bloomington they called the number the mayor had given them for his sister. Rather than have the boys try to muck their way through an unfamiliar city, the mayor's sister decided she would come out to meet them at the truck stop on the highway.

The mayor's sister turned out to be an obese woman named Shirley with a Buick full of Salerno butter cookies for her brother and a six-pack of soda and a bag of baloney sandwiches on white bread for the boys.

"Whenever I ask Richard what he wants from home for Christmas, he always says the same thing," Shirley said, gesturing toward the Buick. "'Salerno butter cookies,' he says, every time. So this oughta keep him from getting homesick."

"A guy wouldn't have to think of home to get sick on all these," Ed said to Stormy as the two of them loaded up three of the auxiliary compartments on the truck with cookies.

The ride in to Peoria was wonderful. It was a bright December Illinois afternoon. The fire truck was getting a lot of attention on the freeway. Truckers would tip their hats, patrolmen would wave, and uncountable kids would press their faces against rear windows and beam at them until they were well out of sight up ahead. The boys had to admit they cut quite a figure on the highway even if they were green.

They cut more than a figure, in fact, they were an absolute spectacle when they pulled the truck up in front of Grandma Storbock's house in Peoria. She lived in a quiet old neighborhood unaccustomed to visiting fire equipment, and many of the good neighbors ran out on the street in slippers and tee-shirts carrying fire extinguisher, blankets, and asking where the fire was.

"There's no fire," Grandma yelled from the front porch. "It's my grandson Stewart, all the way from Alaska in a fire engine."

"We're taking the truck *to* Alaska, Grandma," Stormy reminded her on the way in the door.

"To, from, who can keep track of you kids? Stewart, I thought fire trucks were supposed to be red."

"I did too, Grandma." And the boys were led in to the biggest pot-roast dinner the Central Plains had seen in probably a few weeks.

Ed and Stormy left early the next morning with two fresh thermoses of coffee, leftover pot roast in tin-foil, plus a cedar chest, two dressers, and a dining-room table set tarped and roped down on top of the truck. They blew the siren for the kids waiting at the bus stop and set their sights on Omaha.

They crossed the Mississippi without incident but had to hit the lights to get around Des Moines. They had no trouble finding the Olmstead extended family outside of Omaha. It's amazing how anxious people are to give good directions to a fire truck. Ed and Stormy soon found their rig parked in front of a fine country home and themselves parked in front of proba-bly the second biggest pot-roast dinner the Central Plains had seen in at least twenty-four hours.

After a little get-to-know-you session with a few of Pastor Frank's cousins, Ed and Stormy loaded up ten cases of home-canned beets, tomatoes, and pickles, and with a whoop of the siren headed out to I-80 for the long haul to Scottsbluff and Ed Flannigan's in-laws.

Showing up at your in-laws' unannounced is never a very comfortable entry, but showing up at two in the morning unannounced in a green fire truck loaded with furniture, canned beets, and butter cookies, can be darned near painful.

Emily's parents never thought the world of Ed. They figured Emily was worth more than a road-grader driver and volunteer fireman from the End of the Road. But they always treated Ed decently, and they wel-comed Stormy as well into their modest ranch home within spittin' distance of the highway. They sat around the kitchen table and chatted sleepily about the grand-kids for a short time while Emily's mother heated up some leftover . . . pot roast.

"They eat a lot of pot roast down here on the flatlands, don't they, Stormbocker?" Ed said later, sharing a double Hide-A-Bed with Stormy in the den.

"Yeah, and we still got Grandma's leftovers to eat."

"Threw it away at the Seventy-six outside Lincoln."

"Thanks."

"You're welcome."

"Good night."

The boys endured a short night on the Hide-A-Bed. A kitten dive-bombed their heads at unexpected moments the whole time, and neither one of them could relax enough to sleep, hearing the constant rush of trucks and cars on the highway outside.

"Stormy, let's go home," Ed said, pulling on his pants.

"I'll drive." And the boys headed west with a gray December dawn in their side mirrors and both of them starting to feel like horses headed toward the barn.

The day eventually found them in Montana, where they got their pictures taken by the local paper in Billings with their truck and a troop of Cub Scouts at a Dairy Queen. They looked up Bud Koenig's brother in Missoula, who ceremoniously handed over a wooden crate that must have weighed three hundred pounds, explaining, "Bud would want it."

It turned out to be a bunch of rusty car and chainsaw parts which were being sent as a joke between the brothers, and it's a good thing Ed and Stormy didn't know about the prank at the time because they scratched the paint on the truck trying to heft it onto the top.

They finally topped off that day in Coeur d'Alene, Idaho, trying to find Doug McDoogan's family, who supposedly had something for him. Ed and Stormy spent over an hour trying to find anybody who was related to Doug or even willing to admit they ever knew him before they gave up and got a room for the night.

"Ed, ol' buddy?" Stormy said as he eased into bed.

"Yeah, bud."

"I feel like a pot roast dipped in coffee."

"That's just about what you are, I'd guess. Lean into it, we're almost there." And Ed rolled over in the dark, trying to erase the white lines from his eyelids.

When Ed and Stormy woke up they came to the realization that this was the last day of their "big trip." They intended to take full advantage of it.

The two clean-shaven men were in high spirits as they pulled on their End of the Road Volunteer Fire Department windbreakers, checked the ropes on their cargo, and fired up the big green truck for one final day of highway exhibitionism.

They were the stars of the diesel pumps just outside Spokane, where they had their pictures taken with several friendly truckers and bought some jack-a-lope postcards. Ed disconnected the governor and the boys pulled onto I-90 with sirens wailing to see just what that baby could do.

"She gets quite a shimmy to 'er at seventy-five," Ed yelled over the roar of engine.

"Better slow 'er down before we lose Grandma's furniture," Stormy yelled back, feeling a little self-conscious about the whole affair. Being bright green is one thing. Being bright green with flashing lights and sirens is another. But being bright green with flashing lights and sirens and breaking every traffic law in the books is a whole separate fruit altogether. And a dangerous fruit at that, so Ed shut down to an agreeable sixty miles an hour, switched off the fireworks, and the boys continued the last leg of their journey into Seattle.

When they got to the barge lots at the port of Tacoma, it was with a little sadness that Ed and Stormy gathered up their personal gear in the cab, checked the ropes on the menagerie of cargo on the back, and gave one last long look at their big green baby.

Once the truck reached town it would be everybody's pride and joy. It would be paraded down Main Street, polished by other hands, driven by many people and owned by all. Right now, for these last few minutes, it was the sole property and purpose to life of Ed

Flannigan and Stormy Storbock. Two little boys who grew up to be firemen at least part of the time and took great pride from that fact all of the time.

They turned the keys over to the dockmaster, called a cab to the airport, and shouldered their duffels out the chain-link gate to the port.

On an afterthought Ed turned to call to the dockmaster, "Don't be playin' around with the lights and sirens, ya hear?"

"Yeah, yeah," the man said, dismissing them with a hand.

As Ed and Stormy's taxi pulled up to the gates of Seattle-Tacoma Airport, unbeknownst to them, a half-dozen longshoremen and a dockmaster were crowded around the cab of their big green baby at the port of Tacoma.

The dockmaster hit the strobe lights and threw the switch for the siren. A piercing wail ripped through the barge staging area and seven little boys who would've been firemen giggled and glowed with the glorious sound of a dream come true.

Local salvage dealer Argus Winslow was asked to supply a second junked car for this year's Beluga Lake Ice Classic. Every year an old car is placed on the lake and bets are placed on the day it will fall through the ice in the spring. Organizers jumped the gun a little this year and the first car fell through the ice as soon as they shoved it out there.

We've been asked to caution ice skaters to avoid that part of the lake until the hole heals over.

Kirsten Storbock's blue Chevy Blazer was reported missing after the State Highway Department's twelve-foot turbine snow blower made a pass down Flat Back Road. A Highway Department spokesman denied responsibility. "The snow's pretty deep up there, and I think Kirsten should keep looking," he said. "We've passed Subarus and a couple Fiats through that blower without knowing it, but I think we would have heard a Chevy."

13

Doug's Stuff

DOUG McDoogan's first couple weeks of affluence were not going as well as expected, even though he had every reason to be elated over his new situation.

He'd lived on the road most of his adult life, and the most deluxe accommodations he'd enjoyed to date in his twenty-nine years before this apartment was a driftwood shack he built and called home out on the spit beach.

Doug was content in his new digs for most of the first week and then it started to gnaw at him. Sure, he had hot and cold running water. Yeah, there was a bed and a toilet, a stove and oil heat. All these things and more that he'd never had before. But it didn't take long before the whole thing became, literally, a hollow experience.

It had never occurred to Doug before that he didn't have any things. I guess there's nothing makes you thirstier than an empty cup, and Doug began to thirst for things. All he'd brought with him from the shack was a fire-scorched cook pot, a cracked coffee mug, a wool army blanket, and a change of shirt. Doug had never owned more than two shirts, and he operated on the alternating "wear a day, air a day" system.

His two shirts, two socks, and single pair of jeans had been plenty for him until faced with his very own empty closet. There were even eight wire hangers on the rod, punctuating the point that they were sadly lacking in purpose.

The kitchen, though small in itself, dwarfed Doug's cooking ensemble. He didn't even own a plate or fork, and everything he ate was out of the pot with his jackknife, the most important possession he had and his means to a living.

Everyplace he looked there was nothing. There was a pile of raw driftwood in one corner waiting to be carved, a mound of wood chips around the kitchen table, and his army blanket on the bed. Everything else was exactly as Doug had found it. Empty dresser, empty closet, empty medicine cabinet, empty cupboards . . . and it was giving Doug an empty heart.

Fortunately, just when it was about to get too much for ol' Doug, the blue-haired lady from Anchorage who was buying all his carvings showed up at his door. She looked over the dozen or so pieces Dough had finished, picked out eight of the best, and left Doug standing, mouth agape in the doorway, with four hundred dollars in his hot little hand.

"That woman must be crazy," Doug said, looking after her, "but I like 'er." And Doug McDoogan decided to go shopping.

Doug, being of the financial caliber he was, didn't know a lot about stores or shopping. He couldn't remember ever having bought a new piece of merchandise in his life. The few things he did have were either scavenged, scammed, or stolen outright. New goods were a foreign and frightening thing for Doug. They were things that "other" people had.

So, as you can imagine, Doug didn't search out a Bloomingdale's or even a Woolworth to outfit his apartment. He went directly to the meeting ground of wise shoppers everywhere. He went to the garage sales.

Garage-saling around the End of the Road has slowed some with the coming of winter, but there's always a few die-hard merchants and junkers doing their Saturday trade.

Doug, unfortunately, didn't get started until well into the afternoon, which was a fatal error. As any good garage-saler knows, all the good stuff goes out the door in the first ten minutes if it hasn't already been claimed by friends and early gate crashers.

By the time Doug got to the handful of stray sales that Saturday, they were already down to the potty chairs and bald tires, which was a depressing sight. There's probably nothing more seamy-looking in the world than a picked-over garage sale. There's usually a boxload of chewed-up plastic kids' toys, a bicycle or two missing a variety of essential parts, a shelf of dog-eared romance novels, and a few washed-out shirts and dresses.

Doug sorted through this stuff with keen interest, to the embarrassment of the proprietors. You see, there's nothing more humiliating than watching someone rifle through your old junk. All the dumb stuff we bought ourselves or were given and are trying to palm off on somebody else. Hopelessly out-of-fashion clothes. Post-trendy paperbacks. Frayed bathrobes. This is why neighboring families usually combine their things to have a garage sale. There's always the chance that way that people will think the really hideous leftovers belong to the other party and not yourself.

"Are you looking for something in particular?" one red-faced woman asked Doug as he stood there with a handful of her old brassieres, digging farther into a box he had no business in.

"Nope," Doug said. "Just lookin'."

"All the good things went early," the woman said in apology. "Shoulda been here at nine this morning."

It was the same story Doug would hear at every stop. "You missed the good stuff." "We had some real deals this morning." "Too bad. We had a leather coat your size hours ago, went for two dollars." And on it went.

All Doug found to his liking was a bunch of flannel shirts that were so big for him he only bought four of them, and a handful of forks and spoons. He returned to his apartment feeling less than endowed.

He carefully hung up the four big shirts on the hangers in the closet and arranged the silverware in the top kitchen drawer. It was an improvement, Doug had to admit. Eating beans out of a pot was easier with a spoon than a jackknife, and it was nice to have a shirt on that didn't smell like his boots for a change. But Doug's junk lust was not fulfilled.

It lasted all week. Doug couldn't keep his mind on his carving. He almost always carved animals. Doug's best pieces were of sea lions, otters, eagles, and bears. But this week his head was clouded with pillows, pants, soap dishes, and appliances. He started what he intended to be a Dall sheep on Wednesday, but by Friday it was looking suspiciously like an electric toaster.

A toaster was one of his favorite fantasies. And a coffeepot. An electric one would be best, but any one would do. He made his coffee in the same pot he cooked his eggs in, and he lived in waiting for a cup of joe without grease floating on it. Doug laid back on his rolled-up shirt and dreamt of pillows. He envisioned towels in the bathroom, shoes in the closet, a winter jacket, ashtrays, frying pans, plates, and the most daring fantasy of them all, a clock radio with a dial that lit up.

Doug controlled himself all week and by the following Saturday he still had $350. He woke up at six-thirty in the morning and began to worry. There was only one garage sale that week and it was supposed to start at ten. As Doug sat at his table drinking greasy coffee, he grew more and more anxious. Every time he heard a car go by outside, he assumed it was somebody on their way to beat him to the good stuff. He pictured all his treasures being walked down the driveway under someone else's smiling face.

By seven-thirty he could stand it no more and

started walking in the dark the few blocks to where he'd seen the signs. There was no evidence of life at the house and the big double garage door was shut tight. Doug could only lean up against a tree in the front yard and try to imagine what lay behind it.

As we've mentioned before, Doug McDoogan is not the smartest guy in the world. In fact it has been rare in his life that he's been in a crowd bigger than two when he wasn't operating at a disadvantage. But one mental ability Doug did have was concentration—or fixation, might be more accurate—like a dog who will sit in a car and stare at the door his master disappeared through for hours, even days.

It was this sort of fixated stare that Doug had fixed on the garage door that morning. Around eight o'clock a light went on in the kitchen and his heart started to pound. At eight-thirty he heard some commotion behind the double door and his palms began to sweat. By a quarter to nine Doug could stand it no longer. He walked up to the big double door and gave it an earnest thrashing.

The woman inside, who was unfamiliar to Doug, cracked the door a notch and said, "It doesn't start till ten. We're not even set up yet." And she closed the door in his face.

Doug was a stranger in a strange land and did not have the aggressive impulse necessary to push his point, so he dug his hands in his pockets, wrapped one around the hot wad of money there, and stood four feet from the door staring at it.

At about nine-thirty the woman took a peek through the door, saw Doug standing there shivering, and thought, *What the heck, I'll let him come in.*

When Doug walked inside the door he took a moment to focus on the dimly lit card tables around the garage, then his jaw dropped. The very first thing his eyes lit on was a shiny electric four-hole toaster. Not two feet away was a clock table radio that was at that very minute playing the morning news accompanied by an exquisite glowing dial. There were two pillows off to his left. A pile of towels folded and tied with twine to his right, and dead ahead a full complement of cast-iron cookware. As he ventured in farther his forehead broke out into a sweat and he was virtually squeezing the ink off the money in his pocket. He pulled a big down parka off a hanger to one side and it fit perfectly. While wearing the coat he tripped on a box and looked down to see a complete set of plastic plates, cups, and saucers with a smaller box inside full of spatulas, spoons, steak knives, and other various and sundry cooking utensils.

Doug could stand no more. Holding his arms out and back as if to capture the whole room, he said, "How much for . . . *everything*."

"Everything?" the woman said, stopping her arranging for a minute.

"Yeah, everything. I want it all. It's perfect. I don't want to lose it. It's mine." Doug was flipping the toaster up and down with a wooden cooking spoon and staring into the face of the clock radio.

As it happens, the woman and her husband had set a goal that very morning over breakfast on what they wanted to make at their garage sale. They'd roughly added up the big stuff, allowed a debit for stuff that would be left over, and came up with a nice round number. "Three hundred and fifty dollars," she said to Doug importantly, as if to dismiss the idea.

"I'll take it," Doug said, still staring at the radio. "Can I borrow your truck?"

And this series of events is what found our hero sitting on the edge of his bed gawking at a huge pile of somebody else's things in his apartment. His elation was palpable. Donald Trump couldn't match it if he bought ten airlines. For the first time since Doug haired-over, he had *stuff*.

He hadn't had time to look things over very closely moving it, so he went about his organizing meticulously. He only had one rule: everything stays. He hung up the clothes in the closet, which included a lot of strange shirts and pants that fit well and a few dresses and blouses that meant nothing to him outside of the fact that they were his. He loaded his kitchen cupboards up with pots and pans and plates. He put an aluminum coffeepot on to boil and plugged in his toaster. He dug out his new radio, set it on the table, and turned it all the way up.

He danced around his pile and picked one thing off at a time. The bundle of towels were hung in the bathroom. He found an electric hair-curling iron which he couldn't identify, then figured since it had a cord on it, it must be an appliance, so he plugged it in and set it next to the toaster.

He placed his new pillows on the bed and covered them with a bedspread. A collection of ashtrays was spread around the apartment more for decoration than anything else, 'cause Doug didn't smoke. There were two velvet paintings of bullfighters, which he admired at some length then hung above the bed. And on through the day it went. Everything found its place.

Even the baby clothes, bassinet, and plastic toys were given a place. Doug smelled them, and held them. He folded them into a drawer . . . and owned them.

At last it was done. The only things left out of place were three bald tires to a Subaru, a piece of Formica countertop from a sink cutout, and a box of books. Doug could only read at about a third-grade level, so the books were of about as much use to him as the tires, but he recognized the importance of appearances. He placed the countertop scrap in the corner on top of the tires and neatly arranged the row of books on that.

"Doug McDoogan. Now that you're a rich man, yer gonna have to learn yourself to read," he said out loud to himself and laid back on his new bedspread to take it all in.

Doug used three towels after a long hot shower and sat in somebody else's bathrobe at the table listening to somebody else's radio and eating toast. He looked at the pile of driftwood yet to be carved off in one corner but couldn't pull himself away from his new things to do anything with it. He played with the hair-curling iron for a while, still puzzling over what it could be, and would periodically turn the lights off so he could watch the glow of the clock's face in his radio.

The hands of the clock were set to no particular time, but it didn't matter to Doug as long as they moved forward. And they did move forward. And the music played. And somewhere off in the mist where the accountings of foolery and fools are kept, where the innocent plead guilty and forbidden apples grow like weeds, a giant hand reached sadly out and made a note in a book. A note that Doug McDoogan . . . had arrived.

Animal activist Tamara Dupree was questioned by police on the cannery loading dock after she was witnessed reading poetry to two dolphins and a harbor seal. "It just really gave me the willies," said one witness. "I thought she'd gone crazy." Ms. Dupree explained that she was trying to communicate with what she regards as a higher life form, although she said the seals seemed to be more interested than the dolphins. "Seals are dumber than corks," said Ms. Dupree. "I guess it doesn't say much for this poetry."

14

Ruby's Video
Roundup

WITH the possible exception of Clara's Coffee Cup, the most poignant and interesting discussion going on at the End of the Road goes on around the coffeepot at Ruby's Video Roundup.

Ruby McClay is the moderator of these discussions, or more exactly the "immoderator," as she seems to do a whole lot more of mixing things up than she does fixing things up. She also will use against you what she knows about you, which is considerable if you take into account her fortunate perspective on the town. Knowing the kind of movies people watch is almost as good as reading their diaries for telling personal landscapes.

Ruby McClay is getting on into her late sixties, to look at her, but lookin' never did tell too much around here. A lot of folks have taken a rough road to the end, and Ruby would fall into that ageless class of elderly people who could be anywhere from fifty-five to ninety. It doesn't really matter, but it does give folks something to speculate on during these dark quiet months—speculation being the better part of winter activity, renting movies at Ruby's being the other part.

Ruby's Video Roundup is the only video-rental store in town and caters to everyone equally regardless of race, creed, color, or confusion. The last of which predominates at Ruby's establishment.

You see, on any given day there are two or three regulars plus Ruby sipping strong coffee from Styrofoam cups, greeting customers and commenting on movie selections. They've informally named themselves "the committee," and have become the bane of every End of the Road movie lover, even though all of us at one time or another have served on the committee with Ruby.

As soon as someone walks in the door to return a tape, they come under the committee's review. Ruby will snag the tape from the poor soul's hand and announce the title to the group.

"Hard Sweaty Bodies?" Ruby might say to Ed Flannigan, sheepishly handing his movie over. "Tryin' to put a little'a that ol' spark back in the bedspread, Eddie?"

"It's a dancing movie, Ruby," Ed would say with six colors of red in his face and neck. "Emily likes dancing movies."

"That ain't no dancin' movie," one of the old-timers on the committee might offer. *"Singin' in the Rain, Yankee Doodle Dandy.* Now those were dancin' movies. They don't make 'em like that no more."

Ruby would run with that thought. "All those people are dead or workin' on it, like you are, ya ol' fart. You oughta open your eyes and look at what some of these kids are doing. It's different."

"It's weird."

"Weird is an opinion. Different is a piece of fact . . ." and off the committee would go on that idea until another customer showed up for some ridicule.

Ruby was always the first of the committee to begin a line of derision, but she also knew exactly how far to go with it. For instance, when Doug McDoogan brought back the rental VCR and three movies.

Doug was an undeniably unlikable loner, so the group was on his movie selections like cats on parakeets. Ruby made the triple announcement.

"*Love Story, Romeo and Juliet*, and *Big Bird's Giant Word Circus*. Doug McDoogan, don't tell me, you're falling in love?"

"Yeah," says one of the committee. "Loves a chicken with a gland problem."

Ruby watched Doug closely. He was taking the ribbing pretty well. A little bit uncomfortable, but nothing serious. Doug was a lonely person, that was plain to see. He must take some comfort, Ruby thought, from other people's love lives, for lack of one of his own. But the Sesame Street tape she couldn't make heads or tails of until the next comment came from the table.

"Well, Doug, you're almost thirty years old. Gooda time as any to learn how to read."

Ruby saw Doug flinch and his eyes drop to his shoes. He shuffled over to the counter to pay his bill. *Well, I'll be darned,* she thought. *The little puke can't read, and he's trying to learn from the kids' tapes. Well, good-for-him,* and Ruby came to his rescue.

"Doug just gets those for the neighbor kids. Isn't that right, Doug?"

Doug looked at Ruby a little confused, but being no slouch of a liar himself, fell right in with the program. "Yeah, that's right. They're always comin' over buggin' me, so I let 'em watch Big Bird to keep 'em quiet."

Ruby pointed Doug over to the children's section. "If they like those word ones, Doug, *Bert and Ernie's See and Spell*'s a good one, and *Grover's Laugh and Read* oughta keep 'em busy for a while. Keep the VCR for an extra day and tell me how they liked them. I can order a bunch more like that." And the committee watched in mixed wonder and warmth as Ruby led Doug past the poison council and safely back onto the street.

That was Ruby's way. Give the underdog a break,

and try to knock the high rider off his horse. The End of the Road had its fair share of both, and Ruby has dealt with them all.

Pastor Frank Olmstead of the First and Last Baptist Church probably rides the highest horse around, but "it's got really spindly legs" according to Ruby. Frank and Ruby have had more than a couple run-ins. The pastor has designated himself the local official media censor, and Ruby, being a good part of local media, has had to deal with this.

The pastor would come through the store from time to time and look for movie titles he might be able to object to. His last time around he found two to his disliking, *The Devil on Church Street* and *Satan's Sunbath*. The pastor never watched the movies, he just didn't like the titles, so he started an official protest against them.

This offended Ruby because not only did she keep a tasteful video store, there wasn't even an adult section, but no one hardly ever checked those two particular horror films out anyway. At least not until Pastor Frank started his campaign against them.

He distributed petitions out on the street, addressed the Chamber of Commerce, and even paid for an ad in the paper against it. This went on for a few weeks, then one day he came into the Video Roundup, passed the committee, and marched right up to Ruby wagging papers in his hand. "Ruby, I demand in the names of the seventy-eight concerned citizens on this petition that you get those distasteful materials off of your store shelf."

Ruby pushed the papers out of her face and said not unkindly, "Put a lid on it, Frank. They've been off the shelf for two days. Used up. There's been so many people comin' in here to rent those darn things ever since you started harpin' on it, that they plumb wore out. Never did such a business on a movie before."

The pastor huffed himself up to full authority and said, "That's good. Now they're where they belong and out of the homes of innocent people."

"Listen, Frank," Ruby said. "Everybody in town

except you and maybe seventy-eight others has already seen 'em in the last two weeks. Except for that, I'd replace them. Besides, I watched them both and they're about the stupidest horror shows ever made. Don't know how I ended up with them in the first place. Thanks for all the business, though. I really got my money out of those two. Buy you a cup of coffee, Frank?"

The pastor softened a little. "No thank you, Ruby, I'll be going. I'm glad we could come to an understanding."

As Pastor Frank disappeared through the front door, Ruby shook her head and thought, *Lord, You do work in some mysterious ways.*

Another mystery to Ruby was Argus Winslow. He was the only individual in this town who was completely unaffected by Ruby and the committee review.

They could usually get a rise out of most anybody. Ed Flannigan and his steamy movies. Doug McDoogan and his love stories. They reduced gentle pacifist Tamara Dupree nearly to tears catching her trying to bootleg *Rooster Cogburn* and *Dirty Harry* past the coffeepot. Chief of Police Peter Bindel left empty-handed once rather than try to explain to everyone why he wanted to see the *Woodstock* movie.

The forty-year-old police chief's most closely guarded secret was that he attended that particular rock spectacle back in his youth, and it *wasn't* as a security guard. Ruby knew about it, but Ruby knew about 'most everything. Everything except Argus Winslow, that is.

Argus would come in and make the most unlikely movie selections with impunity. The committee would try to harangue him for picking *Bambi*. "I always cry at this one," the ol' curmudgeon would growl on his way out the door. He'd check out a *Benji* movie and say it was to show his dog Barney. This crusty old junkyard goat would walk out with *Bugs Bunny and Friends* in one hand, *Old Yeller* in the other, and offer no more explanation to the committee than to say he had a long evening ahead.

The committee had two official positions on Argus. One was that he did, in fact, take these goofy tapes home to show to his dog. The other was that he made random selections of off-the-wall titles just to entertain Ruby and the committee.

Ruby knew they were both wrong. Argus took them home and enjoyed them. She could see it in his eyes. A little twinkle of fun and mischief beneath all that gruff and growl. She could easily picture him laughing out loud at Bugs Bunny, or holding Barney in his lap and shedding a tear for Old Yeller. *You can fool a lot of people, Argus Winslow,* Ruby thought, *but you can't fool ol' Ruby McClay.* And Ruby McClay couldn't fool Argus either, and just about everybody knew they were kind of sweet on each other.

Ruby's private life was exactly that; private. She lived in her small apartment behind the Roundup, and as far as anybody knew, all she did was sit back there with her cats and watch videos. You'd see her out sometimes in her little pickup buying groceries or whatnot, but you often wouldn't recognize her. She never looked natural anywhere except leaned up behind her counter at the Roundup. It was her job, her joy, her position, and her strength.

The whole thing started only five or six years ago, when the video craze first came to the End of the Road. She opened with just a handful of pirated films her sister would bootleg off the movie channels down in Seattle. Ruby McClay, being a respectable person in life and commerce, endeavored to make her enterprise aboveboard at her earliest opportunity.

In its fledgling days, Ruby's Video Roundup operated solely out of her kitchen. She lived in a house then, and customers would drop by to look over her selections, drink her coffee, and talk about whatever came to light. This is undoubtedly where the seeds of the committee were planted and why the first thing she did when she moved into her storefront was to put in a big table, a coffee maker, and some chairs.

There may have been better places around town to shoot the breeze, but none with such broad horizons. Down at Clara's Coffee Cup or the Lame Moose Saloon the topics ranged from sports to salmon fishing, politics to pickup trucks. The parameters of Ruby's discussions were firmly rooted in the nebulous world of the make-believe. The world of movies, where nothing is real but the ideas behind them, and everything is equally important.

In a ten-minute span of time a conversation at the Roundup might drift from L.A. street gangs to the rings of Saturn. The merits of the Apache Indians would be touched on along with King Kong, then and now, teenage sex, martial arts, Douglas MacArthur, and was Ginger Rogers a better dancer than Fred Astaire because she did everything he did only backwards. You just couldn't find this kind of reach in a deliberation down at the other watering holes.

And through it all sat Ruby—teasing and chiding, challenging and listening. Making sure nobody came through unscathed, but nobody left bleeding either. That was her role in life, she figured. These people were like her children. She couldn't really tell them what to do. What ideas to have, what movies to watch, or which ones to like. She just wanted to make sure that whatever they did, they *meant* it. And she set up the forum for that at the Roundup.

After-hours at the Roundup would find Ruby curled up in a Naugahyde La-Z-Boy with her cats, watching old movies. The classics were her favorites, although she never recommended any movie over another. Jimmy Stewart, Katharine Hepburn, Spencer Tracy, Bogart, Gable, Davis, Cagney. People who did mean what they said, and good prevailing over evil by wits and courage, not bare chests and automatic weapons. Actors whose lines were overstated with gestures bigger than life, and nobody mumbled or swore. They talked, they fought, they wept . . . and they *meant* it.

Ruby couldn't keep her eyes open to the end of her favorite movie this night; *It's a Wonderful Life,* with a young James Stewart. She watches it every year about Christmastime. It always makes her feel better. And it did tonight too, as she pulled two of her cats in around her neck, leaned back into the chair, and agreed with her movie, *It is a wonderful life.* And she meant it.

PTA president Emily Flannigan expressed regrets and apologized for the Student Dangle Balls Decoration contest downtown. Elementary school students were asked to construct outdoor Christmas decorations from popcorn balls and string to adorn the municipal light poles. The project attracted so many hungry sea gulls and ravens to the downtown area that stores were temporarily closed on Friday. "It looked like an Alfred Hitchcock movie for a while there," an embarrassed Ms. Flannigan said of the scene, and announced that there will be a PTA car wash on Monday at the big garage on Clearshot, free to any offended parties.

The Organization of Fishermen's Wives will have their monthly home-maintenance idea and fudge exchange at OFW headquarters at noon Thursday. This week's film topic, "Why Keep Living Things Out of the Microwave," is a graphic one, ladies, so bring a strong stomach. And don't forget those recipes.

15

*The Town
Tree*

THIS was the first year that we ever had a town Christmas tree. Most of the reason why we never had one stemmed from the fact that there wasn't any place to put one. At least not until Argus Winslow donated some land downtown to the city for a public park. Everyone agrees that Argus probably did it just to cause trouble, and he couldn't have been more successful.

Argus Winslow, our local junkyard tycoon, has a huge salvage yard out by Far Road. But for years he's had a lot downtown where he stores old junk cars, stoves, refrigerators and things. He's always called it his "city branch," but it was actually just an eyesore. He's been getting complaints all along about his city branch and even been taken to court a couple times to force him to clean it up.

No one ever expected Argus to give in, because he never does, so everyone was pleasantly surprised when one week Argus started towing the cars away, gathering up the appliances, and finally bulldozed the rest of it into the ground. What remained was a beautifully groomed flat dirt lot right in the middle of town.

It was three weeks ago this Monday Argus stood up at the city council meeting and publicly deeded the lot to the city. His only condition on the donation was that it be made into a park. Nothing more, nothing less, and nothing else.

You have to understand here that Argus Winslow is an accomplished rabble-rouser, and although everybody in the council chambers was charmed and grateful for the donation, they wondered at the same time what he was up to. It wouldn't take very long to find out.

First of all, as everyone soon realized, if you're going to have a city park, it has to have a name. The council quickly appointed a "Parks Committee" to tackle this chore.

The first meeting of the Parks Committee was a gray day for all involved. Ruby McClay, owner-operator of Ruby's Video Roundup and president of the Chamber of Commerce, thought it should be named the "Argus Winslow Memorial Park." It was a nice gesture, but Mayor Weekly pointed out that you don't memorialize people who are still living.

Sissy Tuttle, of the Organization of Fishermen's Wives, thought the park should be named in honor of fishermen lost at sea.

This was emphatically rejected by Emily Flannigan, who thought it was a totally depressing idea. That a park should be an uplifting experience and a place where families can enjoy a conscience-free afternoon.

Emily, drawing from her misspent youth at Radcliffe, thought that "People's Park" would be the most appropriate name for it, which caused poor Pastor Frank to blow coffee through his nose and come completely out of his chair. "People's" *anything* sounded too much like communism to him, and while Emily and Frank battled over the merits of nonsense, the Good Mayor sat back listening helplessly until this little brushfire had burned itself out. Finally, he pounded his coffee mug on the table to get everyone's attention and addressed the committee in his usual conciliatory tones.

"Ladies and . . . Frank, I've given this matter a lot of thought," he lied. "And my opinion is that no matter what we name this darn thing, that everybody is just going to call it 'the park.' My recommendation is that we name it appropriately. I leave a motion on the floor that we name the new city park, 'The Park.'"

There was silence on the table as lips were chewed, corners of the room were stared into, necks were scratched, and eventually good sense prevailed and Emily Flannigan seconded the motion.

"The Park" was voted on and adopted by a four-to-one margin. Pastor Frank was the dissenting vote, which surprised no one because nothing pleased Frank, and there was little hope that anything ever would.

Argus Winslow was an accomplished fly in the ointment, and he most probably would like to have been a fly on the wall of that meeting just to get a chuckle out of the trouble he was causing with his generous donation. But Argus had something else on his mind. There were other mischievous forces in motion around the End of the Road. Forces directed toward him and in the hands of one Bud Koenig, Argus's nemesis, archrival, and best friend.

These two old-timers were constantly tormenting each other in any number of small ways, and over the years some of them have become traditional. As in the case of Bud Koenig's annual Christmas prank. Every year on Christmas Eve Bud would come up with a practical joke of one awful sort or another that Argus was made to suffer through. Argus had learned to expect these pranks and watch for them, but never has he been able to avoid one. Bud always outsmarted him in the end.

This year Argus was paying particularly close attention. He'd heard through the grapevine that Bud was quietly collecting cardboard refrigerator boxes. This made no sense to anyone, including Argus, but one thing he did know was that it had something to do with him. It kept him alert and occupied. So much so that he couldn't fully appreciate chapter two in the saga of his city park.

You see, as soon as the committee had somewhat unanimously agreed on the name of the park, they went on to the next piece of business, which was what to do with it.

Mayor Weekly quickly pointed out that it was too late in the year to do very darn much with the lot and suggested hopefully that they table the entire matter until spring. That's when Emily Flannigan, in a last-ditch effort to save the Parks Committee, glommed onto the idea of a town Christmas tree.

Oh no, thought the mayor, dreading the debate that was ensuing even before he had a chance to dread it.

Pastor Frank stood up. "I think that the idea of a community Christmas tree is a grand one, and being as it is in celebration of the birth of our Saviour, the First and Last Baptist Church will take the decorating responsibilities."

"Hold on, Reverend," Ruby McClay poked in. "This tree is in the central business district, and the presentation should be the responsibility of the Chamber of Commerce."

Emily Flannigan would have none of this. "Christmas is for the kids. The schools should get together and let the students decorate."

"Oh, they'll just make a mess of it," Sissy Tuttle said impatiently. "The Fishermen's Wives will take charge of the tree, because there's so many of us and we never get to do anything."

The mayor waited patiently until the debate reached its expected four-way tie. Everyone got quiet and looked to him for a solution.

"All right, all right. The city will provide the tree because it seems like the right thing to do, but whoever you decide decorates it has to come up with the money for the electrical service, which is out of my control. Have at 'er. This meeting is adjourned."

Now that there was money involved, the debate took on an interesting twist after the mayor went home. Emily Flannigan now thought that Pastor Frank's church probably was the most appropriate choice for decorating. Ruby and the Chamber of Commerce thought that the Fishermen's Wives should get the honors because they do seldom get involved in community projects.

Pastor Frank apologized for being so hasty earlier, and agreed that it was indeed a children's holiday and that Emily's PTA should do the honors. And on through the December night they continued to nicely recommend one another while the man behind it all, accomplished prankster Argus Winslow, was trying to guess how six cardboard refrigerator boxes were going to figure into his Christmas Eve.

He'd cruised Bud Koenig's place and verified the reports that there were a pile of boxes there. *He'll probably fill them full of any ol' rotten thing he can find and send them to me one at a time like the Twelve Days of Christmas,* he thought, but then rejected it. *Naw, he did that eight years ago.*

I know, he'll build a pyramid out of them down at the park as a memorial to me, just so people can watch it get soggy and fall apart. Nawp. Koenig's crafty, but he's not tacky. Argus just couldn't get it figured, but he drove around endlessly puzzling on it.

Every time he drove by the park it seemed there was something different happening. He saw the tree go up on Wednesday. On Thursday morning Pastor Frank and his Flock were moping around sizing up the tree and kicking dirt clods. He saw all the women from Sissy Tuttle's gang that afternoon measuring the skirt of the tree. Friday morning Emily Flannigan showed up with a vanload of kids who had to be shooed away by Ruby McClay, who was already there testing the reach of a rented boom truck pulled up alongside the tree.

By Friday afternoon everybody was there, and Argus took more than a little satisfaction from the fact that they were all squared off to each other, bickering about something. *Just like throwing a raw steak to a pack of dogs,* Argus thought. *I knew they'd never be able to agree on that park. Two days until Christmas and all they've managed to do is murder a tree and drag it over here.* Argus grinned like the devil and guided his old pickup truck out the road to his junkyard retreat.

Argus stayed home for the evening. He put his dog Barney out for the night to watch for any shenanigans Bud might be up to, and slept a fitful sleep laced with dreams of large boxes.

In the morning Argus let Barney back in the trailer, turned on the radio, and fried them up some breakfast. The local news was the usual fare; trucks in ditches, a chimney fire, and a fistfight. Then right at the end the announcer heralded a special event that made Argus sit up and take notice, "And don't forget that everyone is invited to the first annual lighting of the town Christmas tree at 'The Park' tonight at sunset."

"This I'll have to see," Argus said to Barney, forgetting for the moment his fear of cardboard.

The day was a busy one for everybody but Argus, who sat home with Barney the whole day long lest he fall into some trap. Down at The Park there was a flurry of activity around the tree. Kids in snowsuits were sitting on tailgates stringing popcorn, Sissy Tuttle and friends were braiding lengths of garland, while Pastor Frank and Flock struggled with a life-sized plastic nativity scene. Ruby McClay was riding the bucket of a boom truck, barking orders and stringing electric lights, while Mayor Weekly and Bud Koenig worked out the final connections to the electrical box nailed to the tree trunk.

"Mighty kind of you to pay for the electrical service, Bud," the mayor said.

Bud took a short look out to the road and said, "I had my reasons, Richard." And slow but sure, the first and finest Christmas tree the End of the Road had ever shared began to take shape in the center of town.

• • •

Just as the sky dimmed that evening Argus loaded Barney in the cab and headed cautiously toward town. Just about two miles out he said, "Barney, this year he's really got me buffaloed," and no sooner had he got the words out of his mouth when he saw it. Right in the middle of the road, where it couldn't be driven around, was a plain ol' cardboard refrigerator box flashing in his headlights.

Argus's heart was pounding as he got out to look it over. He stared into the bushes on all sides, looking for ambush. He kicked the box with one foot, holding an arm in front of his face, and finally pulled back a flap to peer inside . . . "Empty," he said, and kicked the box down into the ditch.

Continuing into town, Argus was really stumped. Putting a box in the road is not a Koenig-caliber prank, but maybe, he thought, the old fool was slipping. But just as he had this thought another box revealed itself in his headlights. Same sort of box, same place in the road. Argus got out again, and again looked for trouble. Again he poked it with his foot, and again it turned up empty. "Well, Barney," Argus said, back in the truck. "Maybe he's just trying to give me my exercise," and just about then a third box came into view.

Argus wasn't going to keep playing Koenig's game, so this time he drove right up to the box and nudged it a little with the front bumper. "Ha, empty! Oh, Koenig, this is the dumbest prank you ever pulled," and he stepped on the gas and pushed it out of the way.

A little way farther along there was a fourth box, and Argus slowed down again and gently shoved it out of the way. By the time he reached the fifth box, Argus was feeling triumphant and cocky and he rammed it at full speed, sending it flying up over the hood and cab and off into the ditch. When he saw the sixth one coming up, he even put a little more pedal into it to get a really good hit. As he got closer to it he could see something written on the side in spray paint.

He was only about a hundred feet out when he could finally read it. MERRY CHRISTMAS, WINSLOW, it said. "Well, Merry Christmas to you too, Koenig," Argus shouted as he rammed into one last cardboard box, which had inside it a wooden crate filled with approximately three hundred pounds of rusty car parts.

Argus looked like the point man for the alien horde as he and his dog emerged from the cloud of radiator steam illuminated by the one remaining headlight. He didn't even look back to assess the damages. He had his mind set on only one thing, and that was walking the last mile to town to choke the life out of one merry prankster with his bare trembling hands. And off he marched toward the town lights which glowed like a halo in the light December snow.

Just on the outskirts of town he saw something change in the sky ahead and figured they must have lit the tree.

"Damn park, anyway," he said, knowing his experiment in rabble-rousing had failed. "Shoulda just left the junk on it."

Argus boiled and Barney drooped along by his side with his ears back and his tail tucked in close. Barney didn't like his master's temper fits, and he sensed this one to be of particular potency.

Then Barney's ears perked up, and Argus noticed it. "What is it, boy?" Argus stopped dead in his tracks for fear the pranks weren't over for the evening. Then he heard it too. Sifting out through the quiet snow were voices singing.

He walked some more, and the closer he got, the clearer came the voices, and his mind started to drift. He was listening now, and what he was hearing mixed so badly with what he was feeling that he nearly stopped. But he couldn't stop because the more he went on the more the voices rang and the sweeter it became. And with every step a chunk of bitterness fell away like a cardboard box.

By the time he turned the corner and faced the tree, Argus had forgotten his reason for coming, as sure as his reason for being there lay before him. The tree sparkled with lights, garland, and strings of popcorn. It was skirted by fifty children holding candles and singing to the angel who sat at the very top. And all the townspeople stood all mixed together, blinking into the snow and singing in full fresh harmony.

Argus and Barney walked across the street and stood with the crowd. He hadn't forgotten about his truck, and he knew he didn't own this park anymore. But he also knew there was going to be plenty of time for all that nonsense, and precious little of this. He'd deal with those matters as they came, but not tonight. Tonight, all of a sudden, he just felt like doin' a little singin'.

——— • ———

The State Highway Department informs us that avalanches have caused periodic road closures on the Sterling Highway to Anchorage. Travelers are advised to call ahead, check the road conditions, and be prepared to spend the night along the way if planning a trip to Anchorage.

An organizational meeting scheduled at seven o'clock Monday for the Young Republicans was canceled when it was discovered there weren't any.

——— • ———

16

Yet Another New Year

LIKE every year, the End of the Road New Year's Eve celebration was meant to be a spontaneous affair, and it was. Probably more spontaneous than anyone dared imagine.

For some reason a formal party was never planned and the yearly midnight gathering either took place at the Lame Moose Saloon on Main Street or over at the Yahoo Club on Clearshot. These were the only two taverns in town, and no one has ever offered their home up for sacrifice to the occasion.

The way it usually went was people would start dribbling into the two clubs from their private parties around ten-thirty or so. At eleven-thirty it became a majority-rules situation. Whichever place had the larger crowd somehow got word to the smaller group, and everyone would combine for the toast to the New Year.

This year's plan, or lack of same, would have been no different if it hadn't been compounded by a deathly thick blanket of winter fog that settled over the whole town, showing no inclination to move on. It was the talk of the scattered smaller parties.

Stormy and Kirsten Storbock claimed to have almost gotten lost in the mist on the way over to the Flannigans', who live in the same duplex. Emily Flannigan, laying out the cold-cut tray with rolled baloney, Velveeta, and Triscuits, creased her forehead and said, "Maybe we ought to stay in tonight, folks."

Ed would have none of that. "It's New Year's Eve, honey. We have to set the pace for a whole year tonight. I don't want to spend twelve months paced to sittin' at home."

"And I don't want to spend twelve months paced to sitting in a ditch," Emily said, but she let the argument go, knowing she would lose it in the long run.

Argus Winslow had a private party of two going out at the trailer with his dog Barney. Argus looked forward to New Year's Eve for just one good reason. His annual fistfight with Bud Koenig.

The not-always-quiet rivalry between Bud and Argus reached its pinnacle at year's end. New Year's Eve was the date they'd set to really let the fur fly.

They never fought with the intention of hurting each other. "Sport fighting," they liked to call it. But it usually made a wreck of the general area involved, and clean as they tried to keep it, they always ended up with some dings and dents themselves.

This year's scrap promised to be particularly woolly, owing to the fact that Bud's Christmas prank this time around had left Argus's favorite truck a nearly total loss. Somehow he'd persuaded Argus to run into a crate full of rusty car parts at high speed. But that's another story, and if you missed it, never mind, it won't matter by the end of this one.

So while Argus was out at his junkyard trying to get his hair up for the night ahead, Bud Koenig was doing the same thing on the other side of town. And Bud eyed the thick fog leaned up against his windows and doors, wondering if it was going to deprive him of his last real exercise of the year.

•   •   •

Mayor Richard Weekly didn't look forward to New Year's Eve, but then there are few gatherings of his general constituency that he did look forward to. He liked them all best one citizen at a time. Things tended to get messy when there was a crowd of them, and as he sat sipping a soda with Ruby McClay at the Lame Moose, he hoped with all his mayoral heart that the fog would keep them home just this one time.

Not reading the mayor's thoughts, Ruby looked at her watch and said, "Ten-thirty. They oughta be pilin' in here anytime."

"I'm afraid so," said the mayor, and on cue the door burst open to let in a winded Pastor Frank Olmstead with Fanny in tow.

"Sufferin' celery soup. It's thick out there."

"Why, Frank and Fanny, what a pleasant surprise," said Ruby, meaning at least the surprised part.

"As God is my witness, we wouldn't be here if we didn't have to be. We were following a track in the snow, trying to find our way home from Bible study. It turned out to be left over from the garbage truck this afternoon. We followed it right into the parking lot out front and got stuck underneath the dumpster. We'll have to beg a ride from one of you."

"You can beg all night, Pastor," the mayor said, "but there ain't any of us drivin' anywhere anymore tonight. You can walk along with Ruby and I later if you like, or wait and see what sort of Looney Tunes choose to drive out in this stuff in the next hour or so."

Four such tunes were in prime pitch and piling into the Storbocks' Blazer at that moment. Ed and Emily slid in back, with Kirsten giving instructions to Stormy in the pilot's seat.

"Stormy, you're going too fast."

"We're hardly moving!"

"Moving is too fast. We should stay home."

"We'll make it. We got Lucky Eddie with us," and utilizing a trick he said he learned in the Army, Stormy shut off the lights and shined a flashlight straight down at the ground to feel his way out to the road. Once they made it to the smooth pavement it was fairly easy going at five miles an hour to make their way, shining the light on the snow berm alongside the road.

Meanwhile, on their way in from Far Road, Tamara Dupree and a few of her ragged friends were crowded around the windshield of a VW microbus making their wary way along with headlights out and shining a flashlight straight down at the snow berm. A trick, Tamara said, she learned planting trees in Oregon.

"It's like flying through a big celestial cloud," someone next to Tamara offered to the crowd gathered around the windshield.

"It's like drivin' into a big ol' wad of snot," Ed Flannigan offered to his audience in a Blazer several miles ahead.

And as our revelers made their way through something between poetry and post-nasal drip, Argus Winslow was packing up Barney in the tow truck while contemplating swatting Bud Koenig alongside the head and whistling a merry tune.

Bud, in the meantime, was on his merry way to town, having had the good fortune to pick up on the tail of young Norman Tuttle, who was out screwing around on a snowmobile. Norman, apparently, could see fine through the fog from his low point of view, and as he headed down the shoulder of the road, Bud Koenig happily tagged along in the glow of his taillight. A small warm light in the mist that would have more impact on the direction of the evening than anyone, especially Norman, had intended.

The Flannigan-Storbock brigade was the first to reach the Lame Moose Saloon. They joined the mayor and Ruby at the bar while the good pastor and his wife slid farther out of harm's way.

"It's mighty soupy out there, but we made it," Stormy said, bellying up to the rail. "Where's the rest of the crowd?"

"Home watching television, if they've got any sense," Mayor Weekly replied, already feeling uncomfortable with the new energy in the room. He considered Ed and Stormy to be among the more sensible representatives of the community, and if they were out on a night like this, no doubt everybody was. And he wasn't too far wrong.

Tamara and her brood were heading into town at a snail's pace when they heard a muffled bump in the haze.

"What was that?" Tamara said, but before anyone could answer, they heard it again.

All of a sudden the contorted face of Doug McDoogan appeared in the windshield. "What the heck ya doin'? Tryin' to kill me?" he was yelling. "Watch where you're going. You knocked me down twice!"

Tamara stopped with all apologies and let Doug in the van for the short ride left to the Yahoo Club, where they were met by one solitary soul, Argus Winslow, pacing up and down the length of the bar. "Where's Koenig? You seen Koenig?"

Nawp, nobody'd seen Bud Koenig, but had Argus seen the rest of the group? Nawp. Well, they'll show up, and they all grabbed stools to wait for the party.

At the same time, Bud Koenig was over at the Lame Moose, pacing around the pool table asking after Argus. "Where is that old goat, anyway? Probably lost in the fog or partyin' with his dog. Dad-blame it, it's only twenty minutes left in this year. We got a scrap to scrape. Where is everybody, anyway?"

"Well, half of us is here," said Stormy. "Others are probably over at the Yahoo."

And with that information Bud Koenig headed out into the murk, bound for the Yahoo Club, while Argus was easing his way toward the Lame Moose in a tow truck. Bud went by way of Clearshot Avenue, using an old trick he learned logging in Washington State, shining a flashlight straight down on the road. Argus took Main Street over, with his flashlight on the road, employing a method he thought he'd invented.

"Bud Koenig's lookin' for you," Doug McDoogan said to Argus when he came in the door of the Yahoo Club.

"Argus just took out after you, Bud," Ed Flannigan told Bud Koenig before he could open his mouth at the Lame Moose.

And two similar conversations at two similar clubs ensued. Bud and Argus each told their assemblies that everybody seemed to be at the other place waiting for them, and the aging fist fighters turned on their respective heels and headed back from whence they came.

"I'll bet that old goat took Main Street," Bud said, heading down that way this time.

"That cornstarched Koenig is probably dodgin' me on Clearshot," muttered Argus, easing his way along that street. And in the meantime the clock ticked toward midnight and two separate End of the Road gangs grew uneasy that they were at the wrong place.

"I think we should go over to the Yahoo and watch the fight," Ed Flannigan said to the gang in the Lame Moose and was met with nods all around, including Pastor Frank, who lived along the way.

"Let's go join the party at the Moose," Tamara offered to her gang, who offered no argument in return, and everybody who mattered for the moment at the End of the Road was in motion.

Pastor Frank and Fanny, Mayor Weekly, Stormy and Kirsten Storbock, and Ed and Emily all piled into a blue Chevy Blazer on one end of town while Tamara Dupree, Doug McDoogan, and a grand assembly of Far Road freaks squeezed together in the forward compartment of a VW bus on the other end.

All the while Norman Tuttle was taking advantage of the quiet night to rip through the streets on his snowmobile like he could never do if anyone could see him. The problem was that you could see him. At least everyone who mattered could.

Just as the gang from the Lame Moose was coming to the Y of Main and Clearshot, and the gang from the Yahoo got to the same place, Norman whizzed by on his snow machine, headed toward Beluga Lake to do some high-speed sprints.

"That must be Bud's taillights," said Doug McDoogan in the van. "Follow him to the party."

"There goes Argus to the ruckus," Ed Flannigan

said of the red glow in the fog. "Put away that flashlight and follow him."

So it was that unbeknownst to one another, the two groups tagged along behind a twelve-year-old boy, who thought he was getting away with something, out onto the frozen ice of Beluga Lake.

While all their potential spectators were losing themselves on the ice, Bud and Argus cursed their simultaneous bad luck at having walked into not only bars void of opponent, but bars void of anybody.

"Bud Koenig, you're turnin' yellow on me," Argus said on his way back out to the tow truck.

"Never seen you run from a fight, Winslow," Bud was saying as he inched once again into the vapor.

When Norman Tuttle started doing figure eights out on the lake, it became evident to everybody following him that they'd misplaced good judgment once again. Stormy saw the headlights of Tamara's van just in time to stop, and pretty soon everybody was standing out on the ice throwing snowballs at Norman, trying to get his attention so he could lead them back to the road. "Look at the time, would ya," Stormy said, shining a flashlight on his watch. "Two minutes to midnight, and we don't even know where we are. We're going to miss the fight for sure."

And two frustrated fighters were at that moment making their way along Clearshot Avenue in opposite directions. The batteries in their flashlights had gone dead and each of them had their doors open with their heads leaned out to see the road beneath them. "Koenig, I'm going to knock your block off," Argus said, leaning closer to the road to keep a track on it.

"Winslow's gonna get a whippin' this year," Bud was saying as he opened his door an arc farther and squinted into the haze.

"Twenty seconds to midnight!" Kirsten Storbock yelled to the group out on the ice pitching snow at Norman. "Ten-nine-eight . . ."

Must be about midnight by now, thought Argus,

worried that tradition was going to be broken.

We end every year with a tussle, thought Bud. *I can't believe that old coot would cheat me out of it this time.*

". . . seven-six-five-four-three-two . . . one!" And as Kirsten raised her arms in celebration on the lake, the open driver's doors of two heavy trucks collided about midway on Clearshot Avenue. Argus and Bud fell out of their seats and laid on the road, knocked colder than mackerels. Their trucks lugged to a charitable halt a short ways away, and Stormy finally hit Norman in the head with a chunk of ice.

Norman cruised into the gathering on the lake, shut off his machine, and looked at everybody, more than a little surprised. Mayor Weekly stepped forward. "Norman Tuttle, what are you doing out here this time of the night?"

"What are *you* doing out here?" Norman said back.

"What are you doing out here?" said Bud Koenig and Argus Winslow in two-part harmony in the middle of Clearshot Avenue, holding their heads and looking each other straight in the eye.

Nobody had an answer for anybody else, and such was the way that the pace was set for yet another new year at the End of the Road.

17

A Night in
the Pass

PEOPLE sometimes have the funniest ways of getting together. We're either shy, disagreeable, suspicious, or unworthy, and it often takes something bigger than ourselves to get to know each other. Bad weather has probably introduced more people to one other than anything else in this part of the world, at least that's how Argus Winslow and Fanny Olmstead came to know each other.

Argus and Fanny have lived in this same little town for years. Argus, of course, was one of the first ones here, homesteading out Far Road way over forty years ago.

Fanny Olmstead has been here about fifteen years, arriving as the young bride of Pastor Frank Olmstead. Pastor Frank came to the End of the Road to escape the liberalism he felt was infecting the Baptist faith and formed the First and Last Baptist Church.

Fanny has never displayed any personality that Argus could notice and seemed to busy herself mostly with community booster activities, fussing over her first-class ass of a husband and generally lurking about looking either embarrassed or offended, depending on what she was looking at.

She normally looked offended when looking at Argus Winslow, and such was the case as Argus and his dog Barney burst through the door of the Crest Café up in the pass.

"First time I tried to drive to Anchorage in five years, and they close the cornstarched pass!" Argus growled, shaking snow from his coveralls and stomping his big feet.

"No dogs allowed in here," said a burly middle-aged woman in restaurant whites standing behind the counter. A name tag on her breast identified her as LILLIAN, and she pointed to the door with an authority that would have sent lesser men cowering out into the storm. Her posturing was wasted on Argus, who hasn't been intimidated by anything or anybody since he first grew hair under his arms over sixty years ago.

"Lady," Argus said, climbing out of his coveralls with Barney at his side. "There's an avalanche on the road in front of us, a blizzard behind us, and you're the only place around for forty miles. Me and Barney are going to be sittin' here for a while, and I'd recommend you get used to it."

"I'll have to call the state troopers."

"Call 'em. Maybe they'll bring a snowplow with them. In the meantime I'll have a cup of coffee and Barney would like some hot cocoa in a dish."

"We reserve the right to refuse service to anyone," Lillian said, pointing to a brace of hand-lettered signs on the wall behind her. There was that sign plus, REST ROOMS FOR CUSTOMERS ONLY, NO SHIRT, NO SHOES, NO SERVICE, NO PERSONAL CHECKS, NO LOUD CHILDREN, NO PETS, AND NO SPITTING.

Unimpressed, Argus walked behind the counter, poured himself a cup of coffee and said, "If you got as much coffee as you got rules, we're gonna get along just fine."

Through this whole thing Fanny sat mortified in a

booth off to one side. She did not like unpleasantness, and Argus was the king of unpleasantry. She had never violated a rule in her life, and if Lillian had ordered her out into the snow to perish, she would have gone not only willingly, but apologizing for staying so long in the first place.

She sat so still, with both her hands wrapped around a warm coffee mug, that Argus might not have noticed her for hours had she not gotten up to use the rest room.

"Well, lookee here," Argus said, about to grab a stool at the lunch counter. "Old home week. If it isn't Fanny Olmstead the preacher's lady. At least I'll have somebody to tell lies to all night."

Fanny gave the curtest of acknowledgments to Argus, and while she disappeared into the ladies' room, Argus and Barney took up roost at her booth.

Lillian the Nazi waitress lurked behind the counter sending icy looks to Argus's booth every chance she could. Lillian took the food-service business seriously, and her role as the only lunch-counter hostess in the whole pass gave her more power and authority than she deserved.

Argus respected power when he came upon it, but he didn't see any in Lillian, and as far as authority goes, well, Argus was the final authority on everything.

"You gonna make that cocoa for Barney, or do I gotta do it?" Argus said from the booth.

"I'm not feeding that animal, and no customers are allowed behind the counter," Lillian said once again, exercising her absent authority.

Argus got up from the booth and headed behind the counter. "I guess I gotta do it." And while Argus put together the fixin's for a hot cocoa in a dish, a flushed Fanny Olmstead returned to the booth and tried to blend into the red Naugahyde.

Fanny had been on her way to Anchorage to see a specialist about a particularly sensitive medical problem. It seems over the last few weeks she'd developed a severe gastric disorder which caused her to, well, ventilate at frequent and often indelicate intervals. The prospect of being snowed in to a quiet café in the middle of the night with other people around could well qualify as her own personal purgatory. And being snowed in with Argus Winslow would have to be Hades in spades.

Returning to the booth and setting down the dish of cocoa, Argus dove into conversation with a horrified Fanny while Barney happily slurped beneath the table.

"So, Fanny, what takes you to Anchorage?"

Fanny, being incapable of lying or evasion, could do only one thing, which was blurt out the truth. "I'm going to have some medical tests done."

She needn't have worried that Argus would pry further into her affairs, because he was much too interested in himself to care. "That's where I'm goin' too," he said, taking a big messy swig of coffee. "I banged heads with Bud Koenig last week and knocked a screw loose. I'm startin' to forget things. Ol' Doc says I'd better go have my head examined, which people been tellin' me for years, but this time the cornstarched ol' coot might be right."

Argus told her the story of how on Tuesday he'd stepped out of his trailer at the scrapyard and momentarily forgotten what he did for a living. "I stood there for a minute and couldn't for the life of me figure out what all that cornstarched junk was doing in my yard. I was gettin' ready to call the cops on somebody when I finally came to my senses." Argus laughed a genuine laugh at himself, and Fanny appeared to smile at the story, although it was probably just gas.

She'd listened politely, trying to remain calm, then using the laugh as her point of exit, she fairly bolted from the booth and headed to the rest room. She'd waited just a tad too long, and five feet short of the door Argus and Lillian were awarded firsthand information on the nature of Fanny's particular medical problem.

Fanny stayed in the bathroom a long time. She didn't know if she would find the strength to ever come out again. She went to the mirror and tried to draw herself together. Her face was so red that she looked scorched. Her hair, which had been tied in a neat bun behind her head, had grown tired with the long day and started to fray. She looked terrible, and the awfulness boiling inside of her made her feel like a ruin. A wreck of a human being.

Fanny had little or no self-esteem on her best days, and courage was another commodity she had precious little experience with. She dropped to her knees and prayed with all her heart for both. It was clear to her that divine intervention was the only way she would be able to rejoin that insufferable Argus Winslow and the dreadful waitress.

Lillian did everything that could be done in a look to make Fanny squirm on her way back to the booth. Fanny expected worse from Argus, but was surprised by his expression when she sat down again. He was holding his dog's head in his lap, and his face was covered with what could only be described as fear. You didn't have to be too familiar with Argus Winslow's face to see that this was an expression that didn't fit it.

"Mr. Winslow, what's the matter?" The words fell out of her mouth before she could even think, and instantly her mind was elevated out of her churning insides.

"I forgot who Barney was," Argus said quietly and without raising his eyes from his pet. "When you were in the bathroom that battle-ax behind the counter said something about my dog, and when I looked at him, I didn't even know he was mine. Barney could tell too. I think it scared him more than me."

Fanny looked at Argus and saw him like no one had before. For the first time in her Christian life she felt genuinely flushed with love for a heathen soul. Whatever she had said on her knees in the ladies' room had found its way home, and she reached out and held one of Argus's hands.

"You're going to be fine. I'm sure it's only temporary," she said, and Argus looked at her and smiled. Another expression that seldom graced that rutted old road of a face. Fanny felt another attack coming on, and with grace and some dignity squeezed the gnarly hand and excused herself to the rest room. "I'll be right back."

When Fanny came out the bathroom door this time she was met with the piercing bark of Lillian giving Argus more grief.

"I said I'm closing and you people have to get out of here. Avalanche or not, you can't stay. I'm going upstairs to bed, and you're going outside. That's final."

Fanny waited behind Lillian for Argus's feisty response, and had to peek around her shoulder when she heard none. What she saw raised a heat and ire in her she had never felt the likes of in all her pious days.

Argus sat staring at Lillian's face in complete confusion. His hands were trembling, and she swore there was even a small tear forming in the corner of one eye. He'd slipped his gears again.

Fanny literally shoved past Lillian and sat next to Argus, holding both of his hands. "Argus, are you all right?" She looked into his eyes and saw that the lights were on, all right, but nobody was home. "Argus?"

"I'm tired," was all he said, and he laid back in the booth. Fanny eased him down, dragging his legs out from under the table, and covered him with her coat, ignoring the cross-armed Lillian watching impatiently. She bunched her hat and scarf under his head for a pillow and felt his forehead, more out of reflex than purpose.

"No sleeping in the booths," Lillian said from behind.

Fanny bristled and whirled.

With a tone of voice that had never parted her lips, and poking a demure little finger straight into Lillian's name tag, Fanny had her day in the sun.

"I have heard all I plan to out of you, my dear. Mr. Winslow and I had the misfortune to be stranded at your establishment, and we are staying here until the snowplows get through. If you don't like that, then I'd suggest you go upstairs and worry about it where I can't see you. Mr. Winslow needs to sleep. Good night."

There's no talent like new talent, and it was plain to Lillian she'd better steer clear of this one. Whatever she had to say she saved until she had one foot on the stairs. "I'm going to call the state troopers."

"Call 'em, maybe they'll bring a snowplow with 'em." Fanny turned her back on Lillian and sat back down in her booth. Argus was fast asleep with Barney's worried head resting on his feet. Fanny touched Argus's face once before leaning back into her vigil with Barney.

Argus woke up with a start when he heard the jangle of chains on a snowplow going by. Barney stretched and bowed good morning as Argus threw off the coat covering him and climbed out of the booth. It was six o'clock in the morning by the clock on the kitchen wall, and he was surprised to find himself all alone. He didn't even see her until he was pulling on his coveralls.

Fanny was in the corner of the booth with her knees drawn up to her chest and her hands holding her skirt closed. She was sleeping quietly except for some strange rumbling coming from somewhere inside her. Argus raised his eyebrows at that, and left her as she lay. Lillian was nowhere to be found, so he put a ten-dollar bill on the cash register and headed for the door.

Just as he let Barney out in front of him, though, he stopped short and trned around. Something was trying to occur to him, but he couldn't place it. He looked over to the peaceful Fanny Olmstead and studied her for a minute. There was something on her sleeping face that drew him. A look. A power. Something.

Argus was not a tender man, or a particularly conscientious one, so it was startling to find himself covering Fanny with her coat. He felt like he owed her somehow, but for the life of him he couldn't figure out why.

He didn't know, and he probably never would, but one thing about Argus Winslow is, he knew a friend when he saw one.

PART THREE

— . —

——— • ———

The End of the Road Winter Carnival is the talk of the town this week. People are gearing up for the festivities and looking forward to a break from the winter monotony.

The annual outhouse race and demolition derby will start at ten-thirty sharp in front of the Lame Moose Saloon. This year promises to be a heated contest, with the Lame Moose introducing their dog-driven two-seater and their arch rivals at the Yahoo Club promising that the wheels will stay on their entry this time around.

The cherry-pit-spitting contest was almost canceled because nobody could find any cherries, but the event was saved when Ed Flannigan announced you can spit a canned olive pit just about as far if you smooth them out with your teeth first.

The home-brew contest will again be judged by Stormy Storbock, who swore he wouldn't drink so much of each entry this year and promised to stay conscious through the whole thing. We'll see. Argus Winslow's "Husky Stout" was last year's winner by default because that was the entry that put Stormy under the table.

——— • ———

18

Tamara's Brother

THERE are a lot of reasons why people wind up at the End of the Road, and lots more reasons why they stay. Whatever our reasons for coming or staying, though, almost without exception we came without our families. Those folks back home who, though we love 'em dearly, seem the most appropriately placed a long ways away. At least that was true in the case of Tamara Dupree and her family.

Tamara had grown up in southern Oregon in a working family. Her father had been a logger, and a proud one. Her mother had been a logger's wife; making lunches, oiling boots, taking guff. And her older brother Danny had taken up the family trade and attitudes.

Tamara and Danny Dupree had grown up two years and two worlds apart. Every single thing Danny embraced about the family history, Tamara despised. Where Tamara saw green rolling hills of environmentally correct forest, Danny saw timber and board feet.

Tamara had left her Oregon home at her earliest

possible convenience and went to school at Berkeley, where she was able to cement into place the consciousness she was born with. By the time she reached us here at the End of the Road she was an experienced vegetarian, card-carrying feminist, new-age apostle, and protector of all things living but most men.

Tamara was free to be that way or whatever way she wanted around here, like she'd never be allowed to do back in the small logging town of her youth and family. But that didn't mean she didn't get lonely for it sometimes. Lonely enough to invite her older brother up for a short visit.

Her parents had been worried about her up here all alone, and although they'd never commit to the trip north, Tamara knew that a favorable report from number-one son would ease their minds considerably.

Even though Tamara was nearly thirty years old, her mother and father always assumed she was crazy, and since she moved to the End of the Road, they were fairly certain of it. Tamara looked forward to disproving them, and besides, she hadn't seen Danny in almost five years.

Tamara's most vivid memory of her brother was a bittersweet thought, and she recalled it while waiting for his plane to arrive.

It had been over ten years ago. She'd just graduated from high school. Tamara had fallen in with this "literary" crowd mostly under the guidance of a progressive poetry professor at their local community college. Danny had told her not to get mixed up with that bunch, which had given her all the more reason to do so.

One night she'd gone to a party at the professor's house. All the other girls at the party were much older than Tamara, but the professor seemed to be paying particular attention to her. He was probably twice her age, and to be sitting on a futon with him listening to sitar music and discussing Dylan Thomas was an exhilarating honor. Exhilaration bordering on fear.

She remembered feeling so "hip" when someone lit incense and put on the strobe light. She leaned back into her cushion and let the music and the sound of the professor's voice wash over her. Then she smelled something burning other than incense and her heart missed a beat. *Dope.* She knew about it, but she'd never been in the same room with it before. Oh, this was *so hip.* Then the professor's hand went to her leg and Tamara swooned.

All her alarms were going off, but no one was responding to the call. Too many confusing signals. Was hip better than right? And what was right? She was old enough for this. Was anybody old enough for this? Why did being the ripe old age of eighteen feel so much like the same little girl?

All these quandaries were not resolved, but were at least waylaid for Tamara when her brother Danny stormed through the front door. She remembers vividly his jagged figure moving in the strobe light toward her. "Tamara, get your little hippie fanny out to the car, now!" he yelled over the music.

He grabbed her by the arm and pulled her off the floor. The professor snatched his hands back and started to get up. Tamara turned just in time to see the professor's nose snap under the back of Danny's hand.

Tamara cried all the way home. Danny bawled her out, but promised he wouldn't tell the folks as long as she never went back there again. She screamed at him. What business was it of his? She was a grown woman! She'd party with whomever she wanted! And she swore to his face that she would never, ever forgive him for as long as she lived. But she lied.

When she got home that night she laid on her bed and, in the familiar smell of her own room, she thought of her big brother. How angry he was. And how fast and strong. And what an idiot he was too. But he'd done it for her. He'd done it all for her, and right, wrong, idiotic, or otherwise, it became an important thing. In some disgusting and humiliating way, Danny was her hero.

Having heroes for big brothers is too often the

curse of little sisters, and Tamara stood with every emotion that could be mixed as she watched her potbellied hero step from the airplane into her life again.

"I see you're still a hippie-dip," Danny said.

"And you're still a redneck Neanderthal," Tamara said back. And they hugged close, genuinely glad to be together.

The ride out to the cabin on Far Road was filled mostly with small talk. How's Mom's goiter? Dad's arthritis still acting up? How's work? Gone. Yes. Fine.

Tamara bristled momentarily when Danny raised his finger like a gun and went "Bang!" to a moose they passed along the road. But she bit her tongue and let it go. That was Danny. She also tempered her comment when he remarked on all the virgin forest he'd flown over that day. "You could log this place *forever* and nobody'd know it," he said.

"The Earth would know it," Tamara said gently.

"Oh, that's right. You're still huggin' trees and savin' whales, aren'tcha?"

"Among other things," she said. And all was quiet in the VW bus until Danny asked her to pull over somewhere for a six-pack.

"Can't be on vacation without a little brew," he said, climbing back in. Then he cracked one, guzzled it, and belched. But that was Danny, Tamara thought, and one hour into it she found herself involuntarily counting what was left of the three-day visit.

Putting all that aside for the moment, Tamara got excited over the prospect of showing off her little cabin. It was her special prize. Although she hadn't built the little log house, she had sort of reconstituted it. She'd replaced the windows, scrubbed it down, oiled the logs, patched the floor, installed a woodstove, hung curtains, and done hundreds of other little details that separated the place from the wilderness once again.

She'd spent the last three days lining her pathway with rocks and chopping a fresh supply of firewood. It looked so *Alaskan*, all stacked up neat on the porch like that. She'd cleaned out the woodstove and laid a fresh layer of lime in the outhouse. It was as nice as she'd ever seen her place.

When they got out of the van and walked down the path, Tamara was looking for her brother's reaction but couldn't see any. He stood on the porch, cracked another beer, and looked around. He looked at the outhouse and out to her garden spot and compost pile. He kicked at the neat stack of wood, and finally looked at Tamara.

"Tammy, if Mom and Dad saw this, it would break their hearts," he said, and just shook his head sadly.

Tamara didn't know what to say. She was so completely bushwhacked by this reaction that she didn't know whether to laugh, cry, or bust him in the eye. Instead of any, she opened the door. "You haven't seen the rest. Come on in."

Danny ducked his big frame through the doorway and looked around the small room, still sadly shaking his head. He looked at her tidy drainboard and the ceramic washbasin. "No running water," he said. He looked at the rows of apothecary jars filled with beans and grains, seeds and spices. "No refrigerator . . . no furnace," he said, hardly noticing the woodstove Tamara had just cleaned and polished. He saw her dulcimer, mandolin, and bongos next to the bed. "And no TV. Darn it, little sister, you're living like poor folks. What am I supposed to tell Dad?" Danny looked at Tamara, emanating something between disgust and pity.

She stared wide-eyed at her older brother and tried to make sense of him. She looked at his big ugly boots on his duck feet. She looked at his pot gut hanging over his belt and the four beers dangling from plastic in one big ham of a hand. And she could not for the life of her understand how they could have both been drawn from the same gene pool.

"Daniel," she said with the patented Tamara Dupree frost to her voice, "you tell Dad whatever you want to."

• • •

The next two days went no better than the first. Danny was intent on disapproving of everything Tamara showed him. He insisted on calling her dog Karma "the wonder wimp," because he wouldn't wrestle with him. He wouldn't eat anything Tamara fixed because "it ain't no meal if there ain't no meat," and he'd commandeer her "hippie wagon" to go to town for cheeseburgers and beer.

Tamara took her brother to a coffeehouse and poetry reading at the Natural Food Coop the second night to meet some of her friends. He wouldn't talk to anyone, and he fell asleep and snored during the reading. He continued to point and holler "Bang!" every time he saw a critter of any kind along the road, and could not even find a decent thing to say about the scenery. "Seen one mountain, you seen 'em all." "Can't eat a postcard, little girl." And somewhere along the way Tamara went numb to the whole thing and simply waited out her time.

The last night was as close as they came to a pleasant moment. Tamara brought out her photo album, and they looked through pictures of them together as children, laughing and grinning from wading pools. Sharing a pony ride some summer long gone. They laughed together at Tamara's prom picture with the ridiculous hairdo and chiffon gown.

The closing picture in the album was the last family portrait taken. It was the summer before Tamara left for college. Danny and Tamara sitting. Mom and Dad behind. Everyone's thin smiles frozen in time and still fading.

Danny closed the album and said with all apparent sincerity, "Mom worries about you. She wanted me to ask you when you're coming home."

Tamara took the album and put it back beneath her bed. "Tell Mom that I *am* home."

Danny Dupree's last morning at the End of the Road was a quiet one. He and Tamara had exhausted all possibilities of conversation between them and it was simply a matter of waiting for the plane to leave. Rather than sit one more hour in his sister's cabin listening to her plink the mandolin, Danny jumped up and said, "I know. Why don't we give your dear old brother a proper send-off and pound on down to that Lame Moose Saloon on the way to the plane." Tamara agreed without hesitation. Anything to interrupt the now monotonous tension.

Without a doubt, Danny found his element at the Lame Moose. He dove immediately into a pool game, a pitcher, and a liar's contest with a few stray fishermen killing time between trips. Tamara was relieved to see a smile on her brother's face for the first time all week, and she kicked herself for not thinking of this place sooner.

Tamara sipped a mineral water and watched her brother from the bar. She couldn't help but admire his way with the other men. He met people so easily. So much the opposite of her. Danny was cocky and funny. He was sure of himself with a loud reckless laugh that made you laugh along. And Tamara did laugh a little at his antics around the pool table, which was not wasted on Danny. A minute later, as Danny was lining up a shot along the cue facing her, he looked up, focused on his sister, and grinned some wading-pool grin that warmed Tamara down to her organic toes. Tamara smiled back and tilted her head off to the side in admiration.

One of the other players caught this and said in a beer-careless way, "Hey, ol' buddy. Looks like that hairy-legged whole-wheat cookie's got the hots for ya."

Danny laid his pool cue deliberately on the table and faced the man. "You got a problem with hairy legs?" he said, moving in.

"Danny, don't!" Tamara got up from her stool.

"You got a problem with whole wheat?"

"Danny!" and Tamara grabbed her brother by the arm and drug him from the room.

"I shoulda kicked his butt!" Danny was braggin' on the way to the airport.

"You could have, and it wouldn't have mattered.

He'd still be a jerk and so would you." Tamara said this not unkindly, and Danny reached over just to mess up her hair with his big ham of a hand.

"I want you to stay away from that place, you hear, little sister? That's a bad bunch to be gettin' hooked up with."

And Tamara could only smile at her big brother, who needed so bad to be her hero, and say, "Thanks, Danny. I will."

At the airport they hugged long, genuinely glad to be together.

"I'll tell Mom and Dad you're fine," he said.

"I know you will, thanks."

And Tamara waved at the big head of her brother in the airplane window until it was gone down the runway. She let her arm hang and sighed with relief that he was gone. Gone home. Where she could still love him . . . at a reasonable distance.

— • —

The State Maintenance crew reminds us not to park our vehicles along the side of the road. Ed Flannigan ate another Subaru up on Flat Back Ridge with the big turbine snow blower on Monday morning. "It sprays car parts for a good hundred yards," warned Flannigan. "Somebody's gonna get hurt one of these days."

The crew also asked if anybody was missing a Subaru, to contact them. They have your car in a bucket in the machine shop.

Larry's Lanes is sponsoring its first annual bowlathon on Friday night. There will be prizes for the best series, worst series, most awkward style, and largest shoe size. Proceeds from the bowlathon will go toward fixing the pin setter on lane three.

The public school system with much folderol made the announcement Thursday that from now on only 100% real meat patties would be served in the school cafeterias. The news was received by an uneasy student body, which wondered at some length what they'd been eating up until now.

— • —

19

The New Guy

QUINTON Burrell and his wife Connie Burrell-Boniface arrived at the End of the Road not only with, but to, high expectations. Quinton was to be the new branch manager of the Fair Deal Bank and Trust, and everybody around here was watching pretty close to see what they'd been sent to work with.

The former manager, Honest Fred, had retired after twenty years at the job, and suffered a fatal heart attack a short time later. It's taken the home office in Anchorage a whole year to replace him. Fred was a perfect small-town banker who knew everybody, their business, and their children's names. He'd approved many a risky loan based on character and a handshake, and he'd never been burned on a deal. Fred was going to be a hard act to follow.

Everyone's high expectations for the new manager were knocked down a peg when Quinton and Connie rolled into town two weeks ago. They arrived in a brand-new green Volvo station wagon with ski racks on the roof and Missouri plates on the bumper.

If being from out of state with an expensive car wasn't enough to undermine their credibility, the fact that they appeared to be barely thirty years old knocked the last brace out from under them. It only took a couple days for the word on Quinton and Connie to get around.

Quinton Burrell earned his MBA at Harvard and had been a highly successful investment banker in St. Louis. Connie Burrell-Boniface was an account executive at a large Midwestern advertising firm. Her campaign credits included a novelty chewing gum made from petroleum by-products, organically grown cat-food supplements, and a chain of high-fashion sock boutiques.

Quinton and Connie's combined income was well into the six figures, and they'd groomed an impressive stock portfolio and offshore investment group before they were out of their twenties. What had went astray and brought them to the End of the Road wasn't quite clear but it had something to do with the stock market fall a year or so back combined with a particular brand of chewing gum being placed on the EPA's toxic-waste hit list.

Quinton and Connie decided it was time to grab what they could and go find an "alternative lifestyle." They'd read about the End of the Road in *Outdoor* magazine, and came out to find their place among the slower paces and lower risks.

Taking a branch manager's position was certainly a step down for Quinton's career, and Connie wasn't at all sure what she was going to do. For now, they just wanted to settle in to a small-town life and get to know people. That was going to prove harder than they'd anticipated or dreamed of back in St. Louis.

For one thing, they'd gotten their impressions of far-north fashion straight from L.L. Bean. When they climbed out of their Volvo in matching buffalo plaid shirts, canvas field pants, and rubber hunting shoes, they looked more like the Ken and Barbie Action Weekend collection than they did anyone around here.

Quinton decided that for his first day in the office at the bank he would provide hors d'oeuvres for the customers as a way of breaking the ice. Connie was a little discouraged when she found that the most distinguished cracker in town was the perennial Triscuit. Then she asked after the cheese.

"Excuse me," she said to the clerk. "Where is your Brie?"

"Don't have Brie. We got Tide, Cheer, and Cold-water All."

"Brie isn't a laundry soap. It's cheese."

"Never heard of it. What kind of cheese is it?"

"It's, well, soft cheese."

"Oh, like Cheez Whiz. Yeah, we got that, and Vel-veeta too. Over by the milk."

Entirely disheartened, and a little bit confused, Connie left, but eventually found what she was looking for at the Natural Food Coop.

If the new bank manager was a little nervous about meeting his customers, at least one of his customers was more than a little nervous about meeting him. As you know, Kirsten and Stormy Storbock's new house burned down a couple months back and they were trying to lay the groundwork to rebuild. They'd built the place out-of-pocket and hadn't quite gotten around to the detail of insuring it when it burned.

They'd lost everything, and as Stormy and Kirsten filled out the financial forms and qualifying papers for the new loan, they realized they had little collateral but their steady jobs and good name.

Stormy had been waiting impatiently for the Fair Deal Bank and Trust to install their new manager so that he could deal with this issue face to face. He was certain that dealing with strangers at the Anchorage office would have gotten him nowhere, and now, in light of the caliber of the new manager here, he didn't think he'd get far anyway.

Stormy was proud, forty, and hardworking. Walking up to a thirty-year-old greenhorn in new pants and asking for money was one of the hardest things he'd ever have to do, but he promised Kirsten he'd do it the new manager's first day.

That day came last Monday. Quinton and Connie came early to set out the trays of crackers, liver pâté, Brie, sushi rolls, and a basket of fruit. They were a little disappointed when the other employees arrived and ignored the hors d'oeuvres in favor of the bag of chocolate doughnuts one of them brought from Clara's.

Connie eventually left Quinton alone to his work, which amounted to little more than sitting in his office waiting for someone to come meet him.

Quinton settled in to sort through the memos and operations notes left him by the previous manager. He'd just opened the first folder when a knock came on his door.

"Yes?"

The door opened and Stormy Storbock appeared. He had a few wrinkled papers in one hand and his hat in the other. "Mr. Burrell?" Stormy stammered, wringing his hat.

"Please, call me Quinton."

"Mr. Quinton," Stormy said, stepping in the door and shaking Quinton's hand. "I'm Storbock, Stewart A. Oh jeez, I'm filling out too many of these forms. I mean I'm Stewart Storbock, Stormy they call me, and anyway I'm needing a loan for my burned-down house. Well, I mean I don't need a loan for the house that burned, I need one for a new house and—"

"Please, sit down, Stormy." Quinton offered Stormy the chair across from him. "Today's my first day on the job and we're sort of celebrating. Care for an hors d'oeuvre?" he said, offering the plate.

"No, but I might have something to eat." Stormy

looked through the offerings. "What's that white stuff?"

"Brie. It's a soft cheese."

"Oh, like Velveeta."

"Sort of. Now what is this about your house burning."

And Stormy told the whole story of how they'd built their dream home with their own hands with their own money only to have it burn just weeks after moving in. He told about his good job as a machinist at the boat yard, Kirsten's bookkeeping business, and even managed to squeeze in a mention of the softball championship game he pitched.

Quinton listened with genuine interest to the story. In his short but successful banking career this was the very first time he was actually dealing with a warm body. All the personal contact was handled by the public relations department back in St. Louis, and there were few clients in investment banking who wrung their hats in their hands during meetings. Quinton was fascinated. This was exactly why he and Connie had come to the End of the Road.

When Stormy had said all he could, he handed over the rumpled loan application and financial statements to Quinton and sat back, anxiously waiting for a reaction.

Quinton knew that whatever he did here would be his important first step into the community. He leaned back casually, but with a look of admiration at the preliminary steps the Storbocks had already taken. Without looking up he reached over offhandedly to the plate of food and grabbed a bread square and pâté sandwich with a toothpick through it.

Meanwhile Stormy was watching Quinton like a hawk. He was waiting for the slightest turn of the mouth or raise of an eyebrow to see if he had a snowball's chance in Charleston that this was going to fly.

He saw nothing at all for a terrible long time, then just as Quinton turned a page and took a bite from his sandwich, the bank manager's eyebrows shot up, his jaw dropped, he looked at Stormy in what could only be described as disbelief, and left the office mumbling, "Excuse me for a minute."

It was Stormy's worst nightmare come true. It was their assets sheet. He knew that was going to be trouble. They'd lost everything but their car and truck in the fire, and there was nothing to list. All of a sudden he felt stupid for even trying this. He knew it was pointless to wait around for the answer, so he left before Quinton got back.

What Stormy didn't know was that not only had Quinton not been reacting to his financial statement, he hadn't even been reading it. He was simply posturing and trying to make Stormy feel at ease. He would look at the hard numbers later after he had time to review Stormy's credit history and the bank's lending policy. The whole thing, of course, was short-circuited by a pâté sandwich with a toothpick in it. A toothpick that wedged itself between Quinton's upper and lower gums at the most inappropriate moment.

"How'd it go?" Stormy's friend Ed Flannigan asked him back in the truck outside.

"When he looked at our assets he dropped his jaw and left the room. I didn't wait around for the explanation. Damn, Ed, what are we going to do?" Stormy leaned his head against the truck window and sighed in resignation.

Quinton, back at his desk, leaned his head against his hand in resignation and nibbled absently on some cheese. Boy, he'd really blown it. The whole town probably knew what a goofball he was by now.

He might have sat there the rest of the morning feeling sorry for himself had not another presence appeared in his office doorway. The formidable presence of one Argus Winslow.

"Whatcha chewin' on, Quinton?" Argus said in his patented introductory manner.

Quinton sat up, startled. "Brie, it's like Velveeta, please have some."

"No thanks," Argus said, stroking his ample belly.

"Gotta watch my girlish figure." Argus took a seat and got right to his point.

"I'm Argus Winslow, you don't know me, but you will. You're going to be talking to a young fella name of Stormy who wants a loan."

Quinton cut him off. "He's already come and gone."

"How'd it go?"

"Badly," was all Quinton could say, thinking only of himself.

Argus stood up and leaned over Quinton's desk. "Listen, sweetmeat. Whatever Stormy and his family wants, you give it to them, hear?" And he left.

Quinton sat in his chair, stunned. Argus left behind him an air of oil and metal that still hung in the room with authority. That sort of rough-hewn command that all working people seemed to have over Quinton. The scarred arms and bulging veins of men who could tear his pink little Harvard body to pieces. He'd let these people fix his car and landscape his lawn, but he'd never let them be his friends. That was one of the things he wanted to change. That was one of his reasons for being here, and it was already going so badly. Why would that rough old man come in here and threaten him like that? How could he have gone so wrong so quickly?

To avoid coming to a conclusion about all this, Quinton busied himself by going through some of the files that Fred had left for him. In the first file, clipped to a bunch of audit reports, was a handwritten envelope to "The New Guy."

"Dear Manager," it began.

> *You have just stepped into one of the most important jobs in town, and I sure hope you know what you're doing. It took me*

*twenty years to get the hang of these folks,
and you'd be well advised to look at their files
before you talk to them. Good luck.*

It was signed, "Fred Ferguson."

Quinton was so curious about this highly un-
professional letter from the former manager that he *did*
go to the personal file drawer. There were dozens of
folders all labeled with unfamiliar names, but he knew
the two he was looking for and took them back to his
desk.

The "Storbock, Stewart A., and Kirsten" file was
slim. There was a closed-out car loan, a credit report,
and a few reference letters. But also there was another
handwritten envelope clipped in.

"Dear Manager," it said again.

> *Stormy Storbock is the hardest working
> man I've ever known in my life. He is honest
> to a fault, and a dedicated husband and fa-
> ther. He doesn't believe in borrowing, gener-
> ally, and has asked us for very little. If he ever
> does ask, he deserves every attention you can
> give him.*

Quinton laid the note aside and opened the fat
"Winslow, Argus Winchester" folder. He didn't even
glance at the other paperwork in the file and went
straight to the note, this one marked CONFIDENTIAL in
big heavy letters.

Dear Manager,

> *Argus Winslow is one of the most diffi-
> cult people you will deal with. He is stubborn,
> confrontative, and belligerent to a fault. At
> the same time he has a heart made of solid
> gold and looks after this town pretty close. I
> might also mention that he anonymously
> owns 65% of the stock in this bank. He will
> expect you to know this and act accordingly,*

but if you ever let anyone else know about it, you would not want to live with the consequences.

Quinton sat somewhere between fascination and nausea. In a flash the consequences of moving into a small town came clear to him. How easy it is to leave the wrong impressions on people, and even easier to get the wrong impressions from them.

He tore into the other files with a new excitement.
Flannigan, Edward and Emiline.
Good hard workers, worth a risk, but tend to want things they can't afford.
McDoogan, Douglas G.
Don't loan this guy a bad idea.
Bud Koenig.
If he ever comes in, look for trouble. He's the only other one who knows that Argus owns the joint, and I don't trust him where Winslow is concerned.
Weekly, Richard.
Richard's been the mayor forever. He knows everything about everybody. Get to know him, and use him for advice.

And on it went. Name after name. Each one the piece of a big picture puzzle that Quinton couldn't see yet. After more than an hour of reading his predecessor's abrupt comments on the clientele, he realized he was beginning to understand this bank and he hadn't looked at a single financial statement. *This wasn't how they taught banking at Harvard,* he thought. And he couldn't wait to get home to tell Connie about it all.

He filled his Gucci briefcase with file folders and told the tellers he was leaving for the day. He had things to do. People to meet. Plans to make. But first he had to go find a "Storbock, Stewart A." and give him the good news.

20

Bud's Birthday

I SUPPOSE we might have all helped Bud Koenig celebrate his sixtieth birthday, had any of us known when it was. It was last Monday, and Monday came and went like most January Mondays will: dimly, quietly, and wintry.

Bud's Saw and Chain Shop was closed all through January, as it usually is, so no one had even run into Bud that day to get an indication from him that it was his birthday. Not that he would have given any.

Some people are like that about their birthdays. They either don't need or don't want the extra attention. In Bud's case, he didn't even think about it. He might have missed the date altogether if he hadn't been reminded of a promise he'd made to himself.

It happened Monday night out at the cabin he'd lived in for most of the last forty years. He'd pulled his old chair up in front of the fireplace and settled in for a long evening with his favorite poet and philosopher, Robert Service. He was reading *The Spell of the Yukon:*

I wanted the gold, and I sought it;
I scrabbled and mucked like a slave.
Was it famine or scurvy—I fought it;
I hurled my youth into a grave.
I wanted the gold, and I got it—
Came out with a fortune last fall,—
Yet somehow life's not what I thought it,
And somehow the gold isn't all.

No! There's the land. (Have you seen it?)
It's the cussedest land that I know,
From the big, dizzy mountains that screen it
To the deep, deathlike valleys below.
Some say God was tired when He made it;
Some say it's a fine land to shun;
Maybe; but there's some as would trade it
For no land on earth—and I'm one.

Bud looked up from his book into the fire. *For no land on Earth would I trade it,* he thought. Bud was so easily drawn in by poetry of the North country. Especially Mr. Service. The land itself had always worked like poetry on Bud.

There were times when, standing outside his cabin, he'd look to the white peaks across the blue-gray bay, watch the wind whip the wave tops, and he'd become overwhelmed with it. He'd lapse into what could only be described as inspiration. His eyes and ears would open to new reaches and all his senses would drink in this place. This wild, majestic, and playful world that was his Alaska. It had been happening to him ever since he first set eyes upon the territory.

One day he would write poetry of this place, he had always promised himself. One day far away, when he was an old spent codger with nothing better to do, he would try to capture in verse this vast incorrigible country that gripped him. He'd always figured he'd do it when he turned sixty.

It was his hero and bard of choice, Robert Service, who reminded him of this promise. Bud was delighted and just a little suspicious when the date ran through his mind, and he stuck on the realization that it *was* his sixtieth birthday.

"Where the hell did *that* come from?" he said out loud to the fireplace. He felt that old poetic wash coming over him again, as it often did when peculiar coincidences of the mind and time happened.

Bud laid aside his book and went to the kitchen. *I guess it's time to keep some promises,* he thought, pulling a pad and pencil out of the cupboard and sitting down with a cup of coffee at the big timber table.

Bud stared into the coffee steam, beat the pencil eraser against the pad, and felt his heart banging away in his chest. He didn't know what he was anxious about. Was it sitting down after all these long years to finally commit his impressions to paper? Or was it that the age of sixty had snuck up on him so suddenly? An age he had assumed in his naive youth was too old to do anything but write poetry.

He didn't know which. It was probably a little bit of both, but he did know he meant to keep his promise. If sixty he was, then write poetry he would.

Bud didn't have the faintest idea how to write poetry. He could read the words of other poets and get that overwhelmed sensation. And he could be overwhelmed looking at the land. But how do words put you to it? And how do you put it to words? And what are the words, the words, the words . . .

Actually, Bud knew more about writing poetry than he thought he did. Like any good poet of any time or place, he sat at the table, tapping a pad with a pencil, and sorted through a lifetime of experience, emotion, and happenstance, trying to get a fix on the essence of it all.

He started at the dim beginnings. On a small ranch outside of Missoula, Montana. In the year that would bring Herbert Hoover on as a new president, a few weeks ahead of the St. Valentine's Day massacre, Trigvy Olaf Koenig, ever after to be known as Bud, came into a cold and windy world. Bud wrote:

And born like a lamb
he became like a man
in a land where no lamb dare to be

Bud tore off the page, crumpled it, and tried to conjure up a better idea with a drumroll on the note pad.

Sheep ranching had never been for Bud, and he knew it from the beginning. Too many routines. Too many bad smells. Too many darned sheep. He longed for the great lands to the north. Beyond the border. Beyond Canada. Back to America's last frontier, where a war was being fought and Americans were fighting on American soil, *for* American soil.

He arrived in Ketchikan, Alaska, August fourteenth, the summer after his sixteenth birthday and the day the Japanese surrendered. A great war was over, but after setting one foot on Alaska turf, Bud knew a great life had just begun.

He planted his big young feet in the soggy moss of a Ketchikan streetside and looked out at the endless rolling hills of virgin timber and calm saltwaters teeming with life. With his feet so planted, Bud Koenig had the very first poetic experience of his life. It was like he'd just been smitten by some strange beautiful woman. No, it was even more than that. He felt a power grow up out of the ground and into his chest. With eyes wide open, he fell blindly in love with Alaska.

When he walked again, it was as if he'd been chipped from the land and set loose upon it. Recent memories of home became instant ancient history, and his only thought, however unconscious, was, *I'm going to grow old in this place.* Bud tried again:

From the hills of a land that I knew
to the edge of a wilderness slough
I cast-off my past
Squared-off my back
And charged into what I would do.

"Pretty flaky," Bud said out loud, tore off the page, and took another gulp of coffee, intent on sorting through the possibilities.

"Someday when I'm sixty, I'm going to write poems about this," a rough young man said to himself while cutting timber in Southeast Alaska. It was his second year felling trees, and he'd just completed the section for the day. He looked out over the clear view of Frederick Sound, with icebergs bobbing and distant white peaks dropping straight into the water like the wall at the end of the world.

He looked down to his work and smiled a workman's smile. All the smaller spruce and cedar were laid across the hill and bucked up fine for the rigging. The large, long straight spruce were saved for last. They were the boom sticks and would hold the log raft together. He laid those down the hill and they skated the cross timber all the way to the beach landing.

Bud Koenig was a first-class timber faller. Even at age eighteen they were calling him a chain-saw wizard. "You can drive a stake anywhere, around any tree, and that darn kid will hit it." It was true, and they still say that. Bud knew how to turn a leaning tree around. He could read a twisted trunk and could hear a widow maker coming before the branch had broken. He was something, he was. He put the pencil to the pad:

> *Just a boy and a hat and a chain saw*
> *with arms like a ninety-year spruce*
> *He laid down the forests*
> *and sang out the chorus*
> *of boys in the wild on the loose.*

Bud ripped up the page. "Grow up, Koenig. And quitcher braggin'." The drumroll on the note pad played again as the poet skipped forward through inspirations.

Bud had come to the End of the Road in the late forties, before there was a road here at all. He'd heard about the homestead land here and had staked out his hundred sixty acres. He applied his sheep-ranching past to the spread to grow enough hay and timothy to prove-up on the homestead lease, but he had no interest in farming.

He applied his chain-saw wizardry to building log cabins. First he built his own, which he still occupies, and then went on to build countless dozens of others for other homesteaders. Most of them, in fact. Most but Argus Winslow's.

The young Bud Koenig and the young Argus Winslow became immediate friends. They were among the few bachelors of the homesteader ilk, and used to cut quite a bunctious swath through this quiet little settlement. They were quick to fight, easy to drink, and hard to follow.

Bud couldn't pin down where they'd parted the ways, or why. But it had something to do with the land. Argus looked to the land as his resource. Something to use and develop. He was more likely to shoot a wolf for the pelt than to listen to it howl in the blue winter night. He opened a junkyard and appeared to thrive in the unkempt world of salvage.

Bud had never lost his footing from the first time he'd planted them in this territory. He took great pride in keeping his homestead as he'd found it. He walked often through his spruce trees and ringed for firewood only those trees he could see were doomed from wind or rot to begin with.

In the world of men and the earth, Bud was a gardener and Argus was a strip miner. They differed on everything except their raw respect of the other one's abilities. Bud considered this.

> *Old friends from the first time I met you*
> *Rivals with rucksacks and tools*
> *Wrestlers and rousers and allies*
> *Oh, where did the sport turn to feud?*

"Eee-gosh," Bud said, peeling off the page. "Winslow ever saw that, he'd pee his pants laughin' at me."

Bud sat back once again to think. He tried to organize something of his sixty years. All those faces. All those wonderful places he'd seen. Most of them not so far from where he sat. He thought of friendships and enemies, all good people.

And he thought of those he'd lost. It's a rough land he'd chosen, and he'd paid the price with many a good friend. Lost in those beautiful high mountains. Drowned in that sensuous sea so full of life at the same time it kills.

Bud thought of how many times he'd thought like this. How many times he'd stood and let that power rush up into his chest right out of the ground and tell him things. Things he would write about one day when he was too old to do for the land. When all he could do was sing its praises. *He would write them when he's sixty.*

And a man of sixty stared at a blank page and tried to fill it with the essence. And he couldn't. He couldn't sum up a life that wasn't totaled yet. Sixty seemed old when he was twenty. It even seemed old at fifty. But at sixty it seemed like the same old thing. "There's a lot of fight left in this old goat," he said out loud, and grabbed for the pencil again.

> *Six decades of life in a minute*
> *I said I would do what I can't*
> *I won't strike a verse when I'm in it*
> *I won't rhyme a word I still am*
>
> *I've friends yet to meet and to steady*
> *My foes are afoot and I'm waiting*
> *These poems that I promised aren't ready*
> *I'll try it again, when I'm eighty.*

And a young man of sixty wadded up the sheets of paper spread around his kitchen table. He threw them in the fireplace and sat back down in his old chair. He wasn't disappointed. Young men of sixty are not supposed to understand the essence of life. There are those who've done it better.

To cap off this momentous occasion, Bud simply opened his book back to where he'd left it. Robert Service was doing service to the North country. The country that so settled Bud in life and unsettled him in words. He decided to let the poet speak the words for him.

There's gold, and it's haunting and haunting;
It's luring me on as of old;
Yet it isn't the gold that I'm wanting
So much as just finding the gold.
It's the great, big, broad land 'way up yonder,
It's the forests where silence has lease;
It's the beauty that thrills me with wonder,
It's the stillness that fills me with peace.

Happy Birthday, Bud.

---- • ----

The sewers have once again backed up on homes located below Main Street. It seems that if four households flush their toilets within ten minutes of one another that the problem occurs. The city manager who planned the system has been fired from his position and was not available for comment. The man joins a growing field of ex-End of the Road city managers, which now totals six in the last two years. The city council would not comment on the sewage problem but suggested off the record that it might be a good idea to call your neighbors and check in before you flush the toilet.

All the new harbor lights have been shot out only three weeks after having been replaced after the last time they were shot out. There has been a lot of local controversy over the new bright lights shining, to some's point of view, too brightly at their homes. The police presently have no suspects in the case, but they are looking for someone who resides on harbor-facing property and is a really good shot. "I'd like to shake that man's hand before I cuff him," said Police Chief Peter Bindel. "He hit 'em all dead center, and never missed a one. I'd like to take 'im along on my moose hunt next year."

---- • ----

21

Emmitt Frank

SOMEWHERE in the midst of a vast Chicago suburb where house after house wound side by side on treeless lots along planned streets named for flora and fauna that no one had ever heard of, a man rested his heavy head flat against a coffee saucer on the table of his neat Formica kitchen. Emmitt Frank heaved a sigh of sadness into the plate and let his arms hang between his bare knees.

A trail of business accessories led from the front door to his roost. A briefcase lay sprung and scattered in the entry. A conservative but not badly cut pinstripe jacket lay half inside out beside it. The matching vest dangled from a dining room chair back. A red power tie was draped weakly across the cat's dish, and the trousers lay rumpled under his feet, one foot still in one leg. It had been a bad day.

Actually, it had been worse than bad. Bad days come and go unpredictably like Lake Michigan rain squalls, leaving behind clear skies, fresh smells, and a sense of remedy. This hadn't been a rain squall of a day. It had been a deluge. A tempest. A hurricane of a day. A day that left nothing behind and took all. And worse than that, it was a day he should have seen coming.

In less than twelve hours he had lost his job and his wife. At least that's what he'd been telling himself on the drive home in his practical mid-sized sedan. But now, as he studied the backs of his eyelids and continued to let the weight of the world push his face into a Melmac saucer, he realized that he'd been losing both for a long long time.

Emmitt had been a low-level government bureaucrat of little or no influence for the municipality of Chicago since college. Almost twenty years now. He worked in the planning department. A boring, almost nonsensical, rubber-stamp position that Emmitt Frank was perfectly suited for.

All the engineering, all the studies, all the real planning was done by other people. Emmitt's job was to study the planning studies and determine if they met the municipal-study requirements, state guidelines on city-form procedure, and federal standards on municipal documentation.

In essence, he did nothing. And he did it with a diligence and efficiency that if applied to material things, might conquer the world. But Emmitt's diligence was applied only to the mistakes of other people. He was an auditor of bureaucratic frailties, and the rest of the departments lived in dread of his memos.

TO: Engineering, Mr. Critten
FROM: Planning, Mr. Frank
Your plan file #1879–4 is missing from 971A and permit rider release sequence 1785 through 1791. File must be complete by 4–12–89 for approval review.

Emmitt was good at what he did, and he knew it. Sometimes he went down to the file dungeon to look at the vast wall of filing cabinets he had filled over his twenty years with the city. And not one document was with an uncrossed t or undotted i. Not one form out of order. It would withstand the test of time. He was sure of that. Nothing slipped by him. He noticed everything. Everything, that is, but his life unraveling right before his eyes.

He should have noticed the edges start to fray when they put that young hotshot on as his assistant. That good-looking, square-jawed planner with a ready laugh, a warm handshake, and a master's degree.

He was ten years his junior, and good at what he did, Emmitt had to admit. But Emmitt felt compelled to re-check everything the young man did because he seemed to do it so effortlessly. And he had fun. For the first time in years, people from other departments were dropping their documents by his department personally instead of using the routing service. They'd lean up against the new guy's desk and Emmitt could hear their laughter back in his cubicle. He would be curious to read the efficiency reports on this one.

Efficiency. Planning. Accuracy. That was Emmitt's life.

Even his marriage was a managed affair. He'd always planned to marry just before turning twenty-five, when the life-insurance rates for single men took a decided leap, and he did. He'd even picked the church for the ceremony based on a printout of road miles required for relevant relatives and friends. It was a well-planned wedding, and they had moved into a well-planned subdivision in an efficiently located suburb to plan a family.

That is where a contingency entered the plan. Emmitt and his wife soon discovered that they were incapable of conceiving children. Neither of their faults. Just mutually biologically incompatible. It doesn't happen often: once in 670,000 cases, according to Emmitt's research. But, nevertheless, it had dashed their plans for children, and their sex life soon became a nonissue in Emmitt's life.

They hadn't slept together in two years, that Emmitt could remember, and his wife had started sleeping in the guest room over a year ago. Not long after the young square-jawed guy with the master's degree had come on at the office. These things all came painfully clear in Emmitt's head as it rested deliberately and efficiently in a saucer.

He remembered last year's office Christmas party when his wife had gotten a little tipsy and made a fool of herself, in Emmitt's estimation, with his new assistant. Then how she'd began spending long evenings and sometimes whole nights with her sister.

He didn't remember that his wife had a sister, but then, he'd paid little attention to her family, or her for that matter. It was frivolous. There was little time for frivolity in Emmitt's life. There were too many people to keep track of. Too many mistakes being made.

And as Emmitt Frank sat contemplating mistakes made, a small group of people in a nameless town five thousand miles away were deliberating his future, although neither he, nor they, knew it at the time.

Mayor Richard Weekly called the city council of the End of the Road to order. "Okay, if everybody's got their coffee, we'll get started. Clara, call the roll."

Clara, the mayor's sister, poured the last cup of coffee, took off her apron, and sat down at the long table in her restaurant, locally known as Clara's Coffee Cup even though the sign fell down ten years ago. She proceeded to take roll call.

"Mayor Richard Weekly."

"Yes."

"Lars Luger."

"Ya see me sittin' here, b'golly, I don' understand the fussin'."

"Thank you, Lars. We'll continue . . . Ruby McClay."

"I'm here. You could let a person finish her dinner," Ruby said between swallows of Clara's Monday-night pork-chop special.

"Pastor Frank Olmstead."

"Present, and honored to be so."

"Shut up, Frank . . . and Bud Koenig."

"I'm here, Clara. Mayor Weekly, let's get on with this."

"Okay, okay. There's not much to report except the sewer's still backed up below Main Street. Somebody shot out all the harbor lights again, and we still have no applicants for the city manager's position."

"It's no wonder. We've fired six of them in the last two years." Bud Koenig sat matter-of-factly sipping his coffee.

"I don't like these outsiders coming in here and telling us what to do," Clara said from behind the lunch counter.

"Be quiet, Clara," the mayor said. "You're not on the council, you're just the secretary. Take the minutes."

"I still don't like it," she said, and resumed her crossword puzzle.

"Unfortunately, Bud is right," Mayor Weekly said. "We've fired so many city managers as of late that the word is out on us, and few qualified people are willing to apply. I might stress that we are in dire need of management. Somewhere out there is just the right man for the job, and we need to do everything we can to find him. Ruby, you're on the hiring committee, how do we stand?"

Ruby McClay took out her notes and wiped the dinner off her mouth with the blank side of it.

"We've advertised the job in all the trade journals, sent out form letters to past applicants we scared off, and we just put an ad in *Alaska* magazine last week. It's all we can do."

"You may be right," said Mayor Weekly. "The *Alaska* magazine was a good idea. We'll get some folks who already understand about the place a little bit. Maybe have somebody with a little backbone."

"That's for sure," Lars Luger said, coming momentarily out of his stupor. "I'm tired of all these wimp Glad Bags we've been gettin'. We need us a manager with a little vigor, by golly. No more'a these darn bean counters."

• • •

And as the good council deliberated, in far-off Chicago a newly unemployed, half-naked bean counter ground his head farther into his coffee saucer, trying to fix on one thing in his life that wasn't planned or calculated.

There was nothing. The only thing in his life without design was his current dilemma; the fact that one young square-jawed man had taken his job and his wife away from him without his even noticing. His wife had left a note on his Pop Tart this morning. His boss had left a pink slip in his basket at five.

He had barely made it from the car to the house. Beyond his control, his body had started shedding his identity at the door. As his suit dripped off of him piece by piece, his legs grew weaker, and he could only manage to drop into a chair in the dinette and fall forward. A ship without a wheel. A train without a track. A man without a plan. It was the end of the road.

The End of the Road, Emmitt thought. That rang a bell. There was a place like that. He knew there was. He didn't miss anything. He stirred from his coffee saucer and looked around. *It was that magazine. Alaska* magazine.

The only frivolous thing Emmitt had ever allowed himself was *Alaska* magazine. It was a journal of life on the Last Frontier. The great unknown. The vast untamed. It was almost pornography to a city planner. So much to be organized. So many studies to make. So many plans to draw and file. And approvals to approve. He'd always read it late at night before he went to sleep, and imagined himself Emmitt Frank the Frontier Planner.

He got up from the table and, still dragging his trousers from one foot, proceeded to rifle through the magazine basket in the hallway. *Efficiency Today. Engineering Weekly. City Sewer Update.* Under them all was the one. An irreverently subjectless publication with, of all things, a *dog* on the cover. *Alaska* magazine.

He flipped to the back pages. To the classifieds, where he knew he'd seen it, and there it was:

• • •

WANTED: City Manager. Must have planning experience. Especially sewers. Inquire at the End of the Road, Alaska 99603.

Emmitt folded the magazine back and began to plan. He would need a résumé and reference letters. He would have to sell the house and the cat. No one was more qualified than Emmitt Frank. He had twenty years in city planning, ten of those in sewers alone. He knew every form. Every document. Every single state, municipal, and government regulation known to western man.

Emmitt's heart fluttered. He *was* going to be the Frontier Planner. He knew it. He, Emmitt Frank, would single-handedly stamp and file the wilderness. *Life could be so sweet at the most unplanned moments,* Emmitt thought as he stood back and looked at his grinning face in the hallway mirror.

It was a face of efficiency, a face of accuracy. He would go to the End of the Road and show them how it's done. This he knew. This he planned on. He allowed himself the private pleasure of admiring his reflection as those poor disorganized folk at the other end of the road might one day.

And it meant nothing to Emmitt. Or maybe he didn't notice it, that the impression of a Melmac coffee saucer was crammed deep into his face, two circles, one inside the other, like the bull's-eye of a giant target waiting to be nailed by some unseen, and unplanned for, frontier marksmen.

Snow dominates the news this week. Lots of snow. Over four feet has fallen since Tuesday, and the debates rage around the big table at Clara's Coffee Cup. Argus Winslow says it's the biggest snow since '48. Bud Koenig says '55 was worse, and Clara thinks '67 has them all beat. The annual "Eyeball Deep Snow Lottery" is on again. Guess correctly when the snow will cover the stop sign at Main and Clearshot and win a chance at the big Husky Snowblower on display at Bud's Saw and Chain. Entry forms are available at Bud's, at Clara's Coffee Cup, Ruby's Video Roundup, and the Lame Moose Saloon.

Along with these heavy snows comes the moose on the road. Our goofy forest friends find it easier to walk the plowed roads than muck through the wilderness, so you are advised to keep a sharp eye out for these gangly refugees when driving. Clarence the Safety Coyote is not kidding when he says, "Running into big animals on the highway is a really bad idea."

22

Clara's
Coffee Cup

IT was the twentieth-anniversary celebration of Clara's Coffee Cup, and the regular gang was a little nervous about their gift. You wouldn't think that presenting a brand-new stainless-steel sixty-cup automatic coffee urn to a woman who ran a coffee shop would be a potential problem. But then you'd have to know a little more about the woman to understand.

Clara Weekly is our mayor Richard Weekly's older sister. She was probably fifteen years his senior, and was easily pushing seventy. She was not one of those people who ages with grace. With each passing year she grew more uncomfortable not only with herself, but with everything. A scowl that had always been frequent with Clara to begin with became permanently marked on her face.

The boys weren't really interested in pleasing Clara with their coffee urn. They knew that was impossible. All they were concerned with was getting a decent cup of coffee. For the last five years Clara's coffee urn was malfunctioning and tended to scorch the brew. If you weren't lucky enough to get one of the first six cups out of the batch, it was likely to taste a bit charred.

"Dad-blame-it, Clara," Argus Winslow and just about everybody else had been saying for five years, "this mud tastes like a singed boot."

"Then get yer coffee somewhere else," is all she would offer in reply.

Clara had the only coffee shop in town, and it's been that way for twenty years. She was not conscientious about her business. In fact, she appeared to despise everything about it. She wasn't going to fix anything that wasn't broken all the way to the ground. And even then, not always.

Her sign fell down ten years ago. It hung from one chain for three years and everyone just ducked under it. Finally it went for good and somebody carried it off. Her windows hadn't been washed in years, but any suggestion that they should be would be met with a rag and a bottle of Windex set at your table.

Clara was such a cantankerous individual, the boys were worried that she would see through their gift of the coffee urn and refuse to use it. Then not only would they still be drinking burned coffee, but they'd be out several hundred dollars to boot. It had to be presented in just the right way, and Clara was not an easy person to present to.

The only joy she seemed to get out of life was from the little toy poodle she kept. It's one of those white stiff-legged things that never holds still and never stops barking. High squeaky barks with a question mark on the end of each syllable. She used to bring it to work with her, but Bud Koenig put an end to that by pouring coffee on it every time it walked by his chair. The dog disappeared soon after.

Despite the lack of affection between Clara and her customers, it was a long and steady relationship. At six o'clock every morning the usual gang would pile in and take their places at the big table in the back.

"This mud tastes like an old singed boot," someone would say to Clara, and then the morning discourse would commence on any subject from red salmon to road salt, Hayley Mills to heavy machinery.

The "big table" was sort of the honors club of Clara's Coffe Cup. There were other tables in the joint, but they were rarely used by locals and were there solely for the sake of the tourists who didn't know the hierarchy of the place. The lunch counter was the bull pen for the big table. As honor members drifted off one by one to their jobs and distractions, the relief players at the counter would amble over one at a time to fill their chairs. There was no system anybody knew of to get a permanent seat at the big table, unless somebody died or Clara got a bigger table. Death being the better bet.

Clara didn't like the big table. All she saw in that grand assemblage of local color was a lot of egos with not enough to do. She'd overhear all their stories, listen to them whine about politics, fishing, and potholes, and her scowl would work its way deeper into her sad face. They were all just obnoxious little boys to her.

Nobody knew or bothered to speculate on where Clara Weekly's basic unhappiness came from. Only Clara knew that, and even she never really thought about it that much.

It went back to her youth, actually. Or absence of youth, would be more appropriate. You see, Clara's mother died when she was seventeen. Her father, while not abusive, was, at best, absent, and the responsibilities of caring for her younger brother Richard fell on her.

Richard was two years old at the time, and the terrible twos have known no better participant. He was headstrong and fragile at the same time. He'd go from argument to tears at the wave of a hand. He toilet-trained slowly, and generally consumed all of Clara's energy for at least those first five years.

What happened because of this is that Clara missed her youth. During that time of life when she should and would have been meeting young men and sparking, she was home, mostly alone with Richard, playing mother.

She hated it. She always hated it. The fact that she couldn't have any friends over without Richard being underfoot. The fact that Richard was so much work to be around. Her father died when Richard was only ten, and she became a full-time guardian. What happened because of this is that Richard was really the only male human being she had ever known. In light of this, Clara bases all her opinions of males on her experiences with her brother.

If a complaint came out of a man's mouth, all she heard was a crybaby. If a man asserted himself in conversation, she could only picture a two-year-old's ignorant stubbornness. Even if a man managed to somehow charm her, she would derail the sensation with a thought of Richard's potty training. Or just figure it for a con. Oh, how Richard used to manipulate her. Men are such manipulators.

Clara's relationship with women was no better than the men. This was probably just jealousy, but she wore it like superiority. She couldn't stand to see another woman with a man. She figured them for fools. Ignorant cows who had no idea of the true nature of men.

All this attitude managed to accomplish for Clara was to draw her in on herself. She'd decided at a young age to be miserable, and she's grown into the habit of being that way. Whatever would finally satisfy her did not seem immediately on the horizon.

As the big day grew closer, the boys at the big table grew more and more nervous. Five solid years of bad coffee really had them edgy. They all knew too well that Clara thought every move they made was meant to exploit her in some way. There was no way she was going to sit still for this new coffee urn.

Tense over the whole thing, all the boys could think to do was beef up their coffee complaints.

"You steeped this boot a little too long, Clara. I'm startin' to taste the laces."

"My wife says that kissin' on me's like lickin' an old Red Wing drug out of a house fire."

"Ain't tasted anything this bad since I tried to suck-start my chain saw."

And on they'd go, but it served no purpose other than to wedge Clara's scowl even deeper into her face. Desperate, Bud Koenig even tried the sweet approach.

"You know, Clara, I feel a little sorry for that little dog of yours, always sittin' out in the car like that. Why'ntcha bring him in anymore?"

Clara gave 'im the stink-eye and said, "So you can empty your coffee out on him every time he walks by?"

Bud shut up. He didn't think she'd ever seen him do that. But she had. Clara saw and heard everything that went on in her café. Even though she cloaked herself in a veil of disinterest, it didn't mean she wasn't watching and listening. She'd been hearing their stories for twenty years now. Most of them dozens of times.

She was amazed at how much time men could spend talking about nonsense while the world fell down around them. Like when her sign tore loose back in '76. Those bums let it hang there for three years without raising a finger to help, and it finally fell down and disappeared. And the windows. She considered herself too old and tired to be washing those big windows. But had anybody ever offered to help? Not on your life.

Her worthless brother Richard, the illustrious mayor, was the worst of the bunch. He'd come in there acting all hangdog and beaten like the wimp that he was instead of standing up and taking control of these situations. *Good God in Heaven, these men are worthless*.

What Clara was doing was getting a lack of opportunity to help confused with a lack of desire. Everybody saw full well that her place was falling to pieces. Everybody appreciated too that she was doing everything all on her own. Everybody also appreciated that after twenty years of random tries, Clara has not accepted one single favor from anybody. So they quit trying. Sort of. Just this one last grand time they were going to give it their best shot.

It was about midnight, long after Clara had gone home, that the mayor let the boys in the back entrance to Clara's. Two of them got right on the windows, and two more went out on the porch to hang up the new sign. Richard had gotten Ruby McClay to paint it and it was a beauty. CLARA'S COFFEE CUP, it read in a crescent across the top. And right in the center was a big steamy cup of black coffee.

Good coffee, Richard hoped, as he and Bud struggled with the big new coffee urn behind the counter. They debated whether to take the old one completely out or not, then decided against it.

"Better not to press our luck," Bud said.

After the sign was hung and windows were washed, the gang just wandered around the place doing an odd thing here, an odd thing there. Bud fixed the front door that stuck in the winter. Argus screwed the metal molding back down around the lunch counter. And Richard went through oiling all the squeaky swivel tops on the stools. When they were all done, they hung their banner, turned off the lights, snuck back out the way they'd come, and felt a mixture of panic and accomplishment. This thing could go either way.

They might not have worried as much about how Clara was going to take the surprise if they'd known what she was up to herself that night. Clara, of course, knew all about the surprise. She knew about everything. You couldn't speak into the back of your hand in a low voice a hundred yards downwind from Clara without her hearing it.

Clara was actually pretty excited about her twentieth anniversary and she was going to bring something to the party herself. Something she was cooking up that very night. Something for her boys.

•   •   •

When Clara walked up the steps of her café at five-thirty the next morning, she wasn't surprised, but was pleased to see the big new sign swinging in the breeze. She stopped for a moment to admire it, patting something wrapped in newspaper under one arm.

She turned on the lights and had to smile a little at a crude banner swung across the back wall, HAPPY AN-NIVERSARY CLARA, and at a single glance she could tell every little thing that had been fixed.

"Well, it's about time," she said out loud to the empty room. "Now I have a little present for you guys."

Clara went over to the coffee urns side by side on the counter and put the contents of her package in the old one. She fired up a batch of brew in the new one and by the time the gang straggled in at six, the place was filled with the sweet warm smell of perfectly brewed coffee.

The boys all stood around the counter with their hats in their hands, looking like schoolboys on report-card day.

"Well, Clara?" brother Richard said. "What do you think of it?"

Clara stood with her arms crossed in front of her and looked at her men one at a time. Each one a little nuisance, and each one a nuisance she wouldn't live without. Not letting her scowl leave her face for a second, she said, "I tried this newfangled machine of yours and I ain't too sure about it."

"Whatsa matter? Is it too big?" Bud burst in.

"No, it's a good size. It's the taste. Can't seem to get a decent cup of coffee out of it."

This mystified the boys as Clara made a big show of sipping a sample cup and spitting it in the sink.

"Must be the flavoring," she said. "Ain't got the seasoning of my old pot."

The boys just scratched themselves and worried as Clara opened up her old urn. Their expressions turned to horror as she reached deep down inside of it and pulled out a charred old logging boot she'd been up half the night scorching in the fireplace.

"You see, boys," she said, making the motions as if to drop it into the new urn. "The secret to good coffee's the seasoning." She turned and looked at her boys, and they laughed all together for the first time in probably twenty years.

School bus number 99 had to cancel its route on Tuesday. After sliding off the road at Ten Mile on Far Road, the driver asked his children passengers to get out and help push. What the children did instead was to let all the air out of the tires in an effort to sabotage that day's school attendance. The End of the Road Review is somewhat reluctant to report that it worked.

Pastor Frank Olmstead of the First and Last Baptist Church will be giving a presentation to the PTA on Tuesday evening. "Puberty: Threat or Menace," is the topic, and the pastor will outline ways for parents to keep sex an embarrassing secret from their children for as long as it takes to weasel out of it altogether. That's in the lunchroom at the junior high at seven-thirty. Donations at the door. Visa and MasterCharge accepted.

23

Norman's Secret

THE whole thing started in Algebra class. Right in the middle of a discussion on the Pythagorean Theorem of right triangles. It was a theorem Norman would never remember, but he would always remember the moment he noticed girls for the first time.

Of course, Norman had noticed girls before. He knew pretty much what they were and how they were put together. They just had never done anything for him until now. Norman and his best friend Stan would sometimes look through those magazines his dad kept under the galley seat down on the boat. But mostly they would just giggle at the pictures for a while, get bored, and go back to chucking rocks at sea gulls.

Now those magazines would embarrass Norman. He and Stan would find less and less to laugh about, and as the interest grew keener, so would it grow personal.

And it was a personal moment Norman was having in Algebra class. Time stopped somewhere between the Pythagorean Theorem and *Portnoy's Complaint*.

It was all brought on by Laura Magruder, who sat in the next row one seat up. She'd dropped her pencil and it rolled toward Norman. He pushed it back to her with his foot without even thinking. When she raised up again with the pencil in her hand, she looked at Norman and smiled in thanks.

It was an innocent smile, or could have been. And it was a genuine smile. But it was also a smile that for the first time in Norman's life he recognized as being *sexy*. Norman had been smiled at before with no severe repercussions, but this one was different. Whether it was Laura Magruder's doing or Norman's fantasy, it all had the same effect.

A floodgate opened somewhere deep in Norman's metabolism and a wash of emotion from passion to panic filled him up and glowed red in his face.

At two thirty-five P.M. on January the eighteenth, 1989, Norman Tuttle reached puberty.

Norman spent the rest of Algebra class somewhere east of the planet Venus. By the time the bell rang he had studied every hair on Laura Magruder's head and fallen in love with them individually. He studied the pattern in her knit sweater until it made shapes on his retina wall like some religious hologram. He memorized the folds in her jeans and the smudges on her white running shoes.

He imagined her feet moving, and where they walked, and if they walked home, and what color her bedroom was, and on through the rest of the hour. When she made a movement, no matter how slight, his heart would jump. He bit the eraser clean off his pencil when she turned to look at the clock over his head, almost catching him staring.

It was the first time Norman had ever regretted hearing the school bell ring. It rang like a rude alarm clock jarring him out of a wonderful dream where everything was in color and he was winning.

As the other kids, including Laura, jumped out of their seats and crowded through the door, Norman lingered at his desk putting his things away carefully, hesitant to step out into that world that had so completely changed since he came to class.

Norman stood out in the schoolyard watching the daily chaos unfold around kids loading on buses, some meeting their moms in cars and others just wandering off in twos and threes. He was looking for her. He didn't know why, or what he'd do if he found her, but nothing in the world seemed more important at the moment.

"Well, if it isn't Stormin' Norman." It was his friend Stanley Bindel saying hello and throwing a snowball at the same time.

"Knock it off, Stan," Norman said, brushing the snow out of his hair, genuinely annoyed.

Stanley was momentarily set back by his friend's orneriness, but put it aside. "What'd ya do, flunk your Algebra quiz?"

Norman looked at Stanley with suspicion for a second then said defensively, "Algebra doesn't have anything to do with it."

"Anything to do with what?"

"Nothing, anything to do with nothing . . ." Norman would have stammered on and probably spilled the beans, but just then he saw her over Stan's shoulder.

She was walking with two of her friends, talking and laughing. Just as she crossed behind Stan she looked up from her friends and their eyes met. It was there again. *What* was there again? *It,* that look, those eyes and that smile. That smile that boiled Norman's ears and sent a giggle of energy from his forehead to his big thirteen-year-old feet.

Laura looked away with a snap of her head and picked up the pace of her trio. The whole thing couldn't have taken more than half a second, but it was long enough to set into motion a complex chain of biological and emotional trip switches in Norman.

Without his conscious cooperation, Norman's body reacted to the tripped switches and began an intricate and dexterous series of functions that he didn't fully understand at the moment. With no more control than if he'd been sleeping, a mating rite as old as puberty itself unfolded before Norman. With dreamlike amazement he saw himself fix on the object of his affections, release with deadly accuracy, and hit his target square in the middle of the back with a snowball.

She turned around angry. Her friends tittered into their mittens and they all three ran off.

"What the heck did you do that for?" Stanley said.

"She was asking for it," Norman said back.

The formal courtship of Laura Magruder had begun.

The next couple of weeks would be hard on Norman. He would spend every day at school ignoring Laura Magruder and every night at home worshiping her. While Norman ignored Laura, she continued to ignore and even actively avoid him, so instinctively Norman knew that the relationship was going well.

He found himself racing from Science to Algebra class so he could watch her walk in rather than vice versa. He memorized all her clothes and wondered what she'd wear next.

He hadn't done an Algebra assignment in ten days. He hadn't played cribbage with his dad in a week. And Stanley Bindel had stopped seeking him out after school. For the first time ever, Norman had a secret so personal that he couldn't share it with his best friend. He might have shared it if he'd understood it himself, but he didn't really. Not everything.

He didn't understand why some of those gushy songs on the radio now made sense. Why he even looked forward to a few of them. Norman had never had any interest in music at all before. Now he found himself spending long hours in the bedroom listening to his clock radio.

And it was the same thing with television. He understood so many more things than he used to. Overnight, like he'd taken a smart pill, stories of unrequited love, terminally ill sweethearts, and lonely soldiers rang clear in Norman's head. He could feel it. Comprehend it. He knew something. What was it he knew? And how could he tell Stanley?

Norman didn't think too much about Stanley. He didn't think too much about anything except Laura. *Laura*. He'd say the word in his head but couldn't bring himself to speak it. Who would he say it to? What if somebody heard? Norman took up full-time residence in his own head.

His fantasies kept him awake and went on way into the night. He'd be a battle-bloodied soldier returning from war. His face blackened with combat, his shirt torn, but his shoulders held bravely back despite a bad limp from a festering leg wound. Laura would run in slow motion out to the gate and press into his arms. They'd spin and hold each other looking into each other's eyes, and finally they'd kiss.

Or he'd be in a hospital, terribly torn apart because of some courageous deed on Laura's behalf. She would be holding his hand, making promises as he looked up lovingly and bravely into her eyes. And then they'd kiss.

The later the night the better the fantasy, and often Norman would be a superman. A nearly invulnerable fighting machine who could ward off all attackers with his highly trained hands and feet. And always, in the background quaking with fear and bursting with pride, would be Laura watching super Norman rip his way through a gang of bikers. Or a communist horde. Or a horde of communist bikers. Always with pluck and venom, and always victorious. And Laura would run to her hero at the end of the endless fray and they'd embrace. And then they'd kiss.

Norman always stopped with the kiss because he didn't really know what came next. He sensed there was something there, but he didn't quite have the background to go on to the next step, even in his head.

There was also a "next step" in the real world of Norman Tuttle and Laura Magruder. A serious steady relationship cannot last forever on the merits of one well-placed snowball. They were going to have to go on a date. This is where Norman really ran into a dark and scary alley. The methods of asking a girl out were even more obscure to Norman than what came after a good kiss.

There were few people in Norman's life who had the experience he needed right now. But there was one, one in particular, who just might be able to help him out.

So one night, after the little kids had gone off to bed and his mom had retired to her sewing room, Norman let his dad talk him back into their game of cribbage in the kitchen.

"Well, Normy. Long time no see. What you been up to all week?" His dad dealt the cards.

"Not much."

"Haven't seen little Stanley around lately. You guys have a fight or somethin'?"

"No." Norman hunched his shoulders down and tried to concentrate on his cards.

The elder Tuttle could tell something was amiss but was afraid to keep stabbing for it. Might stick it in the wrong spot and ruin everything. He trusted Norman to talk to him, and he knew he would when he was ready. Norman was ready.

"Dad, if you had to ask a girl out on a date, how would you do it?" Norman just blurted it across the table like a spilled Pepsi.

Norman's father was absolutely stunned with the question, but warmed by it too. He was relieved to hear this easy answer to Norman's strange behavior lately. He'd feared worse things than girls.

"Well, Norm," he said, "if *I* was to ask a girl out, I'd go down to a pay phone so your mother wouldn't find out about it."

"I'm serious, Dad."

"I know you are. Okay—well, tell me, is this girl interested in you?"

"I think so."

"Does she know you're interested in her?"

"Yes."

"How does she know?"

"I hit her with a snowball."

"Oh yeah, that should do it."

The father of the boy sat back and tried to hide his smile. He didn't understand everything that was going on here, but he did understand that his little Norman was growing up fast. Faster than he'd thought.

He'd always meant to have "the talk" with Norman some day. He knew he got into those magazines on the boat, but he trusted Norman to come to him when he had questions. How to ask a girl out probably wasn't the only question Norman had on his mind, but it was a good place to start.

"The first thing you have to understand about women, or girls, is that there's no rules to them. They're all different people. So what's right with one might not be right with another, you see? I could tell you all night how to win the heart of your little friend . . . what's her name?"

"Laura," Norman said.

". . . and it might not work."

Norman didn't hear the last part of his dad's sentence. He was flushed red as a beet, not believing he'd actually said her name out loud to his father.

Norman's embarrassment was not lost on his father, and the veteran Tuttle decided to keep things easy for a while.

"Where would you take Laura?" he said.

"Roller skating, I guess. I've seen her at the roller rink sometimes."

"Roller skating, that's good. Well, if I was to want a girl to go roller skating with me, the way I'd ask her would be to call her up and say, 'Wanna go roller skating with me?'"

"Dad, I'm serious."

"So am I. Don't make it difficult. Just call her and ask her."

Norman had heard this tone of advice before from his dad. What it meant was, "There's only one right way to do this, so do it, and stop asking stupid questions." Norman understood, but somehow wanted more. There must be more to all of this.

Norman's dad sat back and watched his son. He had two of Mom's good plastic-coated cards folded six ways. Norman's skinny knee was bouncing a hundred beats a minute under the table, and he was going to chew a hole right through the side of his face if he didn't hurry up and say what was on his mind.

While Norman's dad waited for the question, he realized he had to have some answers. Pretty soon he had a couple of his cards folded into squares. He was keeping beat with Norman under the table and reaching all the way down inside himself for a little bit of courage and a lot of inspiration.

Finally Norman cleared his throat. "Dad, like, well. Umm, ya know, *after* you go out on a date and stuff, like, ya know, *then* what?"

There it was. Laying right in front of them. *Then what?* The two men looked at each other and the cards hit the table.

A simple fisherman with nothing on his side but a good heart and an obligation was faced with the task of passing along the combined experiences of an entire species as pertains to love, morality, biology, ideology, and disease. It was going to take a while.

"Normy, let me tell you some things about yourself and what you might be feeling lately . . ."

And on into the night it went. Mrs. Tuttle discreetly snuck off to bed without interrupting, and it was well after two in the morning before the light in the kitchen finally went out.

"It's school tomorrow, bub. An' you got a lot to

think about." Mr. Tuttle hugged his son, and a stunned but wiser young man went up to his room.

Norman would never come down those stairs a boy again. His father knew that, and there were some tears shed in the master bedroom that night.

Norman knew it and he never slept a wink. He laid there in the dark alternating between exhilaration and terror, with a good dose of anticipation for the days that lay ahead.

Especially tomorrow, because *boy,* did he have some things to tell Stanley about.

Two local men walked away unharmed from a single-engine Cessna after a failed takeoff from the municipal airport in high winds on Wednesday. The plane, loaded to capacity with cases of soft drinks destined for schools across the bay, crashed and flipped on the tide flat at the end of the runway. The badly damaged aircraft was salvaged but the scattered cargo was left for Mother Nature to do with what the clamdiggers don't get first.

When asked how windy it really was at the airport Wednesday, a local pilot claimed he took off into the wind that afternoon and flew twenty minutes before reaching the end of the runway. Giving it up as a lost cause, the veteran bush pilot was able to throttle down until he was blown far enough back to set down safely in front of his hangar.

The End of the Road was officially declared a Nuclear Free Zone by the city council at their regular meeting Monday night at Clara's Coffee Cup. Mayor Richard Weekly cited tremendous local pressure for the action, led by leading local pressure-person Tamara Dupree. Under the new ordinance it is now illegal to use, store, or detonate any nuclear devices within the city limits. Violators will be subject to fines up to $100, three days in jail, or 400 hours community-service work.

24

Doug's
Opening

DOUG McDoogan was delighted and confused when the blue-haired old lady once again stepped through his door. He had six carvings ready for her this time, and she gave him the three hundred dollars easily while she studied the new work.

"Doug, I'd say you're getting even better." She turned a piece of driftwood around in her hands, admiring the face of a harbor seal. "The detail is astonishing on this one. Did you get a new knife?"

"Nope." Doug looked down at his feet and shuffled; his standard pose when in the presence of any higher life form, including most dogs. "No, same knife. Maybe it's the electric lights and the heat. I hold still better when I'm warm."

Of course, she thought. *He's never worked indoors before. My Lord, what this boy could do if he had decent tools and an education to work them with.* She put that hope aside for the moment and looked once again at her artist.

"Doug, I have some good news for you. I'm featuring you in an opening at my gallery next Friday." The blue-haired lady leaned on her cane and smiled, self-satisfied, waiting for Doug's reaction.

Doug's reaction, not unexpected, was confusion. *Featuring me in an opening at her gallery.* Doug ran the words through his head to conjure up some images. All he could picture was himself standing in some open window at this woman's store where people could look at him. Like in a circus he saw somewhere. His confusion grew dark.

The woman saw Doug's consternation and tried to explain for him. "All of Anchorage is raving about your work, Doug. They've begged me to get more of your carvings and to bring you to town so they can meet you." She reached inside her purse and pulled out an envelope. "Here are your tickets and some expense money. You'll be staying at the Sheraton Hotel." The woman patted the envelope gently into Doug's hand. "Try to look your best too. All the important people in the arts are going to be there to see you."

And with that the blue-haired lady left Doug to his bewilderment. He couldn't have understood less about what he was supposed to do if she'd told him in Greek. About all he got the drift of was that he was supposed to be somewhere in Anchorage the following Friday to meet important people.

Doug wasn't overly excited with this prospect. When "important people" came into Doug's life it usually meant he was in trouble. Policemen were important people. Judges were important people. Great big bartenders could be important people. Doug knew that with important people he always lost, and it was with considerable dread he resigned himself to the task ahead and opened the envelope the woman had left. It made less sense than she did.

There was a fancy card of some kind with raised gold lettering on it, but all Doug could make of it was his own name, an address, and a time, seven-thirty. There was an airline ticket which meant nothing to Doug, and eighty dollars in cash which meant everything to him but explained little.

Doug McDoogan scratched his head. Pulled himself up to his full intellectual height—and decided he'd go ask Ruby McClay what was going on. Doug had come to trust Ruby over at the video store with the secret that he was basically illiterate, and he relied on her to read the garage-sale ads to him in the newspaper or the occasional piece of junk mail that showed up at his door.

It was Thursday before Doug got around to visiting Ruby's Video Roundup, and by then Ruby had already read about Doug's big opening in the Anchorage paper. She lathered praise on him as she explained what to do with everything. "Okay, big shot. Go to the airport at five o'clock tomorrow. This is your ticket, give it to the girl and they'll do the rest. This note says that someone will pick you up in Anchorage, so don't worry about gettin' around. If I was you, I'd take this money and buy yourself some decent clothes for this hullabaloo. Gonna be a lot of important people there."

"I know," Doug said, showing his nerves by pulling his head down between his shoulders a little bit.

This wasn't wasted on Ruby, who held Doug roughly by his hunched shoulders and said right to his nose, "Listen, buster. Remember that this gig is for you. They're all comin' to see Doug McDoogan. You're the most important person there."

This did little to settle Doug's nerves, but he left with at least a notion of what he was supposed to do. The first thing was to go by the Salvation Army and get himself some decent clothes like Ruby said. That didn't take too long because there was a really good selection in Doug's basic taste.

Doug had never had occasion to buy dress clothes before, but he knew exactly what he wanted. Doug walked out of there in under half an hour with a spiffy new outfit plus a flowered suitcase to carry it in.

He tried the whole works on when he got home, and while admiring his reflection in the bathroom mirror, he started to relax a little about what lay ahead.

He'd scored a near-perfect fit on a forest-green double-knit leisure suit, with a Polynesian print shirt and a genuine Teamsters Local 959 commemorative bolo necktie. The slacks were even bell-bottoms, but Doug opted to tuck them into his new shiny-black cowboy boots which were only four dollars because the heel was off one of them. He stood on top of the toilet so he could get a good look at the boots.

He reminded himself of Hank Freeman back in Boise. Doug used to work for Hank at one of his car washes. Hank was a sharp dresser. And he drove a vintage fanny-pink 1958 Cadillac De Ville with a horn that played "The Yellow Rose of Texas." Hank was class. Doug always wanted to be like Hank, and here he was, well on his way. He was so excited about his new look that he didn't want to take it off. So, Doug hobbled over to the bed, sprawled himself across it carefully and slept in his clothes. From the bolo to the boots.

He dreamed of a circus sideshow with a judge in a big pink car and blue faeries granting wishes for pennies.

Doug was nervous as the plane taxied up to the terminal in Anchorage. This was only the second time he'd ever flown, and the first time into a commercial airport. He was fidgeting with his teamster's bolo and fretting when he spotted her in the terminal before the plane had even stopped.

The blue-haired lady leaned on her cane behind the glass with a concerned look about her. The concern melted as soon as she saw Doug's head appear in the doorway, then it returned again as she watched him limp across the tarmac into the building.

"Doug, are you hurt?"

"No," he said, holding one boot up to show her. "Just short a heel. You don't hardly notice if I hold still. Looks good, though, don't it?"

Doug stood holding his flowered bag and grinnin' like a mud shark as the woman looked him over. She could see that nothing short of brain surgery or violence was going to alter the situation, so she said the only thing she could. "Yes dear, very nice. Come along now, we're going to be late."

She took Doug's arm, the blue-haired lady leaning into her cane beside the man stumbling along in a great green suit. The two who might become the toast of the evening were at least, for now, the talk of the C Concourse.

Doug was awestruck as he was led through the front door of the gallery downtown. The big room was completely white—ceiling, floor, and walls. White boxes sat randomly around the room, and clear glass shelves jutted from walls. And atop each box, on every shelf, was a hand-carved McDoogan driftwood with a card placed beside it. *Birth of Innocence*, NOT FOR SALE identified the partial carving of an infant's face. *Life and Ewe*, SOLD, beside a Dall sheep seeming to charge from the wood.

Even if Doug could've read the cards and titles, it would have only confused him further. He didn't title any of these. He didn't even think about them. And now here he was in a room surrounded by dozens of his whittlin's. Every one mounted, lacquered, and lighted. *Ram and Faith. Love of Ocean. Fossil Friends.* Sheep, killer whales, scallops, and snails all represented perfectly and only partially in the grains of wooden flotsam that Doug'd scavenged from the beach. None of the carvings were finished in Doug's estimation; he'd lost interest in them and laid them aside just as he did there in the gallery when he spotted the food table over in the corner.

"Well, Doug, what do you think?" The old woman was standing behind the table, watching Doug take in the display.

"I think I'll have some of that cheese. I'm awful hungry," Doug said, and that was honestly all he thought.

"You're the guest of honor, Doug, you dig right in," she said, taking the lids off of several tray. "There's wontons, spinach frittata, escargot, sushi rolls, and Buffalo chicken wings." And with that the blue-haired lady went to greet her arriving guests, leaving Doug to puzzle over what a buffalo chicken was, or what anything else on the table was, for that matter.

Doug hobbled around the spread sampling a little bit of everything with his fingers, but kept his eye on the "important"-looking people starting to wander the room. The men all wore neat gray suits, not as nice as Doug's, he admitted, but neat. The women were in a variety of fancy dresses, all smelling like scented urinal cakes, or shampoo, or something Doug couldn't quite place.

They huddled around the displays, pointing, nodding, making hand gestures, and talking. Every once in a while someone would look blatantly at Doug and point, then go back to serious talk. Doug was becoming unsettled and began to retreat to the safety of the food table when a hand reached out and grabbed his shoulder.

"Doug, excuse me." A well-dressed man shook his hand. "I admire your work very much."

Doug didn't understand. The guy had never seen him work that he knew of. He offered nothing in return, and the man continued nervously.

"There's a quality of *tension* between your subject and your material that is *terribly* riveting."

All Doug understood was the "terribly" part, and could only think to say, "I'm sorry."

A tall woman, overhearing his question, came up next to the man and added, "Yes, there is a tension, but there's a balance as well, as if all things in Earth are equal. Have you ever worked in stone?"

"Yes," Doug said, relieved that he finally understood a question. "I humped drill bits at a rock pit one summer . . ." And as he was about to elaborate, the woman machine-gunned him with a high-strung giggle, squeezed his chin, and ran off to fetch a companion.

Before he knew it, Doug was surrounded by friendly, penetrating faces. All seeming to admire

Doug while at the same time saying impossible things to him.

"The way you follow the natural grain in *Birth of Innocence* seems to suggest a fatalistic drift. You see innocence as part of the natural order?"

"Doug, what made you choose beach debris as your medium to create these beautiful forms? What's your statement?"

"Mr. McDoogan, why do you refuse to sign your work?"

"Where did you study?"

"Would you consider yourself an aesthetic?"

And Doug stood dumbfounded. Unable to speak. Suddenly off balance and petrified, he stepped back into his missing heel, stumbled, and went clear up to an elbow in Buffalo chicken wings. He pulled back so hard from that he flung two wings onto the tall woman's chest and had to grab his balance on the shoulder of a stranger in a white tuxedo. The man recoiled from Doug's red dripping hand, which sent Doug careening belly down on the floor, where he could only rest his head in total resignation and look at the pretty shoes.

On the way to the hotel the blue-haired lady tried to console him. "Don't worry about it, Doug. You're an artist. You're supposed to be weird."

Doug sat, still licking chicken sauce from his fingers. "I couldn't even understand what they were saying to me."

The blue-haired lady looked over at her favorite imbecile and something came to her. A story she'd heard somewhere.

"Doug, one time there was this incredible dancing centipede. It had a hundred legs and would dance for people all around the world. He'd never talk to the public and he'd never grant interviews. He'd just travel and dance these amazingly complex and impossibly dazzling dances that the world marveled at. Finally, after many years and much attention, some clever reporter finally talked the centipede into holding an interview. You know, Doug, like a reception, like tonight. Anyway, the dancing centipede stood up in front of the press and said, 'What would you ask me?'

"The clever reporter stood up and said, 'Mr. Centipede, you dance a magical dance that the whole world is in love with. Tell us, how do you do it?'

"'Well, it's simple,' said the centipede, lifting one foot. 'First I put this foot here.' He lifted another foot. 'Then I put that foot there, no there, and then I put this foot umm . . . here, no, must be *here* . . .' And the dancing centipede looked up at his audience, down at his tangled feet, shrugged, and never danced again."

"What'd he do, break a leg?" They were at the hotel and Doug was waiting for the story to end so he could get out of the car.

The blue-haired lady sighed. "Never mind, Doug. It just means you don't have to understand what you're doing as long as you do your carving just like you do. Good night, dear."

"Good night, ma'am."

Doug went up to his room and was surprised to find the light on. It was the nicest place he'd ever been in, and he was looking forward to sleeping here. But he saw that the bed was turned down and there was a candy on the pillow with a note he couldn't read. There was a clean white robe folded up across the foot of the bed with another note.

He wondered if maybe somebody else wasn't staying here too. It looked like they had everything set just like they wanted it. Maybe they'd gone out for something. Doug sighed, not terribly disappointed that none of this was for him.

He opened up the flowered suitcase and pulled out his wool army blanket. He curled up on the floor, where his roommate wouldn't trip over him, and went into a fast sleep. The sleep of the innocent.

And he dreamed of a circus with a magical centipede dancing around and under thousands of pretty, shiny shoes on important people's feet.

———— • ————

The roads are breaking up in the lower elevations as spring slogs toward us. The State Highway Department announced that it will leave its orange tractor with the keys in it by the big sinkhole on Near Road. If you get stuck, please help yourself, but remember it uses a little oil and you have to double clutch to get it in second.

The sewers below Main Street are still giving us trouble. And the city reminds us not to flush our toilets more than four at a time or they'll back up. Call the flush hotline and get the order of your turn before flushing. That number is 223-5874. That's 22-FLUSH.

———— • ————

25

The Expert

EMMITT Frank's first impulse upon entering the Great Land was to start counting things. A professional planner's tendency, I suppose. Before you can start organizing, you have to know what's there to work with. He'd driven all through Canada without counting anything. He'd used his idle hours between driving sprees to study the background on his new home.

Emmitt cared little for history or custom. He was after the hard facts. Alaska: area, 586,412 square miles. More than twice the size of Texas. Population 450,000 in the last census. Highest elevation: Mt. McKinley, 20,320 feet. Lowest point: sea level. State Motto: *North to the Future*. The suitability of this motto was not lost even on Emmitt, whose right brain had ceased function and atrophied years ago.

Within days of losing his wife and job of twenty years, Emmitt Frank had applied for and been accepted as the new city manager of an obscure little

Alaskan community curiously called "the End of the Road." It was more than a new leaf for Emmitt. It was a challenge. Not just a challenge to his professional integrity, but to his broken manhood as well. He, Emmitt Frank, the most diligent and appreciative bureaucrat in the Association of American Municipal Planning Assistants, was coming to the Last Frontier to *tame the wilderness,* or at least classify it.

There would be zoning studies galore. He could see that at a glance. The map he had would go on sometimes for hundreds of miles without indicating a district boundary, residential, industrial, military, or recreational-utility zone. His mouth watered at the opportunities that lay ahead. The opportunity to organize and signify these 450,000 naive and shiftless residents, who probably didn't even know what they were sitting on.

He would start with his charges at the End of the Road, but until then, there were things to count.

He counted moose to start with, but that got boring, so he made two moose categories. Moose beside the road and moose in the road. He soon became impatient with that as well, and formed cow moose beside the road and in the road, bull moose beside the road and in the road, and little moose in general.

Emmitt was a thorough and efficient counter capable of handling a lot of data, and he soon began counting mountain peaks, rivers, tributaries, glaciers, rabbits, and road graders.

It was a peculiar mind at work here. A mind that could look at moose after moose after moose after caribou, mountain after valley after glacier, and not once did a sense of reverence, revelation, or beauty enter his head. The only reaction was, *one, two, three, four,* and on.

It hadn't dawned on Emmitt, and it would take some time before it would, that he was a stranger in a strange land. That perhaps a lot of what he knew was wrong, and that maybe there was more to be listened to here than told or counted.

• • •

Emmitt called ahead from Anchorage to let his new employers know that he would be coming in that day. Mayor Richard Weekly was happy to hear it.

"Good, Frank. Glad you called. As long as you're in Anchorage, go over to the Low Blow Truck and Iron on Potter and pick up the air canister they're rebuilding for the snowplow."

Emmitt looked at the phone, puzzled. "Excuse me, Mr. Mayor, but you want *me* to pick up a truck part? I don't understand."

"Don't have to, we'll have the mechanic put it back in. All you gotta do is bring it down."

Emmitt was still confused. "Won't I need a purchase order? Or at least an authorization? Technically I'm not a city employee yet."

"I'll call Henry and tell 'em you're on your way. Remember, Low Blow Truck and Iron on Potter. When you get into town, come on over to Clara's Coffee Cup. We'll be waitin' for ya. Drive careful, Frank."

The mayor hung up and Emmitt wandered back to his car slightly cheered that his new job had begun but vaguely perturbed that his new capacity as Frontier Planner was getting off on such a peculiar footing. Including the mayor being so glib with him. *Drive careful, Frank.* Not Emmitt, or Mr. Frank. Just Frank. *Professional courtesy could use some work at the End of the Road,* thought Emmitt.

The long and glorious drive down the peninsula did little to relax or acclimate Emmitt Frank. He counted twenty-six moose, fifty-nine mountains, three sheep, four road graders, and a car wreck.

When he crested the hill overlooking town and the quiet bay around it, Emmitt pulled over in a turnout. There below him was the End of the Road. It reached out into the bay from town some five miles on the back of a natural gravel spit and just stopped. Surrounding it were the misty coves, wild white peaks, and wind-whipped glaciers of one of the prettiest little secrets in the world, Kachemak Bay.

Emmitt was taking a picture. It wasn't that he was smitten, or that he was even particularly interested. What he was trying to do was get a photograph that featured the spit along with the digital clock in his dashboard displaying the time and date. In case his time of arrival was ever questioned. Emmitt Frank was not one to let details drift far away.

The new city manager for the End of the Road parked his station wagon in front of Clara's Coffee Cup, smoothed his hair in the rearview mirror, straightened his tie, and, as businesslike as possible, he walked through the front door with a briefcase under one arm and a forty-pound rebuilt dynometer air canister for a Kenworth end-dump under the other.

Most of the current and presiding End of the Road city council was present at the big table in the back. Mayor Weekly was the first to spot him. "Frank, you made it. Here, let me take a load off ya." The mayor relieved Emmitt of his truck part and briefcase while the rest of the council stood up to greet him.

The mayor shook hands first, giving Emmitt a warm two-fister. "Welcome to the End of the Road, Frank."

"Thank you, Mayor. By the way, it's Emmitt."

"I know." The mayor turned toward his council. "Bud Koenig, please meet Mr. Emmitt."

Bud Koenig, the calming influence on the council, took Emmitt's hand. "Pleased to have you aboard, Mr. Emmitt."

"Thank you, it's Frank."

"Okay, Frank, good. You call me Bud, and this pretty lady here is Ruby, the president of our Chamber of Commerce. Ruby, meet Frank."

Ruby McClay shook hands roughly with Emmitt. "How-dee-do. How are ya at sewers, Frank?"

"I've had twenty years' experience with sewage proposals. And it's Emmitt."

"I know, Mr. Emmitt, at any rate, this sewer ain't proposed, it's backed up. All over town—" Ruby would have continued but Bud cut her off with another introduction.

"And Frank, this is Clara Weekly, the proprietor of this fine establishment, the mayor's sister and the official secretary of the council when we can get her nose out of the crossword puzzles." Bud gestured Clara and Emmitt together with his hands.

Clara's sour puss of a face sucked in on itself a little bit and she folded her arms across her apron. "I don't mind tellin' you that I don't like outsiders comin' in here and tellin' us what to do, Mr. Emmitt. But I'm pleased to meet you all the same."

"Likewise, Ms. Weekly." Emmitt reached for her hand, but none was presented. He let his flop awkwardly to his side, and Bud let the silence hang just long enough to embarrass everyone involved.

"Nice place you have here." Emmitt looked around uneasily at their spare surroundings.

"No it ain't, Frank," Bud said. "It's a dive and everybody knows it, but it's the only dive we got. Don't mind Clara, she was born ornery and isn't happy unless something is going wrong."

Emmitt relaxed a little in Bud's confidence and addressed the table. "There seems to be some confusion about my name. It's Emmitt Frank. I've been hearing a lot of discrepancy."

"Says Frank Emmitt on your résumé," Ruby said.

"That would have been Frank, comma, Emmitt. Last name first."

"No comma on my copy." Ruby pulled a wad of four pages out of her back pocket and verified that there wasn't.

Mayor Weekly apologized, "Our copier over at city hall doesn't do such a good job anymore. This is going to raise hell all over town with you, I'm afraid. I announced your hiring in the paper last week as Frank Emmitt." The mayor patted Emmitt's arm, fatherly. "But we're pretty savvy around here, Frank. We'll have 'er straightened out in no time."

Emmitt sipped his coffee and began to wish he'd renewed his Tagamet prescription before he left Chicago.

After a little get-acquainted session at Clara's, Mayor Weekly took Emmitt across the street to the city hall and maintenance shop.

"Emmitt, we have an apartment upstairs you can use until you find a place of your own. Go ahead and eat on the city account at Clara's, but plan on cooking in on Tuesdays. That's her chili night, and she makes terrible chili. Pull your car on over and Bud and I'll help you get settled in."

Emmitt brought very few things with him. There were a few suitcases, an ironing board, and several boxes of manuals and directories. The mayor and Bud looked on curiously as Emmitt unpacked a half-dozen suits and hung them. He pulled out a pile of neatly folded white shirts and three pair of shiny black shoes with stretchers in them.

"You won't have much use for those suits, I don't think, Frank." Mayor Weekly sat down on a box. "You'd better get yourself some decent boots and a warm coat. We dress real casual here, and we dress real warm."

"I'm from Chicago," Emmitt reminded them. "I've lived in snow all my life."

"Oh darn, that reminds me." Bud slapped his forehead. "There's something I gotta show you on the snowplow."

"The snowplow?" Emmitt had a suit half out of a bag.

"Yeah, if it snows in the night, you're supposed to go downstairs and warm up the snowplow for Ed. Ed Flannigan works for the State Highway crew, but he moonlights with us during the winter snow months. Part of the deal is he'll do it so long as his truck is warmed up for him."

Emmitt was dumbfounded. "I-I don't know anything about equipment. And how will I know if it snows at night?"

"I've got that all worked out for you. C'mon, I'll show ya."

Downstairs in the maintenance garage Bud climbed into the big Kenworth dump truck the city had fitted as a snowplow and sand truck and waved Emmitt on up to the cab. Emmitt felt clumsy and exposed on the big machine as he stood on the running board and listened to Bud.

"All you gotta do is turn your fuel on with this here switch, got it? Then you hit your ignition here, see? Then you wait for the light and hit the starter. If it don't fire right off, squirt a little shot of this ether in the air stack right in front of you there. Be patient and go easy or you'll wear the battery down. It's as easy as that." Bud talked the easy talk of a man familiar with machinery. Emmitt listened the awkward way of a man who hasn't even driven a standard transmission in twenty years.

"I-I really don't think I'm the reliable choice for this task."

Bud squeezed Emmitt's shoulder on his way down. "Oh, don't worry about not wakin' up in time. Wait'll I show you my invention." And Bud led Emmitt around the truck to show him how he'd rigged a pie pan with a counterweight outside the front door with a wire to the big horn on the snowplow.

"If we get more than three inches in the pan, it sets off the horn which is right under your bed. Ya can't miss it."

Bud looked with obvious pride upon his gadget, which was at that moment sending convulsions of horror through Emmitt's lower digestive regions.

• • •

That evening, after unpacking, ironing, and refolding his clothes, Emmitt took his manuals and books downstairs to the city offices. He found his space, and after arranging his books and sitting back at his new desk, he started to relax for the first time. This was his environment.

He browsed casually through some files and immediately began to see things. Irregularities. Utility bills unposted. Payments filed by name with no cross reference to address. He grabbed one single project file pertaining to the new sewer system and saw that it was missing a Federal Form DEC-1270, a planning-waiver maintenance-contract release #348, and a surety-bond-guaranteed request voucher. *No wonder the toilets are backed up,* he thought. And Emmitt Frank went to work.

Into the wee hours he doddered over file after file. Making notes and stacking up pink memos on the desk of the assistant he'd yet to meet. Emmitt's head shook frequently and with self-satisfaction. The look of a true pro criticizing an amateur's performance. Emmitt felt wonderful.

This *was* going to work out. He could save this place. He alone, Emmitt Frank, would bring management and order the way God intended it to the End of the Road. He had so much to teach these people. So many things they needed to do.

Emmitt finally went back up to his rooms to get ready for bed. Just before retiring he sat in his window and watched the snow fall over the quiet street. It was peaceful, and Emmitt absently tried to count the snowflakes falling past the porch light on Clara's Coffee Cup.

Emmitt felt on the threshold of a new life. A challenging life where he had so much to offer. A life where he was in charge. An authority. The *expert.* All that lay in front of him.

He drifted off in a peaceful sleep, only to be

thrown awake by a sound like none other; the endearing tonals of the air horns on a Kenworth dump truck being tugged at by a pie tin full of snow.

And Emmitt Frank, Frontier Planner, master manager, and outside expert extraordinaire, went downstairs to the garage and ran the battery down on the snowplow.

Activist-at-large Tamara Dupree staged a sit-in blockade on the Spit Road Monday morning, attempting to halt log-truck traffic in a protest over timber cutting in the area. It turned out that Tamara was the only participant and the trucks continued to drive around her until she finally got cold and went home about lunchtime.

The fifth- and sixth-grade classes unveiled their local history project, which traces the End of the Road as a community all the way back to its founding in 1964. Displays included "Frozen Foods on the Last Frontier," "The Origins of Cable Television," and "Appliances of the Pioneers." The exhibit will be available for viewing all week at the big garage on Clearshot.

26

An Officer
and Tamara

SOMETHING came over Tamara
as soon as she saw the handwriting on the envelope. A
piece of memory jarred just slightly, and pleasantly.
She walked the path back to the cabin without opening
it. It bore an Anchorage postmark dated just the day
before. There was no return address. But there was her
name in blue ink. "Tamara Dupree," written there as
she hadn't seen it written in eight years. It was him. He
could have waited thirty years and she'd still have recognized his hand.

Anthony and Tamara were the heart, soul, and
conscience of the Berkeley scene for two years. At
least they thought they were. Quick to picket, slow to
disperse, they had met during a hunger strike protest-
ing the use of MSG in the dormitory cafeteria. It was
love at first sight. The early months of their affair were
preoccupied with boycotting grapes, then it was
straight into a public-awareness group on laboratory-
research animals.

They were arrested together for organizing an illegal "Bummer March" when G. Gordon Liddy was released from prison. They walked hand in hand down the railroad tracks to protest a Navy chemical-weapons shipment, and hung a banner across their dorm objecting to the U.S. offering haven to members of the ousted Nicaraguan Somoza regime.

Anthony and Tamara were something together. They didn't like anything. They agreed on more issues to object to than most people even knew about. It was a match made in caucus, and they were magical times.

Anthony was two years older than Tamara and trying to get into medical school. He wanted to be a doctor. A doctor of conscience. He would single-handedly take on the American medical establishment from the inside. His major was organic chemistry and his idea was that all pharmaceuticals should be made from medicinal herbs and administered by Chinese holy men. Or women, as Tamara was quick to add.

Despite all their political similarities and parallel consciences, Tamara and Anthony were truly in love. They never publicly pawed at each other, but they were always touching somehow. Even if it was just a finger on a shirtsleeve or a pinch of hair, there was a contact. If they were separated, their eyes never had to search each other out. They'd meet the first time, no matter how large the crowd, as if motion had stopped for everyone but themselves.

If they were at a party and one of them was talking, the other would lean their head into the conversation appreciatively, offering pats of encouragement or compliment as points were made. They laughed at each other's wit and finished one another's sentences sometimes. They were sort of obnoxious to be around.

In private they read to each other and meditated a lot. They made love meaningfully and often. And above it all were their issues. Their causes. That great unwashed idealism that would save the world if they just stayed together.

It was near the end of Anthony's senior year that things started to blur. Anthony was having trouble finding a medical school that his parents could afford, and he was having no luck with scholarships. He blamed the stress for his canceled dates and lackluster performances. He started eating lunch at Burger King, and Tamara could hardly stand the smell of him. He claimed that his lower chakra must be all clogged up and if he could just get away for a while maybe he could find the cosmic Roto-Rooter that would fix everything up.

Eventually he left for medical school in Washington, D.C. Tamara received a few letters at first, a few less as time went on, and not another one until now.

Tamara sat back in her cabin in the morning light and carefully opened the envelope. There was a single page of Holiday Inn stationery with Anthony's beautiful flowing handwriting.

> *Dear Tamara*
> *I couldn't find a phone number for you so I had to write. I'm in Anchorage all week with some seminars. I would love to see you if you can make it up. Please call me here.*
> > *Love, Anthony*

Tamara's heart was fluttering. She'd already been through the whole grieving process on this one. Denial, anger, hurt, longing, loneliness, and finally after eight years had come to just missing him. And now he was back. What a twit. What a sweet, wonderful twit.

Tamara drove to town to use the phone with a thousand questions boiling in her. Where did he live? Was he married? Was he a doctor? Where has he *been* for eight years?

She called the hotel and asked for the room of Anthony Tobias.

"Would that be Major Tobias?" the clerk asked Tamara.

"Um, no, probably Dr. Tobias, or Tobias M.D.?"

"It's our only Tobias, please hold while I ring for you."

Tamara was a little puzzled, but had no time to think as the phone was answered on the first ring by a deep and familiar voice. A voice that warmed her like tea and sent a ripple down her neck to her voice, "Anthony, it's so good to hear from you."

"Tamara . . ." And like two streams in the hills, the words tumbled out of them and into one long river of questions, concern, and guilty conscience.

Tamara told him what the desk clerk had said about a major and he passed it off with a laugh. He told her yes, he was a doctor. It hadn't spoiled his handwriting. Was she still a vegetarian? Yes. Was he? Yes. Married? No. Would she drive up to see him? . . . Yes.

Tamara went to the Laundromat for a shower. She washed her hair and clothes and sang old songs the whole time as she loaded her backpack into the VW bus and headed up the highway.

She had four whole hours in her own head to deal with the issues at hand. Was she being a chump? Could a man return like that after eight years of silence and expect this kind of attention from a woman? Obviously he could. Would the woman expect an apology? Probably.

Tamara arrived in Anchorage with the late-afternoon sunset and found her way downtown to the Holiday Inn. She left her pack in the van and went directly to the room. As she stood outside his door her knees were knocking and her heart was faltering. Being pulled in two directions. There was fear, enough fear to activate her flight mechanisms, and there was longing. Longing enough to keep her rooted in between.

Then she heard something move behind the door and a man clear his throat. An acquainted sound that rang to her marrow, and she knocked on the door.

Their eyes met directly and never had to search.

There was a moment of inertia to overcome, but soon eight years piled out of the way and they held each other close and they held long.

Anthony was anxious to get out of the room. "I've been cooped up in here all day. Let's go for a walk and find something to eat."

"Good idea." Tamara let herself be led back into the hall and looked at her old friend. Anthony was in blue jeans and a worn chamois shirt. He wore trekking boots and grabbed a tired old Army parka to put on. "You look just the same, Doctor, 'cept you cut your hair." Tamara grabbed his arm and they walked off down the hall touching easily, as if it never had stopped.

When Tamara told Anthony she still had her same VW microbus, he was thrilled and insisted on driving it. It's the same bus they used to take down to Big Sur for a weekend of sun and meditation. It's the bus they were mobbed and beaten in for distributing food and pamphlets to striking fruit pickers. They were a team; Tamara, Anthony, and the Bus.

And here the three of them were again reunited and cruising the evening in Anchorage. Tamara knew a place where they could get a wheat-grass juice, and later, the best whole-grained bakery in Alaska. They never stopped talking.

Anthony lived in Seattle now. He was becoming somewhat of a heart specialist and had begun traveling a lot to give lectures. He still thought the real key to good health lay with diet and medicinal herbs, but he worked for a fairly conservative organization and he had to move slowly with them.

Tamara told him about her troubles last fall. How she'd almost starved her dog to death trying to make it a vegetarian and how she'd gotten mixed up with a married man before she knew what was going on.

Big talk turned to small talk, and over a cup of camomile tea at the bakery they finally fell silent. Tamara looked at her old friend and lover through the steam, and a feeling of serenity and security locked down on her. "You certainly *are* a heart specialist, Dr. Tobias." She smiled at Anthony and their fingers just barely touched and explored each other between them. "Let's go home," she said with a sparkle and a promise that put Anthony just slightly on edge.

"Tamara, there's something I want to tell you—"

"Save it," Tamara said, and led her man back to the bus.

They stopped for a bottle of wine and sang old Grateful Dead songs all the way back to the hotel.

". . . Trouble ahead, trouble behind. Don't you know that notion just crossed my mind."

They laughed and locked arms, leaning on each other across the lobby to the elevator.

Tamara was happy. As happy as she'd been in many years. She hadn't been with a man in months. She hadn't laughed with one in she didn't know how long. Maybe since Anthony. Men were such baggage to Tamara. Little boys with big mouths and dangerous motivations. It was a rare one that she enjoyed.

And she did enjoy Anthony. She was so completely at home in his presence and in his room. He excused himself to the bathroom and Tamara wandered around the room touching things absently. There were notes to a speech scattered on the table, "Heart Disease in a Modern Army," it was titled.

Interesting, thought Tamara, assuming it was a medical protest of military diets forced upon its soldiers. Anthony always was one for the fringe causes. And she smiled appreciatively.

She could hear Anthony in the shower now. She wanted to get comfortable herself, and opened his closet to see if there might be a robe or big shirt she could wear. But there was no comfort in the closet, only a flash of white. The flash that happens when a perception changes course at dangerous speeds.

What she saw was the uniform of an officer in the Army. A major, to be more specific. A Major Anthony

P. Tobias, M.D., to be exact. Tamara held the black plastic name plate in her hand and a demon was loosed inside her. The all-important demon that runs her.

She turned when Anthony opened the bathroom door. Anthony stood with a towel around his waist and their eyes met without searching. He saw everything at a glance.

"When were you going to tell me?" Tamara's steely eyes sent a chill up Anthony's bare back. "*After?*"

"Tamara, don't think that. I've tried to tell you. I've written letters and never sent them. I didn't know how . . ."

Tamara did not soften a nudge. "How long?" was all she said.

Anthony took a deep breath and leaned against the doorframe. It was show time. He'd rehearsed this speech a thousand times in his head and now he couldn't remember a phrase of it. He just stammered out the words.

How he'd enlisted while they were still together. It was the only way he was going to get the training to be a doctor. How he hadn't intended to stay in the service, but found that he kind of liked it. That he could do some good there, and that in just another twelve years he could retire with a good pension. A pension that would allow him the freedom to pursue his research and continually present his holistic approach to medicine to the medical establishment. He would have credentials. They would listen to him.

Tamara listened without acknowledging anything. Her arms were folded tight across her chest like something might leap out if she relaxed, or find its way in past her demon. "Why didn't you tell me?" she said.

"The look on your face right now, Tamara. That's why I didn't tell you. I was afraid of you. As much as I loved you, I couldn't trust you. You're very prejudiced about these things. I knew I would lose you, and I couldn't stand the thought of that. I thought if you didn't know, you might still love me even if you never heard from me."

"I did," Tamara said, and everybody present took note of the past tense.

Anthony went over and sat on the bed with his hands holding up his forehead. "I used to hate the military too. But we were kids then. I thought you might have mellowed some. It's not such an awful thing, Tamara." He was not really pleading.

Tamara started to pull on her coat. A frozen determination had come over her. Tamara's personal iron gates guarded by a demon that painted everything black or white. It was always this way with Tamara. Black or white. And she was the only cold judge of which was what. This was black, and her demon would not let her see the light even as it burned inside her.

Tamara's heart began beating again, but at a slow and methodical pace. She finished buttoning her coat and opened the door. Anthony looked up from the bed and their eyes met without searching. "Good-bye, Major Tobias," she said.

"I'll write," said the major.

Tamara let the door close behind her, then whispered "Okay" to the barren corridor.

An Army heart specialist's broken heart and soul laid back on the bed and sobbed as Tamara marched down the hall to the beat of her methodical heart. Some things are just so. They have to be. Above it all there has to be her issues, the causes, the great unwashed ideals, that would save the world if she could just stay together.

And Tamara Dupree, soldier of conscience, paragon of wholeness, went out to her bus, looked at the lit, empty window of a Holiday Inn, and fell apart.

27

The Best Sauna Story So Far

THE Storbocks and Flannigans had been best of friends for years. It seems like they'd done everything together. Built houses. Raised children. Played softball. Hunted, hated—God, they'd even gone *camping* together, the true emotional dipstick of any relationship.

But one thing they'd always talked about doing and never got around to was skiing up to the sauna house on Flat Back Ridge just for the thrill and peace of it.

The sauna on the ridge was sort of the local romantic hot spot. Miles off the road on Big Fish Lake, no one really knows who built the place, but everyone who uses the sauna helps keep it up.

They'd get a sitter for their kids, pack some wine, cheese, and bread, and the four of them would take a moonlit ski up to the sauna. It was a good idea whose time had come.

• • •

Ed said he and Stormy could go up earlier on the snow machines with the wine and food, and fire up the stove. That way when they skied up later, everything would be ready to go.

"Oh, this is going to be so much fun!" Emily squeezed Kirsten. "Just the four of us, no kids. What a wonderful idea." Of course, not Emily, Ed, or any of them had any way of knowing what toll the following evening would take on friendships, marriage, and anatomy.

The next day showed no signs of ill will toward the Storbock-Flannigan brigade. In fact, quite the opposite. The sun rose in its full clear-winter-sky glory on a fresh February snow. The calendar promised a full moon that night, and you couldn't come up with a more perfect day for the outing if you'd made up this story and written it yourself.

Kirsten and Emily put together a packload of wine, cheeses, salami, and bread while the boys waxed skis and loaded up the snow machines in the truck. About an hour before dark Ed and Stormy headed up the ridge road to deliver the goods to the sauna.

It only took a few minutes by machine to cover the two miles back to the sauna, and while Ed built a fire in the stove, Stormy chopped a big new hole in the lake, filled the water barrel, then widened it for a dunking hole.

"This is gonna be great." Stormy was looking down the wooded trail from the sauna to the lake, with the fresh snow reflecting the rose of a perfect sunset, on a perfect day, before a flawless night.

"Yes indeedee-do," Ed said. "I'll damper down the stove, you put the wine in the snowbank there to keep it cold. Put the food inside so it don't freeze, and let's get goin'. It'll be dark soon, and the moon rises early tonight."

The boys were loaded up and back in town before the color had disappeared altogether from the sky.

With the sun gone, the temperature dropped a bit to just above zero, but in spite of the cold, or maybe because of it, the group had an ideal winter night for the occasion.

The two halves of the duplex that the families shared since the Storbocks' fire were alive with the sounds of children being tamed and tied for babysitters. Videos were plugged in, toothbrushes laid out, kisses given, and finally four relieved adults sat back into a frosty Chevy Blazer with eight skis on the roof.

"We're going to celebrate tonight with just some peace and quiet," Emily breathed. "Here, here," everyone agreed, and they all leaned back on the hours ahead.

The moon had risen to its full high-beamed luster by the time our quartet was at the trail head clipping on bindings, sorting out poles, cinching down ski bands, and stomping around in the cold.

"Before we get started, everybody gather in here a minute." Emily flagged everyone toward her, and with genuine affection the four locked their arms around each other and touched their heads together. "I just wanted to say for me and Ed, what special friends we all are. There just isn't anything that could come between us."

Ed burped, Stormy laughed, Kirsten shoved them both and fell down herself, and four good friends, for the time being, hit the trail.

It was a magical half-hour ski back to the sauna. Bright as day, with the moonlight glimmering on the snow like ten thousand diamonds. Galaxies of diamonds that couldn't be told from the galaxies of stars that shone overhead in their pure northern clarity.

The four skied single file down the trail, all lost in thought and admiration, not wanting to spoil this flawless tranquility with even a whisper.

They reached the sauna to find it still happily chugging smoke into the night. As everybody climbed out of their skis, Stormy stepped up on the little porch to check the heat. "Good idea firin' this thing up ahead of time, Eddie." He opened the door, and as the wave of heat hit him, he jumped back a step. "SKUNK!" he yelled, wavin' at his face.

Everybody poised to run, but Emily was the first to realize, "Hey, there aren't any skunks around here." Then she caught a whiff of the problem herself and looked at Ed. "You guys didn't put the cheese in the sauna, did you?"

"Yeah," said Ed. "Didn't want it to freeze, so we put everything right by the stove."

Kirsten brushed passed Stormy and looked into the sauna. "That's Swiss cheese and salami, all right. Ooee, it's hot in here, somebody light that lantern."

After Stormy hung the lit oil lamp back on its peg, Kirsten picked up the pack on the bench and looked inside with disgust. Then she looked up at Stormy, shook her head, and in a tone of voice that wives only use on husbands, said, "I can't believe you idiots put this next to the stove. Look at this!"

She opened the pack further to show what could only be described as a Fondue from Hell. There were slices of salami, Triscuits, grapes, bread, and wine glasses all stuck together with three different kinds of distinctive cheeses, including a very expensive Gouda.

"Sorry, honey," was all Stormy could say. "Stinks in here, don't it?"

"Yes, it stinks in here," Kirsten said as she went outside to show Emily the irreversible damages these two knuckleheads had inflicted on their perfect evening.

Trying to save the day, Ed put on a burst of optimism. "Listen, let's stoke the stove some more and pour some water on it. We'll flush out the smell with steam. All's not lost. We still have the wine, and we still have the time."

His mood was infectious and soon everybody was busying themselves with his plan, which didn't even begin to work, but by the time they realized it, everybody had gotten used to the smell and decided to live with it. They put their ski equipment in the snowbank away from the cluttered porch and everybody stripped down.

There's something about nudity in front of even the best of friends that sparks insipid conversation. Big wheel trucks, macrame, politics, anything to keep the mouth moving, the mind occupied, and the eyes averted. Such was the conversation that ensued as the gang settled themselves around on the toasty benches until Kirsten finally came in with something in her hand.

"You knuckleheads froze the wine too," she said, putting it down on the bench under the lamp where everyone could see it. The bottle appeared to be about half wine, half slush.

"Oh well," Stormy said. "Don't get upset. Just put it by the stove. It'll thaw."

And Kirsten, deciding not to cause a ruckus, put the bottle down and settled in for a good old-fashioned sweat.

If public nudity has a way of animating conversations, saunas are just as good at killing them off again. Comments drift away to dangling conclusions, eyes wander closed, and pores open full-steam ahead to baste the body in its own sweet juices. Every once in a while someone reaches out to pour another ladle of water on the rocks, and the heat climbs and climbs and climbs to the limits of endurance.

"Oooooh, that feels good," Ed said from the upper bench. "Don't know how much more I can take. Is that wine thawed out yet?"

And that was the cue for the wine bottle, which had been heating up way too fast for its own good. It gave off a distinctive "clink" and fell into two pieces. As the contents poured onto the rocks and turned to steam, the pleasure/pain balance of the sauna was shattered and replaced with pure pain and toxic fumes.

"Lemme out of here," rang through the woods in four-part harmony as the whole group stumbled out of the vapor onto the tiny porch. Kirsten, the last one out the door, gave it a huge, final, indignant slam. "My gosh, it's hot and stinky in there," she said.

And it was hot and stinky. Hotter and stinkier than any of them knew, because Kirsten's door slam had knocked the oil lamp from its wall peg and broken it on the rocks around the stove. As the failed foursome stood out front watching the steam cascade from their bodies, the sauna was gutting itself in flame behind the closed door.

"Let's run down to the lake and take a dunk before we go back in," Emily yelled, already running down the path.

And everybody joined her for the traditional and masochistic sauna ritual of throwing oneself into an icy pond. Do a dead reversal on your heart to see if it stops or not. The four screamed and huffed and blustered, caught their wind, and finally stood still in the moonlight for what would prove to be the last time that night.

"Funny how that heat stays with you," Stormy said. "I've got ice right on me and I feel great. Let's go back up for another round." And through the trees, the sauna took that opportunity to burst into flames before their eyes.

There was a wonderful magic moment where four misty friends were silhouetted by the fire, frozen in time and space—and the wilderness, clad only in what God saw fit to give them. And then it dawned on them all at once, "OUR CLOTHES," as they became a blur of white buns and elbows flying back up the trail.

When you're naked and wet in the forest two miles from your car and it's five above zero, the first thing to go is your sense of humor.

"You Storbocks really have a way with fires, don't you?" Ed said, referring to Kirsten and Stormy's tragic house fire back in November and only half kidding.

Stormy looked at Ed, warming himself on the remains of the sauna and their clothes, and he had murder in his eyes. Then he did the worst thing you could do to an old friend who insulted you. Not insult back, not get mad, just turn your back and walk away.

"Kirsten, let's go," he said, trying to look manly

and vital putting on ski boots and skis. "We'll freeze to death out here."

"We'd all better make a run for it," Emily said, putting on her gear, and suddenly the urgency of the situation descended on the party. Their clothes were gone, and two miles stood between them and salvation. No matter which way they turned it, or how hard they fought it, they were all going to have to ski naked two miles in the dark.

The trip going out was every bit as quiet as the one coming in, only for different reasons. Everyone was thinking of only two things: how fast they could go, and how cold they were. Kirsten proved to be the fastest skier in these pared-down conditions and she soon pulled way out in front of everybody. Stormy was next in line, with Emily close behind him, while Ed, now regretting his remark at the sauna, slogged along behind.

The night was as clear and riveting as it was earlier, if not more so, but nobody paid the slightest attention to it. All eyes were on the trail and all minds were on varying favorite parts of their anatomies that were surely going to drop off at any moment.

Kirsten reached the Blazer a full two minutes ahead of Stormy and realized a full two minutes earlier that they were locked out. As she went around checking the doors, a car came by and she instinctively ducked out of sight. Just then Stormy came huffing up with Ed and Emily on his heels. "Start 'er up, why don't ya?" Stormy's voice revealed his growing panic.

"It's locked," Kirsten said lowly and sadly.

"Locked? Where's the keys?"

Kirsten didn't say anything. She just looked back up the trail.

"Let me get this straight," Stormy said. "You locked us out of the truck. The keys are in the fire, and you just dodged a car? . . . Why?"

Kirsten just hugged herself and said, " 'Cause I was naked."

"That's just my point! We're all naked! Damn, you can be such a ditz sometimes."

Kirsten folded and cried. Emily was going to hold her, but Ed broke it up.

"Forget it. Forget everything for right now. We gotta go, *now*. Down the road." Ed used a commander's tone of voice. A tone that all men resented and most men followed, and that quick, the four were once again skiing through the moonlight, right down the middle of the road, hellbent for warmth. Any kind of warmth.

And any kind of warmth was at that moment coming in the opposite direction in the placid, pious form of Fanny Olmstead, the preacher's wife. Fanny was returning from a revival meeting up at the mission and she was inspired this particular evening. The speaker that night had been addressing the subject of Satan and his many forms. From a sweet-smelling opiate that tempts and conquers, to cold-blue savage beasts that sweep out of the darkness.

Suddenly, in the middle of her thought and in the middle of the road, illuminated in her headlights like Satan's fire, were four blue, buck-naked, bowlegged beasts sweeping straight out of the darkness upon her.

Ed saw the lights first as they hit the downhill. "Car comin'. Slow down." And everybody toed their skis in to snowplow to a stop in front of the car. "Thank God, we're saved."

Fanny watched in horror as these naked creatures with frost around their eyes and ice dangling from their faces, hair, and even breasts, waved their arms at her. When they came around to her side of the car she could only stare wild-eyed.

"It's Fanny. Fanny Olmstead," Ed yelled as he opened the rear door. Everybody threw their skis off and the four climbed in the backseat.

"Heat. Heat. Oh, sweet delicious heat. I don't think I'll ever be warm again," Emily said to no one.

Fanny turned her head to look in the mirror and found the icy face of Stormy looking back. "Hi," was all Stormy could manage to say, and Fanny's eyes rolled back in their sockets as she passed out cold on the steering wheel.

The gathering in the backseat, putting away shyness and propriety, and despite strained marriages and bruised friendships, wrapped their freezing bodies around themselves. They held each other tight and squeezed and laughter came out. A four-part laughter that built and filled the car, and filled their hearts. And the warm blood flowed back into their veins, and into their lives, and the moonlit night became a flawless thing once again.

ABOUT THE AUTHOR

TOM BODETT burst on the national scene as the spokesman for the Motel 6 chain ("We'll leave the light on for you") and as a commentator for National Public Radio. His weekly syndicated radio variety show "The End of the Road" was heard between January 1988 and February 1990 over 160 radio stations nationwide. Bodett lives in Homer, Alaska with his wife Debi and their son Courtney.